PRAISE FOR

THE GRAVITY OF US

"The first love, first launch, astronaut story I didn't know I needed."
—Becky Albertalli, *New York Times* bestselling author
of *Simon vs. the Homo Sapiens Agenda*

"A big-hearted, witty, and intensely relatable debut."
—Karen M. McManus, *New York Times* bestselling author
of *One of Us Is Lying* and *Two Can Keep a Secret*

"You will want to stand and cheer for Cal at every
step of his heartstring-pulling story."
—Jeff Zentner, Morris Award–winning author
of *The Serpent King*

"Cal and Leon are fierce and sweet, and
I never wanted their story to end."
—Shaun David Hutchinson, author of *We Are the Ants*
and *The Past and Other Things That Should Stay Buried*

"At once a tender love story and an honest exploration
of anxiety, ambition, and family dynamics."
—Caleb Roehrig, author of *Death Prefers Blondes*

"Equal parts thoughtful and heartfelt, this book never misses a beat."
—Julian Winters, author of *Running with Lions*

THE GRAVITY OF US

BOOKS BY PHIL STAMPER

The Gravity of Us
As Far as You'll Take Me

THE GRAVITY OF US

PHIL STAMPER

BLOOMSBURY

NEW YORK LONDON OXFORD NEW DELHI SYDNEY

BLOOMSBURY YA
Bloomsbury Publishing Inc., part of Bloomsbury Publishing Plc
1385 Broadway, New York, NY 10018

BLOOMSBURY and the Diana logo are trademarks of Bloomsbury Publishing Plc

First published in the United States of America in February 2020
by Bloomsbury YA
Paperback edition published in February 2021

Bloomsbury books may be purchased for business or promotional use. For information on
bulk purchases please contact Macmillan Corporate and Premium Sales Department at
specialmarkets@macmillan.com

ISBN 978-1-5476-0568-2 (paperback)

The Library of Congress has cataloged the hardcover edition as follows:
Names: Stamper, Phil, author.
Title: The gravity of us / by Phil Stamper.
Description: New York : Bloomsbury, 2020.
Summary: When his volatile father is picked to become an astronaut for
NASA's mission to Mars, seventeen-year-old Cal, an aspiring journalist,
reluctantly moves from Brooklyn to Houston, Texas, and looks for a story to
report, finding an ally (and crush) in Leon, the son of another astronaut.
Identifiers: LCCN 2019019167 (print) | LCCN 2019022112 (e-book)
ISBN 978-1-5476-0014-4 (hardcover) • ISBN 978-1-5476-0015-1 (e-book)
Subjects: CYAC: Journalism—Fiction. | Family problems—Fiction. | Astronauts—Fiction. |
United States. National Aeronautics and Space Administration—Fiction. | Love—Fiction. |
Gays—Fiction. | Houston (Tex.)—Fiction.
Classification: LCC PZ7.1.S7316 Gr 2020 (print) | LCC PZ7.1.S7316 (e-book) |
DDC [Fic]—dc23
LC record available at https://lccn.loc.gov/2019019167
LC e-book record available at https://lccn.loc.gov/2019022112

Book design by Danielle Ceccolini
Typeset by Westchester Publishing Services
Printed and bound in the U.S.A. by Berryville Graphics Inc., Berryville, Virginia
2 4 6 8 10 9 7 5 3 1

All papers used by Bloomsbury Publishing Plc are natural, recyclable products
made from wood grown in well-managed forests. The manufacturing processes
conform to the environmental regulations of the country of origin.

To find out more about our authors and books visit www.bloomsbury.com
and sign up for our newsletters.

For Jonathan.
You keep me grounded, and you help me soar.

WITHDRAWN

CHAPTER 1

At home, I'm invisible. At school, I'm bizarre. But to the rest of the world, I'm a journalist.

I get this specific feeling—a tug in my gut, a hitch in my breath—every time I craft a news story, open the FlashFame app, and broadcast live to my 435,000 followers.

When I step off the Q train at the Times Square stop and shoulder my way to the exit, I take a moment to collect my thoughts. I pull in a hearty breath and smile. Holding the phone in front of my face, I go over the plan in my head for my weekly New York City update. What to cover, where to walk.

"Hiya!" I shout into the phone and smirk as the commuters behind me dash out of view. "I'm Cal, and welcome to my weekend update. New York's been slow on the news front— murders and Amber Alerts, all normal stuff—but in national news, one thing is a standout: the search for the twentieth and final astronaut to be added to the Orpheus project."

In the front-facing camera, I see the city scroll by in a mass of billboards, shops, cabs, and bikes. I try not to show the strain in my smile, and remind myself that even the most seasoned reporters have to report on what their viewers want to hear most. And according to my comments, there's no contest: people want to know the latest. It's not like I'm surprised—it's all anyone can talk about right now. Six humans will be setting foot on Mars, and it's ignited an interest the space program hasn't seen in decades.

"The astronaut in question will be chosen in the coming weeks, after which they will relocate to Houston to vie for a spot on the Orpheus V spacecraft, the first crewed mission to Mars."

If this performance doesn't win me an Emmy, I will throw a fit. You ever tell someone you're overjoyed by something, when secretly you'd rather vomit in a bucket than talk about it anymore? That's me with the Mars missions. I hate the hype.

However, people are so wrapped up in the drama around this Mars mission, you'd think it was the latest *Real Housewives* installment. Therein lies my dilemma: Do I want to report on things people care about? Yes. Do I want more followers and viewers? Also yes.

"A representative of StarWatch spoke about the search today," I continue, "but the cable gossip network didn't offer any new information about the candidates."

After my brief, obligatory NASA report, I bring the stream back to New York City by offering recommendations for the biggest events of the weekend: parties, farmers' markets, and everything in between. All while watching the live viewer count climb.

I've done local stories, national stories, worldwide stories before. I covered a full midterm election year, attending rallies for Senate and House candidates in the tristate area, even the severely inept ones who thought microwaves gave you cancer.

I used to feel helpless every time I opened up my news aggregating app, but reporting gave me a platform for my voice, and that resonated with people.

While cable news angled stories to fit their followers and pushed sensational bullshit—*Is Trump homophobic? We interviewed this homophobic Trump voter to get his thoughts!*—my reports covered the *real* news. Raw and unbiased.

Like when the Republican candidate for New York senator fell off the grid and refused to debate or see the press until election night . . . but had no problem attacking his opponents on Twitter. One day, it slipped that he'd been seen in the city, so *I* slipped out of school and waited outside the restaurant where he was.

I started incognito with my phone in my chest pocket and asked him some light questions. He obliged, until I brought up his pending embezzlement investigation, charges of sexual harassment, and the recent staffing shakeup that could have been related to either.

In the end, I chased his limo up Fifth Avenue, where he cursed me—and the fifty thousand viewers—out, live.

Needless to say, he did not win the election.

Nowadays, I carefully plan my videos for the week. National news updates one day, a focus on teen issues another, with a few personal stories sprinkled in. Then, there are my NYC updates. Even if they don't get the most views, these streams are my favorites. It's me, the city, and quadrillions of New Yorkers and tourists in the background.

The front-facing camera starts to show just how much the humidity is taking a toll on my once perfectly coiffed hair, and if I don't sign off soon, I'll look like a frazzled maniac.

"Wow, I guess there was a lot to talk about, because"—I flip away from the front-facing camera and give my viewers a panoramic shot of my surroundings, and the tall buildings on all sides blend into a mix of brick and concrete—"we're already at Thirty-Eighth and Broadway."

These updates always start at the northern tip of Times Square, and I usually just walk down Broadway until I run out of things to say, or until my voice starts to crack. And even in the latter case, I've been known to subject my viewers to the true New York experience: buying a seltzer on the street—after haggling the price down to a reasonable amount, of course.

"And that's all I've got. Keep an eye on my FlashFame story to see why I'll be scouring the streets of the Lower East Side." I flash a smirk as I end the transmission, and release a deep sigh as I shed my journalistic brand.

I catch the F train at 34th toward Brooklyn, which is about the only way to get to the Lower East Side from where I'm at. The flair of the city dims as tourists block the subway doors, as the train stops between stations for three minutes at a time, as the air-conditioning breathes lukewarm air down my neck.

The notifications roll in from my video, which was watched live by around eighty thousand people. But somehow, Flash-Fame knows which comments to highlight, specifically the one that will slash deepest into my heart.

JRod64 (Jeremy Rodriguez): Love this! ❤

How long does it take to get over someone you barely even dated? The irony of him "loving" my posts when he couldn't even commit to "liking" me is at the forefront of my mind, and a rage burns inside me.

The anger ebbs as I walk the streets of the Lower East Side, where the tall buildings of midtown have disappeared, replaced with short brick apartments with fire escapes, towering over everything from abandoned bodegas to artisan vegan bakeries. I double-check the address and take the stairs down into a dark, windowless shop.

"Jesus, Calvin, there you are," Deb says. She always uses my full name. She full-names everyone but herself, really— but that's because she says Deborah is a grandma name. "I've been in this store since you signed off, and the owners of this cassette shop *really* like to talk about cassettes, and I didn't have the heart to tell them I was only here to be your cassette wingwoman. I think they know I'm a fraud."

"I would pay to see you pretending to be a cassette fan-girl." The thought makes me laugh.

"It's not hard. I just repeated the bullshit you say—'the sound is much smoother' or whatever. It was going fine until he asked me the model and year of my boom box."

I browse the collection while Deb impatiently waits behind me. I promised her a vegan doughnut—or twelve—from the bakery across the street in exchange for making the trip to browse cassettes with me. Unfortunately, nothing here catches my eye.

I raid a few tapes from the dollar bin based on their covers alone—guys with beautiful, flowing eighties hair, movie soundtracks with old VHS-style covers—and unironically pay for my retro tapes using my iPhone.

"Finally," Deb says as she busts out of the record store. "That place was weird. You're weird."

"I'm well aware of both, thanks."

We meander through the Lower East Side, which isn't all that different from our neighborhood in Brooklyn. Okay, it's a little bit dirtier, and there are fewer toddlers getting in my way, but otherwise, I see the similarities.

"I love this area," Deb says.

"Yeah, it's okay for things like that random pop-up cassette shop," I say with a shrug. "I hear they're putting in a Trader Joe's here."

"Jesus," she swears. "Of course they are."

We duck into a tiny bakery with no more than five stools of seating. The two bakers are cramped behind the counter, and I start to get claustrophobic on their behalf. But as I look around, I see glimpses of the neighborhood in notices plastered on the walls. Yoga classes, babysitting offers, piano lessons, writers' groups. Panning out, I see protest signs, queer pride flags of all varieties, old campaign stickers from the past couple of elections.

New York has a way of making you feel at home, no matter where you're at. You just have to step off the street, and some neighborhood will claim you as one of their own.

"Exactly how do you make a vegan lemon curd?" Deb asks, fascinated, and I realize I'm missing her in *her* element. Before the baker can even answer, she rambles on. "This place is amazing. I'm going to get a dozen, but I think I want literally one of each flavor. Is that too much?" she asks no one in particular.

I'm a vegetarian, but she's a full-on vegan, and she's in heaven. Vegans get a bad rap, but Deb's always been down-to-earth about it. She embraces it, but not to the extent where she's treating it like a cult.

This also means we *have* to go to every new vegan restaurant, bakery, pop-up, and festival the moment it opens, and I am not complaining about that.

"You're sharing these with me, right?" I ask.

"Oh dear sweet Jesus in heaven," she says after biting into a doughnut. "Not if they're all as good as this lemon curd."

We take our time walking toward Brooklyn, with no real destination in mind. It's too far to walk all the way, but it's a surprisingly nice day, and I'm not in a rush. I *know* Deb's not.

"You shouldn't have paid for these," Deb says. "I have a job, dude. You don't need to jump in and save me anymore."

I blush. "I know, it wasn't that. But I left you alone in that cassette pop-up, so defenseless you had to pretend you were one of us to fit in. The horrors you must have overcome. This is the least I can do."

What I don't say is, I know she's saving every penny from her job. Deb works harder than anyone I know. If I could fix her home life, I would. But until we can flee our respective coops, all I can do is pay for her sugar high.

"One World Trade. We're approaching tourist central," I say. "I'll take a few pics for my Flash story, then we've got to get a train."

The sun's nowhere to be seen, but a series of low clouds pass by, getting split in two by the shining tower. It's a perfect New York afternoon, but I feel the tug in my chest that reminds me what's waiting for me at home. As we hop on a train and make half smiles at each other, I can tell we're thinking the same thing. There's a pretty high chance that one or both of our nights are about to be ruined by our parents.

— — —

We make it back to Brooklyn in record time. Anxiety grips my chest as I take the stairs up our stoop, and I know Deb usually feels the same. To be quite honest, I would have been fine spending a few more minutes delaying the inevitable awkward conversations and heated fights that wait for me at home. Not like the arguments are ever directed at me, but they're still all around me. Lingering.

Wearing our family down.

I part ways with Deb at the third floor of our apartment

building, and a tightness balls up in my shoulders—clenching, constricting—when I launch up the stairs to my apartment, taking them two at a time. Before I even reach my door with the shiny 11 on it, I hear the shouts.

It wasn't always like this.

I put the key in the lock, and with a heavy sigh, I turn it.

A frown falls over my face almost instantly. I slam the door to make my presence known, but it doesn't fix things, it doesn't stop them. I want my being home to *mean* something. I want . . . I don't know what I want—to not feel helpless when they're like this. I try to escape into my phone, but my notifications are once again flooded with questions about . . . the astronauts.

I sigh as I scroll through.

kindil0o (Chelsea Kim): Hi, big fan. Um, is it just me or have you stopped profiling the astronauts? I used to love your streams, and I still do, but I'd like to see more of your old stuff. Are we getting to Mars or not? You only spent like 30 secs on the new astronaut search??

I mute the notification. Of course my followers would notice how short my NASA segments are, how my eyes dart away from the camera when I mention the search for the newest astronauts.

Everyone wants to know why, and I'm staring at the reason: my dad just flew back from Houston from his final round of interviews with NASA.

If he has it his way, I'll never escape this mission.

CHAPTER 2

"Stop waiting by the phone," my mom shouts. "They said they'd call you today if you were chosen. It's five thirty. You've used all your vacation days and it's barely June; you're flying back and forth from Houston every few weeks—it's taken over your life. It's taken over *our* lives."

She points to me, and just like that, I'm a part of their game. A pawn left out conspicuously to lure a bishop and set up a checkmate. She makes eye contact with me, and I briefly see the exhaustion on her face. The panic, the stress. But my gaze darts away. I won't give her that power. I won't be a part of this.

"I'm sorry, but it's time to drop this fantasy," Mom says, turning her attention back to Dad. "Just . . . think about it practically. We can't relocate. I have a life, a job."

"Does this really have to happen *every other* day?" I say as I rush down the hallway toward my room.

"It's only four thirty in Houston." Dad clears his throat,

almost nervously. "And you work remotely. You could code anywhere. I know you don't want to hear it, but there's still a chance. A *real* chance this could happen."

"What about Calvin?" she snaps back. "We'd pull him from his school just before his senior year? Did you ever tell him about what this would mean for his videos?"

"Wait. What about my videos?" I spin back toward them, but as I do, the pieces fall into place. If he got the job, we wouldn't only be moving to Houston, we'd basically be stepping onto a TV set.

Every moment of our lives would be monitored, recorded by StarWatch for their annoying *Shooting Stars* show.

They're both avoiding eye contact.

"Well, we don't know anything for sure," Dad starts, "but there was a clause in the paperwork."

"A *clear* clause," Mom says as she slowly massages her temples, "that said no other public video transmissions can be made including people involved with the mission. And as family, they would consider us a part of the mission."

And I'm gone.

"Cal, wait!"

I slam my bedroom door and lean against it.

Within seconds, my parents are back at it, and there's a part of me that wants to turn around and fix this. To make things right again. They still fought before the astronaut thing, but rarely, and not like this. My fists clench as I argue with myself, wondering whether it's worth sticking my neck out, trying to help them, trying to *stop* them.

But that's never worked.

"You're making me dread coming home, Becca. Every time I come back with good news, you fly off the handle!"

"I've lived here my whole life." Mom's hurt voice creeps through my door. It's like they're having two separate conversations. Neither's listening to the other. "This was our first home. I was born here, my . . . family was born here."

I hear what she doesn't say—my aunt was born here too. She lived down the street from us for years. This street, this neighborhood is all tied up in memories of her. No wonder Mom doesn't want to leave.

"You didn't have the decency to run it by me before you—"

That's all I let myself hear.

This is another reason why my dad can't be an astronaut: we're clearly not fit to be an astronaut family.

NASA picked their first astronauts for the Orpheus missions three years ago, in small groups—three or four added each time. Orpheus I through IV tested individual components of the spacecraft, each test more successful than the last.

The families, though, became stars. What they have is flawless; their personal and professional stories follow a story arc that even I couldn't write. It's hard to look at them and not think they have everything my family doesn't.

The astronauts have heated arguments that line the pages of *People* magazine, and sure, sometimes one of the spouses will have a little too much to drink during brunch. But they still smile for the cameras. They know how to make their imperfections seem . . . perfect.

In the end, they stay happy and supportive—two qualities my parents haven't shown in a while.

— —— —

I plug my headphones into my retro tape deck and put them on. I add my new finds and sort through the rest of my eclectic collection of cassettes: Nirvana, Dolly Parton, Cheap Trick, bands and artists I only know thanks to my thrift store finds. I settle on Cheap Trick and jam it in, and let the guitar overtake the voices.

Dad wants to be one of them. The astronauts, that is. Way more than he wants to be who he is now—an air force pilot turned commercial air pilot who wants to ditch the 747 for a spaceship. NASA announced they'd be hiring the final five astronauts for the Orpheus project. He applied months ago, when most of the spots had already been taken up.

I didn't have the heart to talk to him about his chances. I covered them all in my reports: one of the new recruits was an astrophysicist with a social media following nearing Kardashian levels, another a geologist/marine biologist who'd won two Oscars for her documentaries and even a Grammy for a spirited reading of her audiobook—which was a bestseller, of course. And those weren't the most impressive ones.

Dad's a good pilot, I'm sure, but he's not like them.

He's angry. Impatient. Surly. Okay, I'm not painting him in the best light. I mean, he is an okay dad in other ways—he's super smart and gives killer advice on my calc homework. But it's like everything my mom says hurts him like a physical attack. He snaps back, which triggers my mom's anxiety. Their fighting isn't camera ready. It's messy, it's real, in a way that's too raw to be captured by a camera.

If they can't put on a show for me—at least pretend that everything's okay, like Deb's parents do—how can they put on a show for the world?

I get through a few tracks while I sit on the floor and close my eyes. There's nothing else but the music. And a few cars beeping outside. Okay, more than a few. This is Brooklyn, after all.

After a while, a calmness pours over me, drowning out the fear. I feel . . . at peace. Alone and no longer worried about my future plans. Not worried about the BuzzFeed internship I start next week. Not worried about the hundreds of messages in my inbox—replies to the weekly Cal Letter (I couldn't think of a clever name, don't judge)—where I link to my videos along with important news stories, geared toward those who give a shit about the world.

I think about these things, but I'm able to push them out of my mind for a few minutes, then a few more, until I have to get up and switch cassettes. The tension in my chest eases. It's meditation. For me, it's the most effective self-care system in the world.

That is, until I hear a knock.

Through noise-canceling headphones and blasted music, I hear it. Which means it's less of a knock and more of a pound, but regardless, I take off my headphones and shout, "Yeah?"

My mom peers into the room—she's always afraid she'll

catch me doing "something," and we all know what that "something" is, but I'm also not an idiot and can figure out how to do said "something" twice a day having never been caught thank you very much.

But then I notice her expression. She's tearing up, which is not good.

See, she doesn't cry. They fight, they yell, they make things seriously unpleasant for everyone in a two-apartment radius, but they don't cry. They shout, then Mom retreats from the world and Dad goes for a walk. It's how they process. Getting at each other's throats, but not offending the other bad enough to let them carry their hurt to the next hour.

And . . . here she is, crying.

"I, um." Mom comes into the doorway now. I scan her for bruises, for covered arms, for anything—though I know Dad would never hurt her like that, I never see her upset like this, so my mind reaches for options.

Until she speaks.

"Come into the family room. Your father has news."

News.

My mind freezes. Did the phone ring sometime in the past hour? Did NASA interrupt their fight to tell Dad he was chosen for . . . ?

But that doesn't make sense. We're not like them. We're not ever going to be like them. NASA should be able to figure that out, right?

Before I get too far ahead of myself, I stop the tape and make my way to the door, seeing the empty space where my mother just stood. She turns the corner quickly, leaving just a fluttering patch of fabric in her wake. She's running away from this conversation, and away from the face I know I made when she said "news."

Like it could mean anything else.

I make it halfway down the hall when, *pop*, a champagne bottle confirms the fears flowing through my body. My gut turns to mush. My heart rate doubles. I feel it all over my body like an electric shock, but instead of causing sudden jerks of movement, everything is slow. My nerves dance, but my limbs won't cooperate. All is ash and tasteless, and smells are weak, and I can't even come up with metaphors that make sense because . . .

"A glass for each of us—even for you, Cal. It's a special occasion." Dad hands them out, his happy face immune to the terrified, broken expressions on ours. "And a toast, well, to me. NASA's newest astronaut."

It takes a few seconds for the words to sink in, and it's like my brain is the last one to this party. My fists clench. Breaths won't come. I feel the pressure building everywhere, in my back, my sinuses, my stomach. My legs ache as I repeat the word in my head: Astronaut. Astronaut.

Astronaut.

You know how sometimes you say a word so often it loses its meaning? That doesn't happen. The definition sticks in my brain—and it's even in the etymology. Astro-naut. Space explorer. What every three-year-old kid has not so secretly wanted to be since the sixties.

I slam my champagne glass down with a clink and push past my mother. The hallway blurs by as I barrel into our bathroom. I don't know what this means for my dad, my mom, or me. But I do know one thing:

I'm going to be sick.

Shooting Stars
Season 1; Episode 6

EXCLUSIVE INTERVIEW: On this episode of *Shooting Stars*, astronaut Grace Tucker sits down with host Josh Farrow and gets straight to the question we get most from our loyal Star-Watch fans. (First aired 6/15/2019)

"Good evening, StarWatchers, I'm Josh Farrow. Tonight we welcome Grace Tucker: a fierce pilot, a brilliant engineer, and above all else, a determined astronaut. Who knows what role she'll play in the Orpheus project? Will she assist from the ground, or could she possibly leave the first human footprint on the surface of Mars? It's only her third month on the project, after all, but she's made quite a name for herself. We have Grace in the studio tonight to discuss all this and more . . . Grace, thank you for joining us tonight. There are nine of you now, and NASA recently announced they will add up to eleven more to the Orpheus project over the next year."

"Thanks for having me, Josh. You and I know NASA wants the best astronauts. There was a time when NASA's astronauts were only the toughest, roughest white men. Think back to the Mercury Seven and the New Nine—men like Deke Slayton, Alan Shepard, Jim Lovell, Pete Conrad. They were all smart as hell, sure, but in time NASA realized the benefit of diversity. Diversity in skill set; in place of life; in race, gender, identity, and orientation."

"Yes, of course. But we—*Shooting Stars* viewers—also know NASA has not always been at the forefront of these issues. Like how Mae Carol Jemison, the first black woman in space, went up on *Endeavour* in the early nineties. That was, what, thirty-some years after the space program was founded?"

"Which, if I may interrupt, is why diversity in the space program has always been one of my top priorities, and I've made that clear from my first days at NASA. So I fully stand behind NASA's decision here, and I look forward to meeting and flying with the new recruits."

"Let me put this another way: Do you think your chances of leading this flight are dropping, given how many new recruits NASA's bringing on board?"

"I'm not worried, Josh. Nothing's a given in this environment—you must know that. I could be taken off the mission for getting the flu a day before launch. The government could pull funding; your fans could lose their interest. I just do my best every day. It's all any of us can do."

CHAPTER 3

Maybe it's the panic, but Grace's first StarWatch interview plays in my mind. Over and over and over. It's the only thing I can think of. Grace's upright posture, her camera-ready attitude. Her subtle concern.

I flush the toilet and stand to stare at my reflection. My face glistens with sweat, and my panted breaths fog the mirror. I wipe it away and start to brush my teeth, holding my own gaze like it's the only thing keeping me here, keeping me grounded.

My mind fills with more news stories. Local, national, gossip, blogs. The barely covered press release announcing the relocation of all astronaut families to Houston, the rumors of a shuttered mission—why spend money on space exploration when we could better fund schools or infrastructure?

And I remember the moment it all changed.

StarWatch Network announced its partnership with NASA,

complete with a teaser episode of *Shooting Stars* featuring a pilot in a simulation cockpit. Sweat dripped down astronaut Mark Bannon's brow as the narrator explained the test.

During the simulation, as the craft entered Mars's atmosphere, the screen goes blank. As the surface of Mars comes into view, fast, Mark resets the gauges. When this fails, he reaches for a pen and paper beneath his seat. The scene cuts to Mark entering coordinates and new trajectories into the still-glowing command module. As the craft nears the ground, all panels come back to life, giving Mark just enough time to make final adjustments before . . . *thud.*

"Orpheus V has landed," he says between breaths.

Then the screen cuts to a message to tune in weekly to watch StarWatch's new show: *Shooting Stars.*

The uptick in attention the families got from adoring fans was instant. To some, they became American heroes; to some, they became the newest reality show. They're interesting. They're perfect. They're . . .

Not like us.

"Calvin, honey?" My mom's voice is hoarse.

My parents file in after I gain the strength to unlock the door. Mom's got the look of a concerned mother down perfectly, all creased brows and soft eyes. But my dad's got a different expression. His mouth slants, and he seems detached from it all. I can't tell if he's annoyed, or just not tolerating my reaction. Yeah, it was a little much, but I don't exactly have control over when my falafel cart lunch decides to make a fast escape.

"Are you done?" he asks, and all my muscles tighten at once.

"I'm fine," I say. "I—uh—ate too much."

Dad chuckles and takes a generous sip of his drink. "Right. So it had nothing to do with—"

"You overcoming literal impossible odds to become an astronaut?" I force a laugh. "No, not at all. For the record, it's also not about the fact that we have to uproot our lives in a few months. It's *definitely* got nothing to do with how I won't be able to stream my reports anymore. It's just a lot to take in, okay?"

"Maybe they could let him keep doing the videos?" Mom says. "Why don't you ask them when you go—"

"I can't believe *this* is what we're talking about right now," Dad says, splashing the rest of his champagne into the bathroom sink. "Look, I'm sorry you won't be able to play on social media anymore, but this is real life."

I choke back a laugh. *"Real life?* I have to give up my journalism, plus my *entire life*, because a reality show says so. You really think what I do is less 'real' than StarWatch?"

My mom's caught between us in our tiny bathroom. She's wringing her hands and looking back and forth. Not daring to say anything else. When she and Dad fight, she always knows what to say, never backs down. But now, her face is frozen between panic and helplessness. I know this isn't good for her anxiety, so I take a deep breath to calm myself.

I squeeze by her and into the hall and break into a quick walk to my room.

"Cal," Dad says, and I stop. It's short, but not sweet. His voice has an edge of pity to it. "I'll . . . I can ask them."

"No, it's fine," I say. "It's great, actually. Why would I need to do the *one* thing I'm good at and actually enjoy, when I could be out there enjoying the Lone Star State? I've always loved the allure of Texas. Tripping over Republicans every other step, somehow keeping vegetarian in the land of Tex-Mex and barbecue ribs, it's a literal dream come true."

I'm being selfish right now, and I know it. But this whole thing is born of selfishness. Dad didn't tell us he was going to apply. He didn't explain what would happen if he got in. He just plopped a binder on the kitchen table one day. It was his portfolio—I have no idea why his résumé needed to be in a three-ring binder, especially when you could have just as easily scribbled "Delta" on a napkin and used that.

And then we waited.

Well, he waited. Mom and I gave him shit, because that was so much easier than accepting that he could actually make it in. He could change our lives, make us regulars on *Shooting Stars*, which, despite its patriotic and unifying start, slowly devolved into the overdramatic, ratings-hungry reality show it is now. But he never asked if that's what we wanted.

"Jesus. Get it together," he says.

Looking at my mom's eyes, I can tell we're in agreement here.

"Let's leave him alone for a bit," Mom says, voice squeaking, and ushers him away. I can breathe easier, even if just for a second, even though I know what's about to happen.

"It's not my fault he can't process it. Neither of you seem to get how important this is." His voice rises. "I've worked my whole life for this."

"I think you can drop that," Mom says. Her voice is stronger now. Anxiety be damned, she doesn't take his shit. "We've been together seventeen years, and we all knew you loved space, but you never mentioned considering being an astronaut until you slapped us with that ridiculous binder."

I take the opportunity to flee to my bedroom. As I'm shutting the door, though, Dad comes stomping back down the hall.

"Wait!"

I do, briefly. I take a deep breath and push out the nicest response I can muster. "I can't be excited for you right now. I have to go clear out the troll comments on my video, plus my BuzzFeed internship starts on Monday, and I have forms to fill out. We'll talk later."

"Cal, you don't get it," Dad says. He looks nervous now. "We don't have time to wait for you to get on board."

A beat, and all the energy gets sapped from the room. My legs feel wobbly. I feel my heart rate spike, and my hand feels slimy on the doorknob. I breathe, but it's shallow and unfulfilling.

"We need to start packing tonight," he says. "They've got a house for us."

"What do you—"

"We're *moving* on Monday."

My insides stop working. I'm experiencing literal—okay,

figurative—organ failure right now. I just stare, and blink, and stare again. Then I pull back and unfreeze my body for a second. Just enough to clench my fingers around the doorframe and slam the door in his face.

I click the button lock and dash to my headphones. I press play on the cassette deck and let the sounds pump through, blocking out the shouting and the expectations and my frustrations.

I block it all out.

For a few minutes. The music isn't working. I can't concentrate, and everything sounds like noise and makes me tense up. I feel angry and sad, but I don't know which feeling brings the tears to my eyes faster. I start to cry, but I take off my headphones before I let myself do it. I can't let him hear.

My parents resume fighting in the other room. Well, not fighting, actually. It's a discussion. I hear numbers being thrown out, and words like "movers" and "salary" and know they won't be settling this anytime soon.

I pull out my phone and send a text to Deb.

Can I come down? Need to get out of here for a min

She responds in a flash.

Yeah, we heard the stomping. Door or window?

I send her an emoji of a window and double-check that my door's locked. They wouldn't mind me going down to talk to

Deb—it's only one flight down—but I can't bear to look at them right now.

I imagine them coming to check on me and hearing no response. They'd think I was ignoring them, or if they used that little gold key above the doorframe, they'd know I bailed. And they'd stop the fighting for one second, and they'd sigh "oh shit" at the same time. And for once, I wouldn't be the one trying to make things better, to fix our problems.

Finally, something would be about me.

I lift the window, then the screen. I duck out onto the fire escape and feel the wind tear through my body. I welcome the feeling, refreshing and calming, and stretch out on the landing. My eyes scan the world beneath me, all strollers and parents and dogs, rushing home for dinner before the sun finally sets. Bikes and cars and trucks and brick buildings line the avenue. Beyond that, the trees block my view of brownstones.

This might be the last time I stand out here.

This might be my last weekend living in Brooklyn.

— —— —

When I reach the third floor, I hesitate at the open window. Her sheer curtains are drawn, and I see her silhouette frantically darting back and forth—she's probably throwing all her dirty laundry in the hamper so I can find a place to sit.

It hits me so hard I stagger back and lean against the railing: I'm about to tell my best friend that I'm leaving immediately, indefinitely. Probably. Unless there's some chance Dad's being majorly pranked.

She pushes aside the curtains, and I gasp. The moment she sees my face, which must be lined with tears, her jaw drops.

A familiar pang hits me in the chest. I've seen this expression before. I've *given her* this expression before. Last year, I crawled in her window, a panicked mess, to break up with her.

For some reason, I didn't ease her into it with talking about us growing apart or going different directions, or wanting to focus on school or exploring other options. These were all phrases I had rehearsed.

But she was my girlfriend . . . and my best friend. She deserved more than a weak excuse, so I went right to the point:

"I kissed Jeremy."

We talked it out, and—months later—she accepted my apology. The thing was, Jeremy was always there in the back of my mind. He was the unattainable senior, and I was content with Deb. Unfortunately for her, I found something better than content as I sunk into his lips, the taste of Coors Light on our tongues.

I found a fire, a passion that I was missing. My identity seems to change by the minute, but I knew I was queer—and Deb did too. The hardest thing for her to accept was that it wasn't that I didn't like cishet girls . . . I just didn't like *her* like that, and after dating for three months, I wanted to find someone I did like. And I found Jeremy.

Two weeks later, Jeremy found someone else.

"Calvin?" She grabs my hand and pulls me closer. "Come in. What's—wow, last time I saw you looking like this I had to bring you back from a panic attack so you could break up with me. What's going on, babe?"

My breaths aren't coming easily. I'm suffocating, drowning in the overwhelming pink of her room. The pink beanbag chair with the pink fuzzy pillow and the—*why can't I breathe?*—pink rug that I'm somehow lying on now, though I don't remember crawling in through the window.

I focus on a point on the ceiling, and I don't let it go. Breathe in. Breathe out. Slowly, I pull myself together. I'm okay.

"I'm okay."

Deb rolls her eyes. "Yes, I see that."

"I'm leaving. On Monday. Dad's a fucking astronaut."

This is when she busts out laughing. Like, I'm still crying, and she is one-hundred-percent losing her shit. I can see her try to hold it together—clenching, biting her lip—but nothing's working.

"Oh, god, this is bad. Sorry." She pauses to grab my arm. "It's just so fucking unlikely. Your dad's the least qualified person for this job."

I shrug. "I mean, he's a pilot, I guess."

"For *Delta*." She leans on that word like it tastes bad in her mouth. "He's got to be the first nonscientist they've picked since, like, the seventies."

I decide not to tell her that his degree in aeronautical engineering *does* make him a scientist.

"Focus." I reach out to her, and all the air's sucked from the room. She breaks eye contact and starts picking at the chipped paint on her toenail. "I'm leaving, Deb. On Monday, apparently. We're moving to Houston, and I don't know when I'm coming back. Or if I'm coming back."

It's as if the world reacts to my words. A cloud passes by, casting the window in shade. The pink around me dims. Her lips almost pout as she considers me.

She's not laughing anymore.

So, no, I didn't love her like that. But I do love her. From the moment we met at the mailbox downstairs, when I was geeking out about the vintage Prince cassette I'd just scored off eBay. She'd just moved in that day, but that didn't stop her from relentlessly mocking my obsession with cassettes.

That didn't curb my enthusiasm. I started rambling about it, about how much smoother cassettes sounded and how they had a quality she could never find in a digital copy or CD. I talked so much, I kind of forgot that my room was a disaster, even after I invited her up. She sat on my bed, which was totally unmade, and just listened.

She definitely didn't get it. The cassette thing. But she listened anyway.

That whole year was spent falling into an easy friendship with her. One where I never had to ask *if* she was free later; I'd ask her, "What are *we* doing later?" We spent so much time together, it was like we were dating. Going from friends to more was easy too. Suddenly, we were dating, and it all felt the same.

The same, though, wasn't what I wanted. Where I sought fire and excitement, I got the same calm, comfortable relationship we'd always had.

"What about BuzzFeed?" she asks, cutting through my memories.

I pause. After my coverage of the midterm election got picked up by the national news, plus one full year of building my following and reputation as a reporter, BuzzFeed News offered me a summer internship to help with video content for their new local New York City feature.

When I walked into the headquarters, with its yellow walls and couches everywhere, I knew I was somewhere special. With the laughing twentysomethings and their thick-rimmed glasses, phones always up on top of laptops in open meeting spaces. It was a dream. It was supposed to start next week. It was . . .

"Not going to happen." I realize it as I say it. Everything I've worked for. A foot in the door with a career in media journalism. Stolen away by the astronauts. "Fuck, this sucks. What do I even tell them?"

"Tell them you'll cover the Mars missions. They post a new article about the families like every day."

"On the entertainment page. I was supposed to cover city news." I gesture to the window. "And StarWatch has a gag order on any other video, or really anything, coming out of Clear Lake, Texas. Once Dad signs that contract, I'll be a part of the show. I won't even be able to do my FlashFame vids anymore."

"That's (a) not fair, and (b) wait, I just realized you're going to be on *Shooting Stars*. Oh my god, Josh Farrow is going to be saying your name, aloud, on TV."

I groan. "I can't even process that you still watch that show. It's all perfect families, fancy parties, and petty gossip nowadays. We'll never be able to fit in with those people."

The tension balls up in my chest.

"First of all, it is a fantastic television program." She pronounces each word with extra force. "Okay, yeah, it's a little petty. But hey, they're entertaining at least. Don't act like you aren't a little starry-eyed—pun intended. You were just as invested as everyone else until you found out your dad got an interview."

"Sure, I covered all the new astronauts and reported on the months-long debate about financing Orpheus before the Senate finally passed that funding bill. They were news stories that mattered."

"Well, maybe I think watching astronauts get drunk off champagne before falling face-first into a bush matters too," she jokes.

At least, I hope that was a joke.

Either way, I roll my eyes. "I even did that in-depth report on all the drama NASA caused by buying out every house on the market in Clear Lake, and it got picked up by the *Washington Post*."

She nods, sagely, as I ramble through my frustration.

Clear Lake City is conveniently close to NASA's Johnson Space Center. When the Mercury, Gemini, and Apollo astronauts—and, of course, all the related teams—relocated here from their respective towns, Clear Lake and a few surrounding areas became known for being the home of astronauts. American heroes who made their front lawns the Hollywood of the South.

There was more than celebrity appeal then, however, and the same is true now.

"StarWatch thinks people don't care about the science of it," I say. "Plus, the exploration, what it could mean for our planet, anything. It's so scripted and boring. You know a producer is behind the scenes, stoking the fire or asking pointed questions."

She sighs. "We're getting off track. Forget them—let's get back to *you*. At least ask BuzzFeed if you could do the internship from Texas? You might not lose this opportunity if you try. I'm sure they can be flexible. It's not the *Times*."

"I will," I say. "It'll give me something to do on the car ride to Texas."

She laughs and punches me in the shoulder. "NASA won't pay for a jet? Come on!"

"You know Dad wouldn't go for that. He's spent the past decade moving the car for street cleanings twice a week, even though we use it a handful of times a year. He's not going to get rid of it. He's going to make us all load up the car and go. Forever."

She pulls me into a hug, and I reach around her body and hold her close.

"What am I going to do without you?" she asks.

I know the question isn't exactly rhetorical. At least once a week, she'll tap on my window, needing an escape from her family. They fight too. Maybe all parents fight, I don't know. But with Deb's parents . . . their fights are always . . . scarier. More desperate. The echoed sound of a fist breaking through a particleboard door settles in my head.

They break her heart, and I fix it. That's how it's always gone. Whether it's splitting vegan frozen yogurt at Pinkberry or impromptu slumber parties, fixing her pain—or at least distracting her from it—puts me at ease.

A shiver runs through my body as the truth breaks through. Sometimes, it feels like the only thing keeping me stable is the shield I put up. Cal the performer is always put together. Cal the friend is always there to fix your problems.

I try, but I can't even picture the *real* Cal. The one without a carefully planned video schedule and content calendar, the one who has a clear vision of his future, the one without anyone to turn to.

And I especially can't picture any version of myself in Clear Lake, Texas.

I rest my head on Deb's shoulder and fight back the tears. I'm a little more successful this time, so I get the courage to tell her:

"I'm really going to miss you, Deb."

I nod toward the fire escape, and she follows me out there. We take our usual spots, me a few steps higher than her, the wrought iron crisscrossed grate I sit on hurting my ass.

The wind is cutting, though it's a warm day in spring, and my hair is a disaster.

It's all perfect.

The sun's almost set, but we could be out here all night for all I care.

"Everything's going to change," I say.

Deb releases a bark of laughter. "Is that so bad?"

She bites her lip, and her eyes glisten and puff up. I know Deb could use a change. The only reason Deb is okay now is because she's working the register at Paper Source, which means she can avoid her family for most of the day and night, depending on the shifts she picks up.

I know she'd run if she could, but that doesn't make it any better, for either of us. I wish I could bring her along, to have someone with me on this trip who doesn't drive me mad like Mom and Dad do.

"It might not be so bad—god, why am I tearing up right now?" She takes a moment to rub each eye with her sleeve. "I'll visit you, and you'll come back when you can. You'll end up back in Brooklyn eventually, for good, don't you think?"

"Oh, um, probably." I hadn't yet thought about coming back, really, because I never thought about leaving.

Too much. "It's too much," I say.

"Promise me . . ." She points to my phone. "Promise me you won't stop. Keep streaming all your news stories.

"You know how fickle fans are. If you take a year off, I'm afraid . . . once you move back here, you won't have anything left to come back to."

She's right. Her words slap me across the face, waking some fire within me. I have my next decade planned out meticulously. I have the college brochures on my desk, the SAT prep courses scheduled. I knew exactly how I was getting into my career.

If I leave, even for a year, I could lose so much.

"I know it's against the rules or whatever," she says, "but I say post everything you can until StarWatch pries that phone from your hands."

There's nothing I can do to change NASA's mind. There's nothing I can do to stop this move. The only thing I can control is sitting in the palm of my hand.

A spark of rebellion warms my soul. It's not the smartest move, and it could get my family in trouble, but maybe Clear Lake, Texas, has a story out there just waiting for me to uncover.

Shooting Stars
Season 1; Episode 10

EXCLUSIVE INTERVIEW: The Tucker family's house has a reputation for being party central when it comes to welcoming new astronauts, honoring achievements, or celebrating holidays. In this episode, we pay a visit to Grace, Tony, Leon, and Katherine Tucker to get an inside look at their home and to learn more about the sacrifices the family's made for the Orpheus project. (First aired 7/17/2019)

"Good evening to all our viewers. I'm Josh Farrow, and I'd like to welcome you to another new episode of *Shooting Stars*. Tonight I'll be taking you on a very special tour through the Tucker family home. But first, I thought it would be nice to catch up with our astronaut family du jour: Grace Tucker, her husband, Tony, and their children, Leon and Katherine. It's been a few months since we last got to chat, Grace, isn't that right?"

"Yes, and I can't believe how much has changed in such a short time. I want to thank all the viewers for their help. Without your support, and the thousands of calls and emails to Senate and Congress members . . . well, let's just say we might not be sitting here right now."

"Couldn't have said it better myself. So, last time I was here, we did a quick interview with Grace on that couch, but we only talked business. I want to know more about you all as a family. Leon, with a mother like Grace, you have a lot to live up to. However, you seem to be doing so in your own unique way. By this point we all know about your great talent for gymnastics—in fact, Tony was just telling me about your impromptu gym session today. No pressure, of course, but a few of our fans want to know, do you think we'll be seeing you compete anytime soon?"

"I'm . . . not so sure about that. I've only been back once so far. Still looking for the right trainer. Kat dragged me to a gymnastics center in Houston earlier today, and I spent some time on the rings, hit the mat, and . . . face-planted a few times. I'm not quite so sure I'm competition material anymore."

"My brother's being a little too humble. See, back in Indiana, Leon was basically guaranteed a spot in the USA Gymnastics Elite Squad for his age group. But when we moved here, it was hard for all of us to get into the right rhythm. Plus, our new school is a lot more competitive—academically, I mean. Having said all that, we all know he's still competition material."

"That's great to hear—and I love to see the supportive bond you two have. My sister and I are a year apart too, but we've always been far too competitive to have that kind of relationship! Before we go to break, I wanted to let viewers know we've actually acquired some fan-submitted videos of the Tucker kids at the gym. Our viewers can go to StarWatch.TV to see those videos. Once you're there, read on to take a look back on how Leon's promising career in gymnastics may have been cut short years before a potential Team USA Olympics run. As we know, he's not the only family member whose life or career was affected by the Orpheus missions. With a full Star-Watch pass, you'll get access to a new miniseries that takes an in-depth look at the astronauts' loved ones and the dreams they've left behind."

CHAPTER 4

The weekend goes too fast. Way too fast. A few days ago, I never thought I'd leave my nook of a bedroom, with the tiny bookshelf, twin bed, and tape deck. But now, it really hits me.

I'm leaving Brooklyn.

"Look, buddy," Dad starts.

I hate when he calls me that. So I just keep looking into my bowl of ice cream. I shuffle my feet out of habit, feeling them stick to the stone floor just slightly.

This shop's been a part of my life for as long as I can remember, serving the same four ice-cream flavors. Unlike a lot of Brooklyn—new Brooklyn, at least—it's a no-frills kind of place. Ice cream in the summer. Soup in the winter. And really, both foods usually warm my heart.

Today, though, my chest is too heavy. There are some pains even ice cream can't fix.

"I want you to know that . . . I get it. I know how hard this can be. I was a military brat—my parents moved me all over the place, and I hated it every single time. I resented them for it, and I know you will too, but I hope one day you'll understand."

"And I hope . . . ," I start, not sure how to express the jumble that's in my chest . . . how to say it in a way that will make him take my work seriously for once. "I hope you know what this is costing me. I know you've always treated my videos as a hobby, and I'm sure it looks that way for you. You don't even watch them. So you don't see the time I put into my reports. You don't see the folders I have on my drive—portfolios to help me get into journalism schools after I graduate, all my research on writing scholarships to help pay for college. It took so much work to build this following, and having to abandon something like this just . . . sucks."

"I know." Dad takes a big bite of ice cream. I follow suit. "I should have been more honest with you two in the beginning. That way you could have worked this into your plan. I know how you think—though, I have no idea where you got the planning gene, with how your mom and I are. It's something I'm going to work on. But I need you to get on board, and help your mom do the same, okay?"

I shrug. A half-hearted gesture is all I can offer right now.

Pushing aside the rest of my ice cream, I take one last look at the small shop. I'm going to miss the sticky floor, the water-stained ceiling tiles, the enormous plastic ice-cream cone outside the storefront—the paint is chipping, yet it still manages to creepily light up at night.

Right now, movers are loading boxes into the truck. Boxes

containing my entire life are about to be flung across the country. I sigh, and the chill of the ice cream finally catches up to me, until a firm hand grips my shoulder.

Dad's voice is almost a whisper. "I'm going to miss it here too."

— —— —

"I still can't believe you get to meet the astronauts," Deb says while Dad loads our suitcases into the trunk of our car. "You'll get to meet Grace Tucker and Mark Bannon. Like, actually speak to them. Maybe touch them?"

I roll my eyes. "I think we'll take it slow, at first. What with them being double my age, and always on the news."

"Oh, shut it." She slaps me on the arm. "You know what I mean."

The thought of meeting Mark Bannon, one of the first astronauts picked for the project, immediately intimidates me. I did one report on him that focused on his advocacy for the space program, back before we even knew if Orpheus V would earn the funding to get off the ground. It got me a ton of new followers—the same ones who are probably complaining that I don't do *those* updates anymore.

I know him as a Hulk-like presence who still somehow always looks ready for the cameras. He's got an animated, passionate personality reminiscent of the Apollo astronauts, and I wonder if the rumors are true, about him and Grace vying for the same spot on the Orpheus V mission.

I think back to Grace's *Shooting Stars* interview—which I

only watched for research purposes, and maybe because I was a *little* interested in these new pseudocelebrities—and something about her stubbornness inspired me. How down-to-earth she was, when Josh Farrow wanted her to reveal some tension between the astronauts.

Maybe there's more to this mission. Maybe there *are* real people under this facade. A real story. The rush creeps back inside me. Blood pulses through my veins.

I pull up the latest issue of *Time* on my phone and see the Tuckers' faces beaming up at me. Deb, a notorious space invader, creeps up behind me.

"God, they're beautiful," she says.

My gaze drifts to their son, Leon Tucker. His smoldering stare makes my pulse spike. She's not wrong.

"Could you imagine us on that cover? Me and my parents? We'll never pull this off." I clear my throat. "You know where you watch a movie or read a book or something, and the main character switches schools and is worried about not fitting in, or making new friends? I'm not . . . I'm not feeling any of that."

She considers me softly, with a subtle arch of her brow. So I continue.

"I'll make friends—or I won't, I don't know. People generally suck anyway—but my *family* won't fit in. Mom's anxiety's gotten so bad she barely leaves home anymore, except to go walk around Prospect Park. And they've been fighting so much since Dad applied. The other astronauts are all on another level, and their kids are too. Am *I* a near-Olympic-level gymnast like Leon Tucker? I just feel so . . . inadequate."

"Calvin, you have like half a million FlashFame followers. You've given reports that literally helped sway an election. And even if you have to give it up, you still got the chance at a BuzzFeed internship as a seventeen-year-old—they don't just give those out." She places an arm on my shoulder and lets her words sink in. "You're *more* than adequate, babe. You'll fit in. All of you. But you'll have to let them in too. You've got to get behind this mission—I mean, after the shitshow America's become over the past few years, we all actually have something to rally behind and be proud of. We're going to fucking Mars. And in whatever way NASA deems appropriate, you, your mom, and your dad are going to help us get there."

"I know," I say. And I do.

In this moment, just barely, the sparkle of the mission leaves me breathless. To be a part of history, to play a tiny role in this massive scientific undertaking.

I keep my voice low so my parents can't overhear. "I thought if I ignored everything that's happened over the past year . . . I don't know, I guess I thought that if I didn't put any faith in it—"

"Your dad wouldn't get picked?"

"No, not that. I thought if I could stay grounded and make this feel unreal for all of us, then I could be the realist who helped . . . put Dad back together when he eventually got the crushing no."

"Noble," she says. "But that's not your job."

"It's a compulsion," I say. "I want things to be . . . right. People to be happy."

"But sometimes that bites you in the ass. Like when you told me about Jeremy," she says unflinchingly, "and then I had to hold *your* hand and coach *your* breathing after I found out you cheated on me. But you wouldn't leave—you needed me to be okay, you needed to fix our relationship."

"Are you still pissed at me?"

"Oh my god," she says. "You're doing it again! No, I wouldn't be this flippant if I was still holding a grudge, Calvin."

Deb throws her arms around me, and I'm enveloped in a floral scent. Not like roses or lavender, but like a fall-scented candle in the middle of a potpourri bowl. It's comforting. But I can't bring myself to hug her back.

She continues. "But you couldn't magically fix us. I just needed time. And you can't fix your parents." When I lay my head on her shoulder, the tears soak into her shirt.

"So let's make a game plan," Deb says after a moment of silence. "We've only got one year left of school, unless you fail out, which would fuck up all my planning, so don't do that. Depending on when our graduations are, we can find a place as early as May. I've got a job, and maybe your family would be rich by then, so we could find a place together in Brooklyn."

"What kind of place are we going to find?"

"I don't know, some closet in Bed Stuy? We can live in Coney Island for all I care. I just need out."

The desperation in her voice hits me. "Deb, what's going on?"

There's a pause, where my heart makes its way down into my stomach. She doesn't hesitate. She's not like this.

"It's just not great at home lately," she says, and I get the feeling that's the understatement of the millennium. She drops her voice to a whisper. "Okay, well, it's awful actually. My parents have been around all the time since my pa got laid off. Unemployment is only going so far."

"I thought he was going off on his own?" I ask. Her dad was a designer for a big corporation and said this layoff was the perfect excuse to start his own design firm.

"That's it. He's got a few clients, he has business cards, he's draining his unemployment buying new computers and software, but he's not even registering his company. Mom's always fighting with him, because having income and taking in unemployment is illegal, but fuck, we still barely have enough money to live off." She clears her throat. "They've been using my money. Some of it, for groceries and rent and stuff."

"That's not fair!" I shout. "You work really hard for that."

"I know, I know, but they kind of have a point—I'm the only one with a steady income, and they've taken care of me for so long, I should help a little, I guess. But Cal, I don't even know if we have *health insurance* anymore."

"And you think you'll be able to just up and leave them next year? How will you even save up the money if they're taking it?"

She sighs, long and slow. "I don't know yet. But I'll figure it out, even if I have to crack open my radiator and hide it in there."

"Don't worry," I say. There's one way I can fix this situation. "I'm coming back as soon as I can. If you can just wait until I graduate. I'll be eighteen; there are plenty of schools up here on my list. NYU, St. John's, Columbia—I'd need a scholarship, probably, but I think we could actually make it work."

"Cal, honey?" Mom joins our conversation and gestures lightly toward the car. Her face is strained, almost like she's in pain. I know she's sad. I know she hates the thought of leaving our home. I see the way she tenses her shoulders and grits her teeth.

And I hate that I want to beg her to stay and keep me here. Let Dad do this on his own.

"Are you almost ready to say goodbye?"

"We don't have to do this," I say. It's almost a whisper, and I feel Deb's embarrassment from here. But I have to say this. "NASA's making *Dad* move there. Not all of us too. It's not fair—have you even googled Houston? It's a cesspool."

"Believe me, I have. Clear Lake City is different, but it's beautiful in a suburban way. And I think I understand it. Why they're making everyone move to the same town where the first astronauts lived. I can't even go on Facebook without seeing all my college friends post about them. And though I'm so sad to be leaving my hometown of forty-three years, it's something I have to do. It's something *we* have to do, for your dad." Her feathered brown hair covers half her face. She places a palm on my shoulder and gives me a smile that never quite reaches its full potential.

"Plus," she adds, "with your dad's temper, I give it a week before he gets kicked out."

We laugh, but once the laughter fades into awkward silence,

I know it's time. We're one drive away from a new life. Which means I have three days and a twenty-four-hour drive to figure out how to exist in the town of astronauts.

— —— —

Outside the car, I give Deb a hug and a kiss goodbye. Both are short, and awkward, partially because of the move and partially because of my mom's eyes lingering on us.

"Love you," I say.

Deb smiles. "I know."

I settle into the back seat and roll down the window, savoring the last couple of minutes with my best friend. But we don't say anything. Really, what is there to say at this point? Except, just, goodbye.

Once we're on the road, I busy myself by pulling up all the information I can find about the Orpheus program. Its goals, what it means for our country—outside of the entertainment factor, that is. Orpheus V will take six astronauts to Mars, where they'll build a temporary Martian base, execute some elaborate excavation plans, and perform scientific experiments. Not long after that, Orpheus VI and VII will be on their way, bringing supplies to Mars to set up a permanent base, while Orpheus V sweeps back toward Earth, carrying a ton of soil and rock samples.

I switch to the full *Time* story and see variations on the Tucker family portrait. Their eyes stare back at me; their faces hide all emotion behind them. Where I look for panic, I see reserved excitement. Practiced excitement. Grace Tucker's two teens play their roles well—Leon, the serious, Olympics-bound brother (who is *supremely* hot, if that wasn't clear), and Katherine, the precocious sister.

It makes me wonder . . . what role will I play?

The article has a few more pictures spread out of the family together, posed on sets from the sixties. It reminds me of some of the old magazines I've seen. A wholesome family candid, with the family around the small box television with its wooden frame and obnoxious antenna.

"Do you know much about the sixties? Like, the Apollo missions?" I ask.

Dad fake swerves the car and gasps. I roll my eyes. Mom shakes her head but doesn't start a fight.

"You're asking about the sixties? You're asking me and not Siri?"

"Dad, no one actually uses Siri. And whatever, I'll just look it up," I say, knowing he will absolutely not let me do that, now I've shown an interest.

"So clearly, I wasn't around then, but the sixties and early seventies were the golden age of spaceflight." I catch his eye, and I can see the sparkle from here. "See, the astronauts moved to Clear Lake and the surrounding areas, and they all lived together, partied together, mourned together, and, eventually, some of them took America to the moon and back. It was a scene, like nothing that's ever happened before. I know you don't care for *Shooting Stars*, but even back then, the town was always swamped with the press. You couldn't get a car down the street to save your life on launch days because of all the news trucks and fans. It was like Hollywood or something."

"You showed me those articles once before, I think."

"I have all the good ones in the storage unit. Not doing much good there, I guess. But the country was obsessed with the astronauts. The whole country held their breath as mathematics and sheer brilliance brought back the Apollo 13 crew from the explosion that could have taken their lives. And they mourned when the Apollo 1 flight crew were burned alive on the test pad, thanks to a vulnerable wire and a pure oxygen atmosphere." A silence fills the car. "They were the true American heroes, all of them."

I listen to him talk, and I'm mesmerized. He cares so much, but I never really knew. I mean, he had a few books on this; he obviously loved flying planes . . . which is also why this eight-billion-mile road trip was utterly confusing for me. Was this really his dream all along? Was I never paying attention?

"That's cool, Dad."

"*You* think so?"

My mom laughs at this and places her hand softly on my dad's leg. I feel the connection in the car. It's warm, and for one moment, we're all smiling. I can't even think of the last time we were content to be around one another. No shouting. No slammed doors, no loud music to drown it all out.

I know it can't last. I know my parents, and a part of me wonders if this truly is happiness or defeated acceptance. But I savor the moment as I pull up old paparazzi photos and *Shooting Stars* clips. I start taking note of everyone's expressions:

crisp, practiced, perfect. Are they all that good at faking it? Or do they actually buy into all this? I'm looking for a flaw, but I can't find the reality behind the show. Until I come upon a candid shot from one of the parties—looks like another mixer at the Tuckers' house. Grace has on a sleek, formfitting red cocktail dress; her laugh looks so pure it makes you want to join in. But in the background—

"Leon," I say.

Mom turns around. "What's that?"

"Oh, I mean, nothing." I return to the image. "Just thinking."

He's sitting on their couch, the glow of his phone illuminating his face. But he's looking up at the spectacle of it all, just past the camera. And there's a brooding there that pulls me in.

I'm interested in him purely from a journalistic standpoint, I remind myself, even as his narrowed eyes and sharp jaw pierce through my chest. It's easy to crush on him for being insanely good looking, sure, but what appeals to me the most is his expression.

There's a fire that burns behind those eyes, and I cling to hope that maybe he's a cynic, like me. My breath catches, and my hand reaches out to the picture. I might be imagining it, but I still cling onto the hope that *someone* in that suburb could actually be my ally.

Or maybe . . . maybe something more.

CHAPTER 5

Praise me, for I have lived through a twenty-four-hour car ride. I have lived through two nights in crappy hotels—believe me, the best hotel in Higginsville, Mississippi, is roughly a negative-three-star hotel by New York standards. I survived staying in the same hotel room as my parents, in tiny rooms with thin walls and two double beds.

I have lived through figurative hell, and my reward? Arriving in literal hell. Clear Lake, Texas, at ninety-two degrees.

I step out of the car and survey my new hometown. The heat is wet—the humidity clings to my body, to my lungs, to my eyelids. We've pulled into a park to stretch our legs as we wait for our NASA rep to come show us to our new house.

There's a swing set, a few of those rocking ponies, and an old metal slide all on a bed of wood chips. I try to imagine the kids of the Mercury astronauts from the early sixties—Astrokids, I think they were called—playing in this same park.

I imagine a picture-perfect mom holding an infant in her arm while pushing a toddler in the little swing that looks like a plastic sumo uniform.

Standing here in this swampy mess of a day, I wonder how much they had to fake it for the cameras. Put on a happy face, retouching their makeup between diaper changes and photo shoots. The astronauts had their jobs—to get us to the moon—but their wives had it even harder. They had to fit in, raise their children, take care of the house, the lawn, the gardens, the cooking, the baking, the parties, all while caking on the makeup.

The Astrokids must have played their parts just as well—rambunctious when the magazines wanted them to be, calm and pensive at other times. I groan when I think about playing that part now.

"Cal!" Dad shouts. He's in good spirits, which is the only positive thing to come from this sweaty nightmare. "The NASA guy is pulling up now."

Dad's smile reminds me again of the absence of fighting between all of us. It's like we're back to the pseudonormalcy of our pre-NASA days. Dad has plenty of reasons to be happy, but why is my mom smiling too? Does she not want to shatter his fragile happiness? Is she pushing down her feelings? Her angst about being taken away from Brooklyn, her irritation for the duties that are about to be added on top of the fifty hours a week she spends coding? The spouses aren't like the astronaut wives of the sixties—prim, perfect, calm, sober—but there's still an expectation.

Or is she actually . . . happy? Hopeful?

That thought makes me nauseous. She was supposed to be on my side.

The "NASA guy" gets out of his car, and quickly makes his way to Dad. He's supremely put together, with his short but styled blond hair, checkered shirt buttoned to the top with no tie, and gray slacks that fade into brown boots. The fact he's in anything but shorts makes me sweat doubly on his behalf. Are Texans just immune to this?

He shakes my hand as soon as I get to the group.

"Brendan," he says. "You must be Calvin Junior."

I offer a faint smile. "That's Calvin," I say, pointing to my dad. "Call me Cal."

"Got it. Well, do you want to see your new house?" he asks. "Get ready for it. NASA's been big on bringing back the retro appeal."

He rolls his eyes briefly, but his smirk says it all: it may be over the top, but it's worth it.

The town's not awful. It's even kind of cute. There's a different kind of history here. *Modern* history. Brooklyn has homes that date back 150 years—even our apartment had the original hardwood floors from the early 1900s.

We pull up to our house, and I take in the pristine lawn, which fades into the precisely cut bushes lining the house. It's been so recently painted you can see a glossy shine. The windows sparkle; the mailbox has our last name etched into it.

There's something so real about this place, and it counters everything I got from the park. Seeing the pictures, reading the stories, it all seemed perfect.

And this kind of . . . *is* perfect. I watch my dad take it all in, his smile gone—his expression replaced with a look of pure wonderment.

If I'm feeling this way, I can only imagine the thoughts going through his head.

"As I'm sure you know, we've got a little . . . media problem here," Brendan says as he unlocks the door to our new house and steps inside. "Mostly local news, people looking for anything to trend. A few amateurs who want to sell footage to StarWatch, which is a whole other beast you'll need to prepare for. But there are strict rules, even for StarWatch: They get full filming rights inside the astronauts' houses—within reason, of course—and at the space station, but at the end of the day, it's your home. You decide whether to let them in, keep them outside, or *kick* them out."

Brendan and I share a smile, and there's a strange comfort in having clear boundaries and a little bit of control over our new life.

"So why isn't anyone here now?" Dad asks, disappointment hitting his face. Like he's actually looking forward to getting assaulted by the press.

Brendan laughs. "NASA's holding a press conference now and mentioned *important updates*, so every camera in the city is there. The media team tricked them into thinking we're announcing the final astronaut, basically, so they didn't swarm you right away. Don't worry, we'll let you settle in first."

I hear my mom's sigh of relief from here. When our eyes

meet, a quirk of a smile hits her face. Even if Dad doesn't end up on a flight, this is going to be a wild ride.

"Does everyone who works at NASA have this problem?" I ask.

"Well, I don't. Since the news isn't very excited about the soil samples I work on." He chuckles, and ends with a high-pitched huff. "But the astronauts have to deal with it, all of them. They're—*you're*—the interesting ones."

"I mean, soil can be interesting, I guess?"

"My team thinks so, but I doubt the general public does. Not yet at least." He shrugs. "Rovers send back a ton of great data, but they can only do so much—we'll get the first samples back after the Orpheus VI flyby, where we can do real tests, study the soil in a lab, that stuff."

If there's one thing I know about the "general public," it's that no self-professed media pro actually knows what the public is interested in. Sometimes trial and error is worth a shot, but it's not surprising StarWatch would choose glamour and prestige over . . . dirt.

After following him inside, I take my first refreshing breath. The cool air makes my skin prickle all over, in the best way. The place is sterile, new. Foreign.

My dad paces around the living room, where a brand-new television sits on a midcentury-modern sideboard. A light-colored plush couch faces a retro coffee table flanked by two accent chairs.

Okay, this is a pretty cool house.

The whole place balances vintage personality with modern appliances. A record player sits on a bookshelf, with a collection of vintage records at its side. They really went *all in* on this retro thing. If you replaced that record player with a tape deck, I might be kind of here for it.

"Your lawn is your own. There's a special number for the local police on the fridge. The media isn't *that* bad, usually. But they'll only get worse as we get closer to Orpheus V launch."

I take in this moment of peace, knowing it'll be my last in a while, and follow Brendan to my room. I throw my bag on my new bed, say I'm going to change, and shut the door. I find my dresser—this is where my cassette deck will go, I've decided—and I sit and lean against it, slumping down.

I take a few deep breaths. Admitting I like our new home, even this town, feels like I'm abandoning my old life.

I pull out my phone and open the FlashFame app. Then I close it. I know the rules, I've read Dad's contract—*to stay consistent with the narrative arc set by the Shooting Stars host and producers, no streamed or recorded video is to be shared publicly without prior consent and guidance from StarWatch Media LLC.*

Meaning, they don't necessarily want me to shut down my accounts. But they want to control it—which is even worse. The pang in my gut gets stronger as I type out a text to Deb.

I think I'm going to do it. I mean, technically, I haven't signed anything, right? They can't sue me or whatever, right? . . . right?

I planned on updating on the way down and telling my followers I was going on a brief social media hiatus, but I wasn't able to do it in the car, and the rest stops and hotel rooms only provide so much privacy—meaning, none at all.

But now that I'm here, knowing that my dream is flickering like a dying candle, I can't go on any hiatus. I can't—no, I *won't* let StarWatch control me.

I clear my throat and stare at myself in the camera. My dark hair covers my eyes, a cowlick pushing my hair up in the back. Not my hottest moment, but this will be short.

As soon as I hit the LIVE button, the viewers tab starts climbing. I let it pause for a minute, allowing my followers to react to the notification they all got on their phones before I start. I smile and point to my cowlick comically as the hundreds of viewers become thousands. In the middle of the day on a Wednesday. *Who are these people?* I wonder. *Why do they care?*

And then I don't care why they care, because I enjoy being a little famous. My core tightens again, at the thought of being forced to shut my account down. To give up everything I've worked for. By the time I got back to New York, I'd have . . . nothing.

"Hi, everyone," I say, voice squeaking, after the viewers tab hits two thousand. "I, um, have one hell of an update for you all, so sit tight."

I feel the rush flow through me. Once again, there's a story out there to break. And I'm doing it myself.

"Let's cut the intro," I say, deciding to rip off the bandage.

"You've all started to notice I've been dodging questions when it comes to NASA and the Orpheus missions, and it's time I told you why. The twentieth and final astronaut added to Project Orpheus is none other than . . . Calvin Lewis. No, not me, my father, Calvin Lewis *Sr.* I'm coming to you live from Clear Lake, Texas, where we've just relocated. Recognize this dresser? This room? No? Well, I don't either, but if I have my way, both of us are going to see a lot of it in the future, so get ready."

I get up and walk around the room, collapsing on the foam mattress. I hold the camera high above my head.

"So, yes, I may have broken a big news story just now, but if you all don't mind, I need to turn this into a personal story. My father—an airline pilot turned astronaut, apparently—forced the family on a three-day road trip to Texas instead of putting us on a plane. I don't get it either, but I do have a very thorough review for the Higginsville Holiday Inn off Route 49 in Mississippi. As much as I love family time"—I pause for effect—"I can *not* handle another road trip like this."

I spend the next five or ten minutes recapping my road trip from hell in all its gory (boring) detail, until my mom peeks her head in the door. "Are you . . . ?" she mouths before taking in a sharp breath. "Never mind. Put that down and come outside with us. Now."

"Please stand by," I say robotically to my phone and peek through the window. A few cars line the streets, staying out of our driveway, and my dad and Brendan stand there staring at them.

"Well, that was fast. I should have mentioned this earlier,

but I may have just broken a lot of rules. I'll give you the full update tonight . . . if StarWatch doesn't murder me by then. Wish me luck."

I stop streaming and leave the room, ignoring the gnawing in my stomach that I'm not ready for whatever's coming.

The mood shifts when I step outside.

The air-conditioning that cooled me off apparently gave me temperature amnesia, because I'm shocked by the curtain of heat I just dipped under.

Standing on the blacktop driveway by our car, a little stunned, is my dad. He just stares at the street while reporters buzz around their news vans like flies, making cameras appear as if from nowhere.

Mom sighs loudly. We make eye contact, and I can see the strain on her, the tension in her facial expression.

"You should go. I'll get Dad." I nod to make her feel confident I can take care of this, and she darts back inside.

I can't tell my dad's expression from behind, but I see him go rigid. He's never been the center of attention, outside of making the announcements as copilot on his flights. And for that, he can hide behind the cockpit. He can't hide here, where the sun highlights every flaw and accents every doubt.

He had the foresight to wear a clean shirt at least.

"Crap," Brendan says. "Okay, um. I'm not usually the person who deals with this. I'll make a call."

The realization hits me in waves. *I did this.*

I broke a national news story.

It was a small act of rebellion, which is not entirely

uncharacteristic of me—like when I slipped past guards at City Hall to attend a press conference to grill the NYC Housing Authority on a mass of broken elevators in their public housing projects.

But that wasn't for purely selfish reasons. The pang in my gut turns to fire. This is my calling, and I won't let StarWatch get in the way. Sometimes, you have to take your future into your own hands.

And one way or another, I just did that.

Only, I didn't think about what that would mean for my family.

"What do you want to do?" I ask Dad. There's a firmness in my voice that I didn't know I had in me. "Should I get Mom back out here? Or should we hide inside?"

My shallow breaths start to make me feel light-headed.

Dad turns to me for a second and considers my question as one producer starts her report.

"We're here at the house of the newest astronaut for Project Orpheus, Calvin Lewis Sr., whose son is widely known thanks to his following on the social media platform FlashFame. Calvin—senior, that is—is assumed to be the final astronaut selected before NASA launches its preparations for Orpheus V. The lucky six astronauts on that mission, poised to be the first humans to set foot on Mars, are still to be determined."

My stomach sours, and I feel the tension claw through my shoulders. We need to move fast if we want to get out of here with no notoriety. A solid smile. A brief wave. And we duck inside. But they're recording, and I can't shout that instruction to my dad, who's stopped, standing like a dope with his head pivoting back and forth from me to the camera.

And I see why.

And my chest falls.

I knew they saw my FlashFame video. But I was wholly unremarkable with my almost-half-a-million viewers in New York City. Not here. Not to these small news stations. They know what happens when they put a clip of me online: all my fans will watch it. The cameras are on me.

Which means, they didn't come here just to see my dad.

They came here for me too.

CHAPTER 6

To hell with a graceful exit, I think as Dad rushes past me and into the house, slamming the door so I'm stuck outside. *That was on camera!*

So I smile and pretend it's one of my videos. I smile because it's the only thing holding me and this family together, and I hope the cameras were too` focused on me to get the full effect of Dad's tantrum. If he loses his cool in there, which he will, the mics might pick it up.

Please don't shout.

Please don't shout.

Without putting too much thought into the matter, I go into damage-control mode. I force my legs to move—they're stiff and they ache from being held so tightly. I paste a smile on my face. At first, it's strained, but as my limbs loosen, my face does too. By the time I'm at the end of the driveway, I've got as close to a natural grin as I can pull off.

The reporter stays on the sidewalk—she knows she's not allowed to come closer—so there are a few feet between us. She's got that Hillary Clinton look, with an immaculate solid blue pantsuit. Her smile is practiced; her arm is outstretched.

"Cal Lewis, I'm Gracie Bennett from KHOU-TV. We were thrilled to see your announcement about moving down here, as Houston doesn't get many viral superstars in our midst. Congrats to your father and the family on this exciting adventure. So, we've got to ask—can we expect any Houston weekend roundups in your future? Are you going to give us the inside scoop on the astronauts' lives?"

I chuckle—it's forced, but everything's forced right now, so give me a break. My mind scrambles for a way to redirect the conversation back to my dad, and NASA. "I, well, I'm not sure yet. All I know is my dad's so excited to join the ranks of great astronauts like Jim Lovell, John Glenn, and to be living in the same town as they did—it means a lot. To all of us."

She gives me that soft head tilt and pleasant smirk that you get when the other person starts to see you as some teddy bear. *Adorable*, I see her thinking. I groan internally.

I'm not sure what else to say, but I'm stopped short when I notice someone approaching the cameras from the corner of my eye. As her shoes clack on the sidewalk, her lavender sun dress billows in the soft breeze. It's Grace Tucker. She takes off her sunglasses, and even I'm a little starstruck. She turns to the camera.

"Grace, hello! What do you think about—"

Grace cuts in. "We're all so thrilled to have the Lewis

family joining us. We'd say more, but I'm too excited to introduce my family to them, and I can't wait any longer. 'Bye, now!"

I wave goodbye, and Grace reaches for my arm.

"You're welcome down at the station anytime, Cal!" the reporter calls after me. "Remember, K-H-O-U!"

I let Grace guide me back into the house. I stop short at the door when I hear the yelling. We make eye contact, and I don't want this to ruin her first impression, so I say:

"Sorry, we didn't realize they'd be on us like that. It really surprised them."

She nods and smiles and we pretend she's accepting my words at face value, but then I step inside and announce over Dad: "We've got a visitor!"

Silence.

Recognition.

Awkwardness.

I see Dad go through these phases like they were the five stages of grief. That's two embarrassments for him today. I wish I could tell him that it's not my fault the cameras panned to me. That I didn't want him to have to share the attention. I only wanted to tell my story, and not let some contract he signed get in the way of that.

"Grace. Or, um, Mrs. Tucker." My dad crosses the floor to the doorway and offers his hand for her to shake. "It's nice to meet you."

"Same, same. And please, just call me Grace." She takes a look around the house, and she runs her finger across a recently polished vintage typewriter. "How do you like the decor here? It takes a while to get used to, but it really is beautiful. Anyway, it's a pleasure to meet you all."

"It's, well, better than I could have imagined." Dad gestures to us, briefly. "This is Becca, my wife, and Cal, my son."

"Becca," she repeats. Then she turns to me and smiles. "And I actually know this one. My daughter Kat has been a follower of yours for years now. I heard they were bringing your family up here, but I didn't know it would be today. Lucky that Kat saw your video and told me. I came as quickly as I could." She turns to my parents. "The—for lack of a better term—paparazzi can be hell here."

Dad glares at me. "You posted a video? Is that why—why they knew we were here? You know the rules about that."

"I decided to sidestep the rules," I say weakly. My cheeks flush, and I suddenly realize there are three pairs of eyes aimed right at me, judging me. I want to take a walk, but I can't even escape with all the news vans out there. Maybe I can outrun them. "But I can fix this. Let me go out and see if they're still here. S-sorry."

As I'm leaving, I hear Grace warn me not to go outside, but I don't care, and my speechless parents don't protest. I can't be in this house anymore.

I know I can fix this, even if I'm not sure how just yet.

When I open the door, I'm struck by the media circus in front of our place. The number of cars, vans, cameras, and reporters has tripled. I freeze as they all point their cameras at me, but a thrill pumps through my veins. It's the same rush I feel when I give my reports, but it feels bigger somehow. Why would America care about *me*? Just because I'm the newest character on this obscene reality show? Because my dad has a one-in-four shot at making it on Mars?

It doesn't make sense.

"Hey, um, Cal?" a voice calls out from next door.

A second person's gasp falls out behind him. "Oh my god, it's really him."

My cheeks flush as I turn and see the two teens from the Tucker family portrait staring at me. Both of them are immaculate and prepared for this life, with easy smiles and a confident gait. They're wearing pressed clothes, dressed up a little too much for school.

"I'm Leon," the guy says, extending a hand. His posture is too tight, his expression too practiced. "It's nice to meet you."

His voice is a little loud, and I guess it's so the microphones pick it up. It makes me cringe, but when you're standing in front of perfection—even when you look like a sweaty mess who hasn't showered in days—you just have to do your best to fit in.

"Good to meet you too."

An uncomfortable pause lingers between us. We're making eye contact, and I'm so lost in his gaze I almost forget about the hundred thousand people who will be watching this interaction.

"We came as soon as we heard," the girl says. "I'm Katherine, a pleasure to meet you."

Though there are three of us, they've naturally angled their bodies out in a way that makes them look like they're in a stage performance—all our bodies tilt toward the cameras.

In this moment, I wonder how many rounds of media training they had to go through to act like this. So composed and polished next to each other.

My smile starts to fade, as these don't seem like the people I want to be friends with.

The thrill's long gone now, and all that's left is this awkward energy.

"Right," I say. "So we've all met."

Silence cuts through us for a split second longer, until Leon bursts with laughter. His sister and I follow closely behind, and for one brief second, Leon hunches over and puts his hand on my shoulder. I feel his grip, even after his hand leaves my body, and despite the heat, a chill goes straight down my back.

"Sorry," he whispers. "I know it's awkward with all the cameras."

"Anyway," Kat says, regaining some of her composure. Her voice is soft, like she's no longer performing for an audience. "The van at ten-o'-clock? That's StarWatch. And they're going to insist on interviewing the family."

StarWatch is here. It takes a while for it to settle in. Will their cameras be on me? How is Mom going to handle the constant attention? How much will it take for Dad's composure to break?

"And we were thinking," Leon says, "there's a path that goes between our houses that the reporters can't use. We can sneak away and hide out in the playground just off the trail. That is, unless you want to be subjected to StarWatch on your first day here . . ."

I look back and forth, and my head starts shaking a clear no without my brain giving the command. The only way I can fix this and give the focus back to my dad is by leaving.

Okay, and partially it's just that I want out of here as soon as humanly possible.

"Is Mom in there?" Katherine asks, and I nod. "You two go around back. I'm going to let her know what's going on."

In a blink, she's gone, and I'm following Leon around the side of my house. His profile catches in the sun, and I wonder how he's not sweating at all. He's got these high cheekbones and bright eyes, where he could smile without even moving his lips.

"I'm Cal," I say. "I know we did this already, but I think we need a do-over. Because that was . . . weird."

"Leon." He leads me down a grassy slope and to a path lined with trees. It's not like the old woods you see in the parks in New York, but it's equally manicured.

We follow the path until we come to a little swing set. He veers off and jumps into a swing, immediately kicking off and soaring high. I sit in the other and rock back and forth slowly.

"Your mom kind of saved me from the reporters." I kick some of the dirt beneath my shoes. "It's a lot to handle."

"I get that. People are obsessed with us now. It's like Star-Watch makes our lives seem so dramatic—well, our parents' lives. They usually stay out of *our* way."

I chuckle. "Maybe that's why they didn't seem so interested in my dad. I think his chances of getting on the first mission are low."

"Why do you say that?"

"He was a pilot for Delta."

I say that, like I always do, but Leon just stares at me.

"Is that so bad?" he asks.

"It's not bad, it's just . . . everyone here is so cool. My dad's smart, sure, but he only knows how to fly a plane."

He laughs and slaps at the chains above my seat. I twist back and forth.

"Only knows how to fly a plane. So, I'm guessing it takes a lot to impress you?"

I pause, because even though I'm having a good time, I want to ask him if he really does buy into all this. The veneer cracked a bit when he laughed and when he kicked up on the swing set, but . . . the covers, the interviews, the relocation, the decor. How can he just be okay with it, when I'm all scrambled up?

Or maybe I'm all scrambled up because I might be okay with it too.

"There you guys are." Katherine bounds toward us and sticks out her hand. "Okay, wow, I'm Kat, and I watch your feed religiously."

I pull back, just slightly, then shake her hand.

"That was creepy," she says. "I mean, your show and the Cal Letter are the only ways I get my news. I started watching when you covered the election, because you were the only news-ish person who didn't make me want to punch them with their analysis."

"Oh, thank you. I don't . . . think anyone's ever said something so nice," I say with a smirk.

She shakes her head. "I swear, I'll stop fangirling soon. Just. Seriously, you're great. Your interview with the woman who developed FlashFame was my favorite, by far. I wanted to *be* her."

I twist my swing and my gaze meets Leon's. "No raving compliments from you?" I smirk, and he busts out laughing.

"You caught me—see, I'm the opposite. I just can't stand your political analysis or whatever." He rolls his eyes. "Joking. I've seen your videos, but only over Kat's shoulder."

"Hmm, no feedback," I say. "You're not very helpful."

Katherine leans in, reducing her voice to a whisper. "The only feedback I ever hear is that he thinks you're super cute."

I pull back and almost fall out of my swing, while Leon makes a guttural gasp that makes Katherine jump back in laughter. His composure's shattered, and I bet he'd flip if the cameras were on him now.

"Kat, what the hell?"

She smiles broadly at this. "So you have two fans, is what I'm trying to say."

"This is a lot of information," I say. I look between the two of them, and Katherine starts walking backward, away from our house.

"Anyway, the reporters should be giving up soon now that StarWatch has got a grip on the situation," Katherine says. "There's a party Friday night, at our place, and Mom is going to invite your parents. You should come, if they even give you a choice in the matter. You'll meet some of the other astronauts, and once you get incredibly bored of the science talk, you can find us at the back of the house with a bottle of champagne we've lifted from the stock."

"Kat!" Leon snaps.

I nearly gasp—the prim, poised, and always proper Tucker kids. I imagine them in a backyard, sneaking out a bottle of champagne and staring into the sky. It reminds me of summer nights with Deb on the fire escape, with whatever we could lift from our parents' alcohol stock—usually craft beers (meh), red wine (double meh), or scotch (quadruple meh, but wow it works fast).

"Oh, calm down—Cal's cool!" Kat does a quick, excited jump as she clasps her hands together. "These parties get boring *fast* without any other teens around. The astronauts all have young kids. We only come because, well, we live there."

I imagine how annoying it would be to be stuck around a bunch of drunk adults.

"I can see why you would turn to champagne to fix your boredom," I say with a laugh.

"Oh, please," she replies, "we end up pouring half of it out."

"Your mom won't notice a bottle missing?" I ask.

They both pause to consider me, and by the smirk on my face, they must be able to tell that I'm far more entertained by than appalled by their champagne heist.

"You'll understand when you get to the party," Leon replies. I stand and dust myself off. I think about her words and sneak a glance at Leon before he can look at me. I think he's cute too. Really cute. "See you soon, I hope?"

His gaze meets mine, and an ache pulls at my chest, reminding me of Jeremy, of Deb. Of crushes, and of falling.

Shooting Stars
Season 2; Episode 6

EXCLUSIVE INTERVIEW: Our producers meet Calvin Lewis Sr., the final astronaut picked for the Orpheus missions. He takes a break from unpacking and starting a new life in Clear Lake, Texas, and joins astronaut Grace Tucker to chat with us about the space program, Calvin's chances of making it to Mars, and the announcement that took us all by surprise. (New episode airs 6/10/2020)

"Welcome to a new, and exciting—albeit rushed—*Shooting Stars* interview. I'm your host, Josh Farrow, and I am enthused to be bringing an exclusive interview to you with the final astronaut chosen for the Orpheus missions. And here he is: Calvin Lewis, along with a soon-to-be close colleague, Grace Tucker. Welcome to Clear Lake, Calvin."

"Well, um, thank you! Hope you don't mind the boxes; we kind of just got here a couple hours ago."

"I assure you our viewers are not bothered by that. They're interested in Calvin Lewis—Calvin Lewis *Sr.*, I should say. Many of our viewers, of course, know all about Cal Junior. I must say, we were taken aback by his surprise announcement today."

"I think we were all a little caught off guard by that. Look, we're really sorry about—"

"We're so happy to have Calvin on board at NASA. I know how hard it was for my family to adjust—pulling Kat and Leon out of school, Tony's job transition. We want to make sure they have a smooth, *conflict-free* transition, don't you agree, Josh?"

"Right, of course. Now, I'll be honest with you, I usually go into these interviews much more prepared, but I've barely had time to review the press packet. So why don't you talk to us about your experience. I see you most recently worked as a commercial pilot with Delta, is that right?"

"Yes, I flew for Delta for about a decade, but I started in the air force—that's where I met my lovely wife, Becca. She was working in cybersecurity, so our jobs never overlapped. But we happened to cross paths, and, you know, sparks flew."

"Fascinating. You know what I love most about interviews? It's digging in and finding all the fascinating pieces of a person the world doesn't get to see. And hopefully we'll see that side later, but I am curious . . . what do you think your specialization is here? What do *you* bring here that no one else does?"

"Oh, wow. That's a big question. I feel like I'm in the job interview again, only there's literally a spotlight on me now. Hah."

"Josh? If you don't mind, I wanted to cut in."

"Of course, Grace. Go ahead."

"We were just discussing our experience, and I have to tell you—he's genuinely knowledgeable and passionate about NASA, and I can't wait to have him in flight simulations with us. During his time at Delta, he trained more pilots there than anyone else in the entire company. You know when you meet someone and automatically know they'll go above and beyond to reach any goal? I haven't seen that kind of determination around here since I met Mark Bannon! But there's a personal connection too. Calvin, why don't you tell them about when you first discovered you wanted to be an astronaut?"

"Oh, sure. It's a simple story, really. When I was ten or so, I watched this documentary on Apollo 11. Everyone knows Neil Armstrong, and we all know the glory those astronauts received, but I remember thinking of how innovative we must have been. They said the RAM, the memory, for the guidance computer matched that of a digital watch—and that was back in the early nineties, way before smart watches. I looked down at my own watch, which could barely do anything but blink and beep at me. And it hit me that . . . somewhere at the intersection of sheer human intelligence and determination—and a little bullheaded bravery—we made it to the moon. I can't think of anything more inspiring. Nothing gives me more faith in humanity than seeing something like this come together. So, yes, I bring a lifetime of experience and enthusiasm, but I also bring a deep appreciation of the history and tenacity that made NASA what it is today."

CHAPTER 7

Dad mutes the television.

"So as you see, you missed a great interview."

It's sarcasm. And I deserve it. We watch the show in its entirety, which starts out with a surprisingly in-depth look at all the new astronauts who have been brought on. The final astronaut, my dad, was barely covered.

"They didn't talk about you much, but that's probably because they knew you had that interview with Grace," Mom offers.

He laughs. "I enjoy your optimism, but it's pretty clear that Josh guy hates me. He said, maybe, three words to me?"

"He said way more than that, Calvin." She pauses to massage her temples. "Cal, he came in pretty quickly after you left with the Tucker kids. He was clearly pissed, but he thawed as soon as your dad told that story. Your dad's got a little bit of that charm left in him."

Mom flicks Dad's ear playfully.

"Ew, guys. And I've told you, I'm sorry. I was just tired and grumpy. I didn't think about what would happen. And really? Screw Josh Farrow. He just tried to make you look like a fool on camera, and you knocked that question out of the park."

"Thankfully Grace was there to lob me that softball of a question," Dad says. "She was actually very nice to us, don't you think?"

Mom sighs, kind of wistfully. "I don't know how she does it. As soon as you left, she snapped into media-training mode. She taught us so much in so little time. Thank god they didn't want to see me, though. I was a mess."

"They will someday." My voice is soft, but it still sucks the joy out of the room. "They're going to be everywhere we go for the foreseeable future. Every public event. Every party. Was Josh Farrow really that angry?"

"He was," Dad says. "About time someone wiped that smug look off his face."

It breaks the tension in the room, momentarily, even though we know we're not out of the woods yet. It's day one, and we've already angered the wrong people. But for once, our family is gelling, and maybe that's because we're in this together. We don't have any distractions—my only real friend is thousands of miles away, and I still haven't unpacked my things, so I can't even escape into my cassette collection.

As I go to my empty room, I feel oddly free. The coils of tension in my back have snapped, my breaths are stronger, deeper. I slide under the sheets and squeeze my blanket. The heaviness of the day finally starts to set in as I plug in my phone.

But just before I set my phone down, I see a new email in my "professional" inbox—the one I keep public so my fans and haters don't clog up my personal email. One look at the subject line, and all the anxiety sucks back up into me, pulling my muscles taut and pushing an ache through my nervous system.

StarWatch Media LLC: Letter of Cease & Desist for Calvin Lewis Jr.

"Fuck," I announce to the empty room.

— —— —

"I'm getting sued," I tell Deb approximately two milliseconds after she answers the phone. "I'm getting sued!"

"It's seven thirty. In the morning." She's panting. "What is wrong with you? I closed last night."

"Oh, you closed a Paper Source in Park Slope? When? At, like, eight thirty?"

"Nine, but I'm still tired. Damn."

There's a pause on the line, and it hits me that just because I've been up half the night panicking and rereading the email I got doesn't mean seven a.m. phone calls are appropriate. But *I'm getting sued!*

"Elaborate. Please." Deb still sounds mildly irritated, but she's decided to put up with me, and I love her for it.

"I got an email from StarWatch's lawyers last night. I'll spare you the legalese, but it basically means if I make another video, they're going to pursue legal action. Their lawyer has an official letterhead and everything!"

She sighs. "So, you're not getting sued."

"Well, not yet, but—"

"You aren't being sued. You're being threatened. Just lie low for a bit and have your parents look it over. Maybe they won't even sue—I mean, that wouldn't look good, would it? A big media company picking on a teen FlashFamer like that?"

I consider her appeal. It makes sense, but how can I risk that? And the cease-and-desist letter was so broad as to include *ANY* video with me in it, regardless of location. In one minute, my career just vanished before my eyes.

"I can't risk streaming anything now. I knew they were pissed, but I didn't think they'd do something like this. I've got all this nervous energy now, and I can't sleep, and I don't know what to do."

"Take a run?"

We both laugh.

"No, seriously," I say, still chuckling at the prospect of physical activity, especially in this heat wave.

"I don't know. But I wouldn't panic. You just got on their radar, and they want to scare you away. And Calvin?"

"Yes?"

"Never call me this early. Ever again."

I sigh. "Understood."

After I hang up, I pull up the map on my phone. There's not much around me, and I don't feel like exploring the city with our junker of a car today. I'm stuck with only one option—the Starbucks half a mile away.

So I put on a deep-cut tank, mesh shorts, running shoes, and sunglasses. It's a quick ath*leisure* look, and it'll have to do. I step outside, and the refreshing air of an early summer morning hits me. The humidity seems to have disappeared, dew's still on the grass, and things feel better already.

While I'm walking, I feel myself picking up the pace to match my "city walking" style, but here . . . there's nowhere to be, I have all the time in the world, and best of all, there are no tourists who need to be shoved out of the way. Win/win/win.

So I slow my pace and read through the email in my mind. The letterhead was fancy, but was it there just to look scary? And the verbiage they used to explain what rule I broke, it didn't even apply to me. The only thing I signed was a release form saying that StarWatch could post any videos or photos taken of me—that was required of everyone.

"Hiya, friend!" someone shouts from the other side of the street. "Welcome to the neighborhood."

It's Stephanie Jonasson, another of the candidates for the Orpheus V mission. I can't remember what she does, but I know it has nothing to do with the actual navigation, so she's not in the same field as Dad and Grace are.

"Hi, Stephanie, right?"

"Yep. And this is Tag," she says, pointing down to her miniature Pomeranian, who is currently pawing my leg. "Say hi to Cal, Tag."

I bend down to pet the tiny dog. "Oh, right. I've seen Tag before—they did that Animal Planet documentary on him, right?"

"Oh boy, you've got a fan!" she says to Tag.

It's weird when people talk to their dogs as if they're humans, but I don't say anything. The documentary comes back to me—it was a miniseries on famous pets, and an abnormally large amount of time was spent on Tag the Pomeranian.

"Can I ask you . . . did StarWatch have any problems with the documentary? I know Animal Planet filmed on your property."

She laughs. "They have a problem with everything. But yes, I was forbidden from appearing in the documentary, my voice or face. They have a strict policy with the astronauts."

"With just the astronauts? I thought the families couldn't join either."

"Well, they still threw a fit, but my wife Heather's a lawyer. She pushed back until they eventually gave up, which is why she got to be in the documentary with our little boy here." She pauses, and I see understanding dawn on her face. "Oh, let me guess, they're not too happy about your announcement? I watched *Shooting Stars* last night and almost died when that jerk tried to show your dad up. But I was in tears by the end of it—I really can't wait to meet your dad. He seems like a genuine guy."

"He is." I smile, and the smile lingers for a bit as I bend down to give Tag a few more scratches.

"StarWatch is, let's say . . . a necessary evil. They make us look good, and they bring a lot of interest into the program. It's easier to get projects funded by the government when a subset of the country passionately cares." She laughs. "I mean, sure, I wish America cared for better reasons, but I won't complain. Don't worry too much about StarWatch. Their bark is worse than their bite."

We part ways, and I'm still a little terrified, but there's this energy pulsing through my veins. It's the same one I felt earlier as I leaned against the dresser. Rebellion. If it worked with Heather Jonasson, it'd work for me. It *will* work for me.

At least, I hope it will.

With a surge of inner strength, I pull out my phone and open the FlashFame app. Sure, no one else is going to be up now, but I have to document this so people can watch it later. As I look into the front-facing camera, a confident grin hits my face.

"Good morning! If you aren't already subscribed to the Cal Letter, you're going to want to fix that now, because tonight I'm going to send you the full text of my cease-and-desist letter from StarWatch. Yeah, that's right. StarWatch is threatening to sue me, of all people, but unfortunately for them, I didn't sign any nondisclosure agreement." I shake my head. "This mission's screwed up my life enough as it is, and I'm not going to let a jerk with fancy letterhead keep me from sharing the truth with you. Keep an eye out for more updates soon, and if you're in the mood for passive-aggressive statements about me, I'd keep your television set to the StarWatch network—they don't take 'no' very well."

CHAPTER 8

While I'm no stranger to mild fame, I've never seen myself on the news doing something as innocuous as getting Starbucks or shopping at The Container Store. *The Container Store!*

Only a handful of days have passed since I called out Star-Watch, and since then, it's like a target's on my back. My daily Starbucks runs have been documented everywhere from Houston's eleven p.m. news to *Teen Vogue,* and every site has their own version of the "drama" my rebellion has brought to Clear Lake.

The real drama's that every pic they snap shows me in a daze, with my hair eight kinds of fucked up. It's not a good look for me. Sure, I'm being vain, but I've got a brand to protect.

An equally bad look for me? Bright yellow gloves, dirt-stained jeans, and sweat dripping off my face. The hand shovel in my grip shrieks with strain every time I shove it into the ground, and I don't blame it.

This is not my idea of a great Wednesday.

Kat walks toward my section of the community garden, and I guess she admires my work by the way she stares at it.

"Is this the pepper patch?" She kneels to get to my eye level, then jumps back. "Are . . . you okay? You look like you're struggling."

I wipe sweat off my brow with an equally sweaty forearm. "Gardening isn't my favorite activity."

"Oh, I see that." She fails to stifle a laugh. "If it makes you feel better, Mrs. Bannon has Leon checking the melon leaves for fungus or something."

I plant another pepper seedling—a tiny, insignificant little patch of leaves—and try to knock the dirt off my gloves by clapping. It doesn't work.

"Leon's here?" I ask, trying to sound three parts nonchalant and one part eager. I think it comes out the other way. "I wanted to thank him—well, you both—again for stepping in and sneaking me away from the reporters last week."

"Don't worry about it. And, yeah, I'll show you where he is." Kat pats the dirt around the last seedling I planted. She looks down the line of tiny leaves, hesitating, before taking my shovel. "Once we fix this. Sorry, these plants are too close. At least, based on what Mrs. Bannon told me when she asked me to come check on you."

"Not a chance. I followed instructions exactly," I say. Kat's gaze presses into me, and I give in. "Okay, there's a small chance I wasn't listening to *all* the details."

"It's fine, I'll just take out every other one and plant it farther down the line." She looks to me for confirmation, but I just shrug. "Sorry, I've been taking this online coding class, and I think it's spilling into my real life. Like I'm troubleshooting your gardening mishaps or something."

Laughing, I dig in with my hands and help Kat fix my mistake, while also trying not to damage any of the seedlings.

"I didn't know you code," I say. "I don't know why I would have known that, but still. My mom's a developer. If you need any help, I'm sure she'd be up for it."

"Oh, I will definitely talk to her about it. Mom and Dad are no help when it comes to this stuff. I've been trying to start slow, but I have all these projects I want to try out. I write down ideas when they come to me . . . just have to wait until I'm actually good enough to code them."

The heat is sweltering, but a few clouds have gone by. Between that and conversing with someone who's not barking instructions at me, I'm a little less crabby.

A little.

"So, do you do this often?" I ask, gesturing to the infant peppers. "Dad never told me volunteering at the community garden was a big thing for the astronaut families."

"Yeah, they don't tell you about that when you sign up," she says with a laugh. "But I think it's great. Really. I mean, the parsnips I planted a few months ago should be ready to harvest at any time now, and that's"—she hesitates—"not . . . even a good vegetable. Damn, you're right, this sucks."

"I'm going to take a break," I say. "If anyone asks, say I'm confirming the proper seedling spacing or something—it'll buy me ten minutes at least. I just need a breather."

If she's figured out I want to *also* stumble upon Leon's fungus search—which sounds gross, but I'm sure he could even make fungus look cute—she doesn't let on about it.

"A break sounds good. I might go look for your mom. I'm really curious what coding languages she uses," she says before we part.

The park is expansive by Clear Lake standards—at least the length of a couple of football fields. Apparently, they rent out small patches for personal use, and the crops from the bigger gardens go to the community food bank.

I come up to a sprawling patch of vines, and my gaze falls across the guy who's closely inspecting each leaf. Leon. My heart does an extra pound for good measure, as if I wasn't already aware of my feelings.

When I get to him, I give my mouth the command to speak, but nothing comes out. I'm just standing there, with the smile on my face growing by the second, like a creep. When he looks up at me, all disheveled and covered in dirt, I doubt I'll ever be able to speak again.

Thankfully, I find the words.

"How's the fungus?"

They're not the best words, but they're words nonetheless. My cheeks flush with heat.

"No sign of it yet," he says, "but Mara is having me check again. She thinks the 'cold spell' last week brought the soil temperatures down."

"Cold spell?" My laugh is too loud, too awkward. "What'd you get down to—seventy?"

"Seventy-five, maybe?"

Leon stands, and for a second, we just smile at each other. There's a peace in being alone with him, even when we're not saying much. The nuanced expressions, the rising pulse rate, all bring a rush, a high all over my body.

But the line between sweet and creepy is especially thin when crushes are concerned, and there's only so long two people can stand in silence before it gets weird.

"You look nice," I say.

". . . How is that possible?"

"I don't know. Dirt suits you? I have a thing for gardeners?" I pause. "I'm awful at this."

"You're fine." With a soft quirk of a smile, he points to a shaded spot under a tree, and we take seats in the grass as he pulls out a water bottle. He offers it to me, and I take a sip of the cool water. But it doesn't cool me off. It doesn't calm me down.

"We didn't really get to talk earlier," he says. "It's kind of weird getting to know someone who you only know vaguely from the internet. I mean, my sister probably knows every detail about you."

"Eh," I grunt, "she only knows a specific part of me. I give my personal updates sometimes, but I really care about my reporting. Either way, the guy on the screen is just . . . a version of me. The version I want people to see. A brand, almost."

I want him to see all of me.

"That's got to be hard," he says.

"It's hard to always be *on*. I always feel pressured to have the cheekiest take on an issue, or to know every cool thing happening in the city. It's a lot of work to keep this up, and I think, because it's 'just social media,' people don't see that."

He starts to reply, but I'm distracted by the vibration in my pocket. When I pull the phone out, I gasp. "*Shit.*"

"What is it?" Leon asks. "Everything okay?"

"I . . . I had an internship for BuzzFeed—to cover local events in New York and boost their video content. It was going to be my first real chance to break into the business. Do something close to what I really want to do."

"It . . . *was*?"

"Obviously, coming to Texas wasn't in my plan at that point. My friend Deb convinced me to email them to see if they'd consider a remote internship or some other collaboration. I was desperate, so I did, and . . . now I'm too scared to read the response."

He inches closer to me, and the place where his arm meets mine shoots electric currents through my body. As he leans closer, I smell the comforting aroma of earth and spice. Whether it's his deodorant or cologne cutting through the smell of the park, I don't know. What I *do* know is, I'm so caught up in the scent, my heart is struggling to keep the blood pumping through my body right now.

"Come on, read it. What'd they say?" he asks, his voice an excited whisper.

I clench my phone, still holding it facedown. I am not ready for this. Not here, not now. But with Leon next to me, I find the courage to turn over my phone and open the email.

Hey Cal—I talked it over with my boss, and we definitely want to work on something in the future, but unfortunately—

That's all I allow myself to read. I stand up, wanting to duck out somewhere. But there's nowhere to go. Cameras fill the exits, astronauts and their families prowl the gardens . . . this is as alone as I'm going to get.

"I'm so sorry, Cal." Leon pulls me toward him and puts an arm around me—just quick enough for his scent to fill my lungs, but not long enough for me to come to my senses and hug back.

"It's fine. It's fine," I say, even though it's not fine. "I knew this would happen, I just didn't expect it to sting so much."

"You'll find something else."

"But this is what I wanted. This was my plan, my way in."

His hand slides down my arm, gently but deliberately, and I feel the support pouring out from him. "Then just come up with a new plan."

I laugh, because that's one thousand times easier said than done. After a few breaths, I start to believe it, though. There are other ways—I just have to figure them out. This is a minor setback. I suck in a breath and hold it in my chest, steeling my core.

"I'm still really bummed," I say, releasing the breath, along with my confidence.

He places an arm on my back and leads me back toward the gardens. We have been gone for a while, and they're bound to notice if we don't come back soon. Plus, they seem to be setting up a stage for an impromptu press conference.

Leon clears his throat, dropping his palm from my back. "Can I ask you something?"

"What do you want to know?" I ask. "I'm an open book. Kind of."

He laughs and scrunches his eyebrows to look like he's deep in thought. "So . . . is that why you do it? The app and the fame?"

"I want to be a reporter." He just keeps his eyes on me, and the words fall out. "But it's more than that. I *am* a reporter now, however amateur it might seem. I want to make a name for myself. I want the mainstream media to know that this new form of reporting matters, and that it can make a difference."

"Those sound like good reasons."

"I guess I just like telling a story. I like challenging people's thoughts, starting conversations. And, I don't know . . . I kind of like when people listen."

"Wow . . . it must feel good to know exactly what you want." He rubs his shoulder in an awkward, almost self-conscious fashion. "That's got to be validating, though. It's like you have all this power. People really care. They listen to you."

He won't make eye contact with me now, and I see the boy in the magazine photo again with his distant stare, his sullen expression. I wonder what I did, or what I said, to make this version of him come out. I want to make him feel better, but I don't know what he needs.

I reach out to him, but a shrill screech comes from the amps that circle the rickety stage set up in the center of the park. Our attentions shift. Unresolved tension balls in my chest.

The moment's passed.

After a quick sound check, and a few posed shots for the local news photographers, astronaut behemoth Mark Bannon approaches the stage. At the podium, five or six microphones intertwine, and I assume that's because one is hooked up to the amps around the stage and the rest go to all the local feeds or StarWatch.

"Speaking of damning emails . . . have you heard anything else from StarWatch's lawyers?" Leon asks. "I, uh, noticed you didn't cease . . . or desist."

I chuckle as we both sit cross-legged on the ground. "Nothing yet."

"Are you nervous, though?" Leon's hand reaches out for my elbow for a second, but he pulls it back. Even in this heat, my arm hairs prickle at the phantom sensation. "I would be. StarWatch is . . . well, they have a grip on us in a way that not even the bigger players like CNN or the *New York Times* do."

"A grip?" My voice is thin, the bravado vanishing by the second.

Mark Bannon's amplified voice breaks through our conversation.

"Friends, thank you for being here. And a special thank-you to Mara Bannon, my perfect wife, who somehow has the patience and the energy to coordinate these volunteer days."

There's a chuckle, followed by applause.

Mark clears his throat. "This is a great week for NASA. After five years of searching, the core team of astronauts for the Orpheus project has been assembled. We're finally a complete unit. Now, we still don't know the first six to be scheduled on Orpheus V"—he winks to a camera to his right—"which I know is dirt my friends at StarWatch have been especially eager to uncover. But what we do know is this: in twelve months, six of us are going up into space, and we're not coming back until we touch Martian soil."

Leon scoots closer to me on the ground and nudges me with his elbow. "Get ready—Bannon's a bit of an . . . idealist."

"As we approach, oh, T-minus thirty-one-million seconds until liftoff, it's worth thinking about why we're here. Why we're doing this. Why should *you*"—the way he says "you" makes you feel like he's talking directly to you, to all Americans, and all humanity at the same time—"care?"

Another dramatic pause, and I think I hear Leon snickering beside me.

"Progress. It's another giant leap, yes, but it's more than that—it's about developments in solar energy, medical technology, climate research. Getting humans to Mars to set up the Orpheus Martian Base is the first step to unlocking all these secrets. When we land—I promise you'll all remember where you are on that day for the rest of your lives."

More applause as he gets off the stage, and Mara nearly tackles him as a greeting. I look to Leon, and he's more expressive than I've ever seen him: rolling his eyes, an incredulous look on his face.

Kat returns and sits next to me. "He really knows how to hype up a crowd."

"It's all nonsense," Leon says.

I stay quiet. Truth is, I felt Mark's passion through his speech. My heart's pounding in my chest, and I get that rush. I get the way he tells this story.

Off the podium, Mark and Mara speak to the local news, who can't get enough of the action. When the Bannons hold hands, even I get the urge to go interview them and join the media frenzy.

"I don't know," I say. "I think Mark really believes what he says."

They stay silent, probably because they moved on to another topic while I spaced out. When the Bannons tire of the interview and take their leave, the cameras fan out to get some shots of the other families.

A photographer breaks off to get some candid shots of Mom and Dad at one of the gardens. Leon grabs my shoulder, hard, and I nearly jump—but when I see a StarWatch producer and cameraman hustling toward us, I get why.

We stand and dust ourselves off as the producer gives orders to the cameraman to hold off on recording for a few minutes. She turns to me.

"You're the one with the social media or whatever, right?"

"I . . . guess so?"

She looks so uninterested, I can't tell if she's happy, sad, or has the capacity to feel human emotion at all.

"I'm Kiara. I'm from Brooklyn too."

She doesn't ask for my name, but I guess that's because she knows it, or she doesn't care. Even with her attitude, there's a part of her that comforts me. She's cute and familiar. Like, Brooklyn cute, which makes sense.

She's got ankle boots and tight black jeans. She's got a mostly see-through white blouse on with a plaid shirt overtop. Her unnaturally black hair falls down past her shoulders, and she looks out at me from behind bug-eyed reflective shades. Somehow, she pulls off the look *and* stays sweat-free.

And I can tell her attitude isn't directed at me, or anyone for that matter. She just seems . . . over it. Which I have to admit is also a comforting emotion, given how expressive all these Texans are.

"These events are just the worst, aren't they?" she asks.

"It's my first event," I say with a shrug. "But hopefully I'll be conveniently sick for the next one."

Leon snorts, but says nothing. She chuckles too, and the snarky Brooklyn chord that still strums within me resonates with hers.

Kat moves closer to us just as the camera starts rolling, and the three of us pose awkwardly in front of the camera. After a heavy breath, Kiara's personality flips. She's on. She's smiling, engaged—I'm drowning in her passion.

"I'm here with all three teens of the Orpheus astronauts,

and fast friends since day one: Cal Lewis Jr. and Leon and Katherine Tucker. So, what did you think of that speech?" Kiara asks. "Pretty amazing, huh?" We hesitate. Her eyes narrow, and I see the real Kiara flash behind them.

"Oh, yeah," I say quickly. "Listening to Mark will always get you inspired."

"That's *so* true," she replies. "Do we have any budding astronauts in this group?"

She smiles and tilts her head like we're puppies, which *definitely* isn't condescending or enraging at all—I have to physically strain to hide my disgust on camera.

But even I can't form words. I know these interviews are fake; they're expertly cut to fit whatever narrative they find most entertaining. I've seen it happen so many times, but to watch StarWatch do it in person to me? That's when I start to feel icky.

Thankfully, Kat saves the day. She launches into a seemingly prepared response about how she can see herself becoming one of NASA's programmers someday, but would *never* go up on a spaceship.

She smiles. She giggles. The camera eats it up.

"And Leon, we assume you're not following in your mother's footsteps. Everyone's wondering when we'll learn more about your gymnastics career. Do you think you'll steal the spotlight from your mom and make it on the US Olympic Gymnastics Team?"

"I, um, think that's a bit of a stretch." Leon's posture's changed; he seems unenthused to the point of exhaustion.

"That's a good point. Can't get cocky yet! You've got a long road ahead, and we're so glad there might just be a whole family of American heroes here. And you—"

The camera points to me, and I hesitate.

Kat's all in. Leon's all out.

And I'm somewhere in the in-between.

CHAPTER 9

In the past few hours, I've listened through four of my cassettes, changed into three different outfits, and ignored two heated arguments (Dad unpacked all the kitchen boxes; Mom can't find anything) all to prep for one party. But it's an important one. It's our welcome party.

However, I can't find an outfit to save my life, because Leon texted *"excited to see you tonight :)"* and my body melted into a puddle on the floor, and now I can't even button up a shirt right because my entire body is tingly.

I tear through my closet, knowing nothing I own will impress him.

I pull out my phone, without much thinking, and dial Deb. If anyone can calm me down, it'll be her.

"Astrokid, what's happening?"

I scoff, and consider hanging up on her to prove a point,

but I say, "Shut it. I need your help. Wait, maybe this will work. Or does it look like I'm trying too hard?"

"Do you want me to stay on the line or . . . ?"

"Yes, hold on, sorry."

The outfit I've settled on is simple. Well, it's one of those that isn't really simple, but *looks* effortless. Black jeans over worn boots. A light jean jacket over a tan-and-gray-plaid shirt, over a black tee. Each time I look in the full-length mirror, I feel self-doubt gnaw at me in a way I don't usually experience. Is this right? Is this *too* Brooklyn? I already ditched the John Mayer hat and infinity scarf—because let's be honest, Clear Lake ain't ready for that.

"Sure, okay, whatever, let me drop everything," she says.

"What could you possibly be doing right now?"

The silence on the other end is palpable, and I realize I'm being pretty rude. I've always thought of Deb as mine, as in, you never had to make plans with her because she was always free (and vice versa).

"Okay, I'm being rude but I'm also freaked. We have our first party tonight. Like, with all the astronauts. StarWatch will be there."

"Have they said anything about the cease and desist?" she asks.

"Not yet," I say. "But I know they will soon. My videos have been getting a lot of traction lately."

"Yeah, I've already seen you on the news twice since you moved. This has been an eventful week."

"Exactly. Plus, I'm doubly freaking out because Leon Tucker

said I was cute, and I also think he is cute, and it's not like I can run to my parents and talk about this because, as you can probably hear, they are always shouting about something."

"If you really wanted me just to say everything's going to be fine and you'll be great, we could have done this over text."

Her voice is bitter, and it reminds me of the few times we passed each other in the stairwell or saw each other in school after I broke up with her. But just as our relationship was inevitable—she was the literal girl next door, with the wit and charm to make anyone want to be around her—so too was the rebirth of our friendship.

Our dating relationship was easy, until it wasn't, for me at least. But our friendship always seemed to transcend our petty fights or obnoxious habits.

"I'm . . . sorry?" I say.

A sigh from the other end. "Fine, sorry. Guess it was my turn to be an ass. I just have a feeling this is going to be one of those catch-up sessions where you talk the whole time and then say 'I gotta go' and dash when I have things to tell you too."

"That's not true," I say before glancing at the clock. "Shit, well . . ."

"You actually do have to go, don't you?"

"The party started five minutes ago. I just don't know how fashionably late we're going to be." I clear my throat. "I'll call you later, okay? Maybe not tonight, but soon."

"Fine, fine." A beat. "And Cal?"

"Yeah?"

"Everything's going to be fine and you'll be great. You can text me a picture of your outfit if you want me to approve it, which I will, immediately. Just call me later, okay?"

"Okay. Thanks." I take a long breath and let it hiss out of my teeth.

"Love you," she says.

"I know."

— — —

We drive up to the party at eight fifteen, though if the party is as champagne-fueled as I've been led to believe, we will be walking back.

I pause inside the doorway, and my eyes widen at the sight. The walls are all wood with teal and gold details. The glassware is out, dozens of champagne glasses—bright, sparkling ones like the expensive crystal flutes my parents bring out every year on their anniversary. Copper serving trays are being passed around, with deviled eggs and other more questionable meat appetizers.

To the side, taking up an entire kitchen island, are the bottles of champagne sitting in a copper tub full of ice. Leon and Kat were right: no one would notice a bottle—or ten—missing from this supply.

Everyone's dressed up in their own interpretation of the term. From air force uniforms to sleek dresses, to bow ties and blazers over jeans. Glasses clink; the scent of vanilla candles fills the space between the tightly packed bodies.

I navigate around the pockets of chatting astronauts, their families, and media types. I can't discern the music that plays, but the strumming of a rhythmic guitar floods the room. It's coming from all around—the record player's hooked up to a surround sound speaker system. It's a heavy-handed metaphor for the whole night, but it works.

When I turn back, my dad comes through the door and freezes. "This is just like . . . oh my god."

Tears start forming in his eyes, but he rubs his eyes quickly to shrug it off. We're all dazzled, but thankfully everyone's huddled in the kitchen, and they haven't really paid attention to us.

"You remember those *Life* magazines I've showed you?" Dad asks. "With the astronaut parties with the families? This is it. It's real." He clears his throat as a tear rolls down his cheek. Mom puts a hand on his back.

I'm feeling something here. Some bizarre nostalgia for an era that came half a century before my existence.

It's all beautiful. And overwhelming.

Until I hear the whisper-yelled commands of someone to my right. "Closer," the voice says. "Did you get the tear?"

In the corner of the room, Kiara's got her sights set on me and my dad, while Josh Farrow—"the face of *Shooting Stars*"—stands next to her with a clipboard, directing her every move.

Dad doesn't notice, but just being in the same room as Star-Watch makes me uncomfortable, so I slip away as Mom introduces herself to the families who were lucky enough to get out of gardening duty. As I reach the kitchen, Kat runs up and gives me a big hug. I did not think we were hugging friends. Or, maybe hugs are just a Texas thing.

She pulls out a Tupperware stocked with deviled eggs and starts placing them on the tray.

"I made these, so you better like 'em."

"Why are they . . . green?"

She laughs. "Fair question. I add avocado to them. It's my secret ingredient, though I guess when it completely changes the color it's not so secret."

"No, not exactly."

I take one anyway, thankful there's at least one meatless thing I can eat here. I scan the crowd, and my chest aches as I look for Leon. This isn't a totally new feeling for me. There were sparks with Deb once. And something with Jeremy too.

But something about this feels different. Deb was my best friend, and we just fell into a comfortable relationship. Jeremy was new and exciting, and he was there as I took a self-guided tour of my own queerness—something I may never fully find the right label for.

But with Leon, the burning in my chest has never been so perfectly bright. So clear. It's like when I spend hours picking background colors for the teaser images before my shows—when I hit that perfect shade of bluish-green, and I could never describe *why* it's perfect, but it just is.

With my crush on Leon, it so clearly *is* right.

Every time I close my eyes and let my mind drift for too

long, I see his face giving that side-eye smirk with those perfect teeth. Those teeth that rarely see the camera—back at the swings, it felt like he'd stocked up all his smiles for me, for that moment.

And something else—no, not his ridiculously sculpted gymnastics muscles—draws me to him. It's the hesitant quality that the camera *does* get to see. The side I saw in the gardens. Everyone else here is so sure of themselves, so overconfident. But he's different. Real.

I'm jerked out of my daydreaming by a palm on my back. I turn to see a woman in a dark blue blazer, and I'm caught off guard by her intense body language. She's too close for comfort, and now her hand's outstretched, and I wonder if my face reflects my shock.

"Donna Szleifer," the woman says. "I'm NASA's deputy social media manager, and this is Todd Collins, who directs our public affairs team."

She pulls another suit next to her, and the man in it smiles briefly.

"Hi," I say. Because I have no other words to say to these people right now. Because I should not be the one interacting with NASA staff. "I'm Cal."

"We were surprised to see that you broke the news," Todd says.

"But we shared your clip right away on Twitter and Facebook," Donna says, "and tied it in with our press releases, and it's gotten a lot of attention, which is great. Just great."

I reach behind my head and rub my neck, just to give my

hands something to do. My cheeks grow warm, and my shoulders form into a shrug.

"Yeah, look, I'm sorry abo—"

"Calvin Lewis," Dad cuts in, and appears beside me, and I sigh as I'm saved from a potentially awkward conversation.

"Rebecca Lewis. But you can call me Becca," my mother says and offers her hand. Her shyness is in full force, and she clutches her purse to her body as if someone here was going to snatch it from her. But she's taking the lead in introducing herself. She's putting herself out there. She's really trying. Either that or she's stocking up on stories to tell her therapist.

Out the corner of my eye, I see Kat by the back door. It's a sliding glass door that's propped open, though no lights or anything seem to be on. She nods toward the door and widens her eyes to give me the hint.

I slip out of the conversation, remembering the promise of champagne and time with Leon and Kat. Thankfully, it's not too hard to go unnoticed.

But then I feel a presence behind me, a mammoth one, and it sends chills all over my body. The kind of chills that spike at your neck and raise hairs you didn't even know you had, then rush down your back in shuddered pulses.

Craning my neck, I recognize the star of the astronauts' volunteer day: Mark Bannon. Up close, it becomes even clearer that he is the tallest astronaut of all time.

That's not an exaggeration. It's his claim to fame. He's six foot five, the exact tallest an air force fighter pilot can be, way taller than astronauts used to be allowed to be. But the Orpheus capsules are bigger, and he has the room to exist there.

His smile is huge, unmoving, like his face is made of stone. Actually, his whole body might be made of stone. I have a feeling that if I were to punch him in the gut, I'd be the one hurting.

"Mark Bannon," I say, as if he doesn't know his own name. "Um, Mr. Bannon. I mean, Mr. Mark Bannon. I enjoyed your speech at the park."

"Just Mark is fine," he says with a heavy laugh. "Thank you, thank you. You Calvin's boy? I suspect we'll all be getting to know each other quite well."

"I guess so. Maybe you'll get to fly with my dad someday."

Mark laughs. "That's not likely."

"What do you—"

He holds up a hand. I obey his rock-palm and stop speaking. So much for my meaningless small talk.

"You know how long I've been here, right?" he asks somewhat condescendingly, as if I'm supposed to do anything but agree with him.

I do. He was one of the first.

"But there are six spots."

"The role your dad would play in a mission—it'd mostly revolve around maneuvering the ship. Your dad's a pilot, just like me and Mrs. Tucker. Only one of us will be picked for the mission. The other two will be alternates, so we'll all be working the same drills, day in and day out."

"Oh, well, that's nice," I say. "Look, it was great meeting you, but I have to go find someone."

He lets me go after a firm (almost painful) handshake. Once I finally get outside, the music and the noise of the party all die down and I'm able to breathe, even despite the humidity.

The moon's glow lights the backyard, enough for me to see that there's no one back here. I walk around the yard, taking in the brief respite, wondering when Kat and Leon will join me, when I hear a noise.

"Cal!" someone says. I turn to find there's a pathway to the side of the house that I hadn't noticed before. Their yard is fenced in, which leaves a little nook for a few chairs, a bottle of champagne, and a small shed.

I walk quickly over, nearly breaking into a run, and stop to smile when I see Leon. He smiles back and gestures to the seat next to him.

"Good to see you," I say. "Everyone else is fucking weird here."

"You're including Kat in that?"

"Your sister put avocado in the deviled eggs. She can't be trusted."

He laughs at that. A soft laugh—more strained than light. The moon illuminates his features, and my brows furrow to match his.

"Hey, you okay?"

He makes eye contact with me, briefly. "Oh, hmm. Yeah. Sorry, I guess I just get antisocial at these things."

His sullen expression floods into my body, and I consider

asking about it, but something stops me and tells me we're not *there* yet.

I don't know where we are, but I like the journey so far.

I take the unattended, opened champagne bottle on the ground and bring it to my lips. The tart, fizzy liquid burns my throat as I swallow it down. The taste isn't great, but I could get used to it.

"I like this little hidden area," I say, which makes him laugh. "No, I'm serious! This was the size of my bedroom in Brooklyn. It's comforting."

He looks dramatically from left to right. "This was your room?"

"Well, it had a ceiling, but yes."

We pass the bottle, and the flavor gets better. The burning is less noticeable at least.

"So, Houston," I say. "Anything fun to do downtown? Shows or anything?"

"We don't get a ton of bands that play here. We'll get stadium tours sometimes, but those are a little more mainstream— Elton John, Nicki Minaj, Justin Timberlake. People like that." He smirks. "It's probably not your scene."

"Excuse me? You think I don't like mainstream music?" I don't bring up my cassette collection.

He shrugs. "You've got the Brooklyn hipster vibe, what can I say? You're telling me you don't go to indie shows?"

"Well, I never said that. Back home Deb and I saw a ton of indie shows. But the reasons for that are twofold: First, it's Brooklyn, so indie shows are everywhere. Second, those tickets are cheap. It's not like either of us could afford to see shows at Madison Square Garden."

I take a swig from the bottle as he starts laughing again.

"You think you know me so well," I say, wiping the foam from my lips. "But let me guess—you haven't been to a concert since you came here. Oh, wait, I know your type. You listen to the radio, because you like a lot of different music, but you don't really stan for anyone."

"Wow, almost none of that was correct." He pats my back condescendingly. "Really good try, though."

"Fine, who do you stan for?"

"Dear god. I will tell you if you stop saying the word 'stan.'" He keeps my gaze, and the reflection of the porch light makes his eyes shine. "I don't have a favorite, but I literally couldn't go to the gym for practice without my K-pop playlist."

I hesitate, and he must see the confusion in my face, because he follows it up quickly, tension straining his voice.

"I mean, I like mainstream music like SZA and Khalid and whatever Calvin Harris song is currently at the top of the Billboard charts too."

"No, K-pop is cool, I just never pictured you a fan of it. I haven't listened much, but I've watched a few music videos before. They are super entertaining."

He thaws a bit, and as I pass the champagne to him, I scoot a little closer. Almost imperceptible, but from this angle, our knees softly brush against each other. He doesn't pull away, and the heat from his touch makes me melt.

"The music's great, and there are so many artists I love in the genre, but there's just something about how every song is high tempo and exciting—K-pop knows how to hit hard. It kind of makes me feel invincible. And I don't get hung up on lyrics since, well, I don't know what they're saying."

"Makes sense to me." I offer him a genuine smile, and he returns it.

My smile widens, and a laugh comes out.

"What was that for?"

"Just, you and I are different in so many ways, but . . ." I drift off, formulating my thought. "We're kind of playing the same role. We have this massive public presence, but we've got this whole life that the public doesn't see. I can't believe you're that stoic, almost regal cutie from the *Time* magazine cover."

He sighs, and a distant look takes over his expression.

There are a dozen more questions I planned on asking him, about the astronaut families, about his mom, about Clear Lake. But there's one that, maybe it's seeing him with his guard down like this, that I *need* to ask.

"Can I . . . be real with you for a second?" I hiss a long sigh through my teeth. "How do you all stay acting so perfect?"

I see the skepticism behind his eyes, so I pull back.

"Why do you ask?" he says. "This isn't, like, for your show or anything, is it?"

I avoid eye contact and feel the blood rush to my head. "No, no. Of course not. I just . . . my family is . . . I don't know, it was an idiotic question, sorry."

He puts a hand on my knee, and I breathe in so fast it's almost a gasp. It's unfair that there are enough nerve endings stored in my knee to make a simple act like that leave me breathless.

Our eyes meet, and suddenly I'm the insecure one.

"My dad isn't like yours," I say. "My mom isn't like yours. I'm not like you. We can't carry ourselves like you do. We aren't built to deal with this, no matter how much Dad thinks we are."

"Cal, we're not perfect. We're far from it."

"Come on, you are literally America's family right now. You were on the cover of *Time*—all of you."

He shakes his head. "Don't treat me like that, please. I see it in your eyes right now, this awe of my perfect life. It's not perfect. We can pretend, I guess. I can pretend better than I thought, actually. Well, maybe not—near the end of that *Time* photoshoot the photographer made us all do a serious pose because he said my smile didn't look 'right' in the other shots. I can fake a confident, serious pose, but I can't fake happiness."

We're close, but I want to lean in even closer. His melancholy buries itself into me, and I want to stop it. I focus on his face in the moonlight, and it's then I realize I want to kiss him. I want to fix his insecurities and make it better, even if the happiness and rightness lasts only a couple of seconds. Or a few minutes. I bite my lips, subconsciously, and his gaze drops to them.

But it's too fast. Or is it? He can't deny this connection, the one I know buzzes through both of us. The fire's not strong, but something's there, smoldering.

I lean forward, just slightly.

And he stops me.

He puts a hand to my chest, and his eyes soften to almost a look of pity. My chest aches with awkwardness, and I want nothing more than to jump over this fence and never look back and—

"I think you're cute," he says. "I know we just met, but there's something about you I really like. But I need to make sure you understand something first."

I clear my throat and look past his ear. Anywhere that's not his perfect eyes. "Oh, um. What's that?"

"If you want to kiss me, kiss me because you like me. Not because you think it'll make me happy."

"But I—"

"You can't just kiss away all the bad feelings I have. You can't kiss me and make me better. I think you know that, but . . . I have to say it."

There's a part of me that wants to deny it. To say that I really just thought he was cute and super kissable and wanted to go for it—not that all those things aren't true, but that's not what made me lean in. I wanted to help. I wanted to kiss him and see him smile again.

He doesn't deserve that, which is why I say, "I'm sorry. You're right."

"Thought so." He sighs. "You had that 'poor puppy' look. It was cute, don't get me wrong, but I don't like being the one who makes you look like that. Like you think I'm some broken baby bird or something."

It's silent for a bit. I wait for the awkwardness to set in, but as we pass the bottle back and forth, I feel myself worrying less about the silence and enjoying his company more. It's a bit cooler out, and a nice breeze cuts through the humidity.

"Sorry if I made things weird," he says. "I'm not usually so upfront about my, um, depression." His voice dips, low and soft, like it's a foreign word he knows he's pronouncing incorrectly. "It's something I've been trying lately. I'm not always my strongest advocate, you know?"

I nod. "For the record. I do want to kiss you, at some point. And not just to make you happy."

He smiles at that, and the tension in my shoulders melts away.

"Someday," he offers.

"Yeah, someday."

I want to tell him I'm here, that he can talk to me if he needs to. Or I can sit here, inches from him, listening to him breathe. In, and out. I want him to know how remarkable it is that, of the billions of people in the world, I am the one who's sitting next to him, under stars and the champagne's haze. I want him to know the improbability of two people meeting like this. That it's astounding, no matter how inconsequential it is. Sure, strangers meet all the time. It's the universe's way to say we don't matter. None of this matters.

Our eyes meet. And it's clear that, sometimes, the universe is just wrong.

I almost lean into him again, but I hear someone open the sliding glass door. It's Kat, and she's around the corner in a flash, taking up the third chair with a sigh.

"You guys are missing a hell of a party. They're all sucking down the champagne. Cal's dad and Stephanie Jonasson—" she turns to me and adds, "the one who brings her yappy dog to parties—are currently battling for control of the record player."

"Good." Leon laughs. "I hope they break it."

Kat turns to me. "So this record player came with the house, because everything *has* to be sixties and seventies themed, I guess, and Mom kept bringing home these records after work. She would bring like ten home a week. One day she comes in with a big stack, and Dad is like, 'Hey, what's going on? Are you raiding a record store on your lunch break?' First, she laughs because she doesn't get much of a lunch break, being an *astronaut* and all, and then she says, 'They just keep giving them to me. I can't say no.'"

"You mean NASA is buying your mom records?" I ask.

"Dozens of them," Leon explains. "They know Mom and Dad throw most of the parties here, and I think they think it sets the tone, or whatever. During one *Shooting Stars* episode they asked what Mom's favorite record was. She got so flustered, it was great. I guess I get the retro appeal, but I don't know why NASA won't let them stream like normal people."

"Ha, right." My voice cracks.

"It's total nonsense," Kat says, then gasps. "Oh! Sorry, your cassette thing is totally different."

I look down, and heat flushes my face.

"What?" Leon asks. "What did I say?"

"I—it's embarrassing." I never thought it was embarrassing before, until I heard those words come out of his mouth. "I have a tape deck. A cassette player, I mean. I get a lot of old cassettes, and whatever new ones come out. I've got a big collection now. The sound's smoother, I guess."

"We didn't mean to make fun of you." Kat laughs. "Well, we didn't then. Now, I kind of do. How old is that cassette player I see in all your vids? Can I remind you that you were not alive in the eighties or nineties, and even if you were, you'd have no right collecting them?"

"Ohhhhh," Leon says. "It's a *Brooklyn hipster* thing, isn't it? So, I think that means I was right."

I laugh at that, and I slap at him to get him off my back.

"What are you two talking about?" Kat asks.

I roll my eyes as Leon launches into an explanation of our earlier conversation.

"Oh, you told him about the K-pop—that's usually info you drop during the *second* date."

Turning to her, I narrow my eyes.

"Uhhh," Leon says. "We'd need a first date for that to happen."

"Look, I'm just saying I ran interference for thirty whole minutes so you two could have some alone time. Champagne, the moon, the stars—all looks like first date material to me."

The way my heart is beating . . . this isn't a date, it's on a totally separate plane. Do you need a first date when you can hide from gardening duty together under a tree, or get to know each other under a perfect night sky?

"Dating is overrated," I say. "I like whatever we're doing."

Kat squeals, which makes Leon groan. After a few more minutes, we're able to polish off the rest of the bottle.

"Oh, guess what? Cal's mom said she'd start giving me some coding lessons," Kat says while chucking the bottle in the recycling bin. "She's awesome."

I laugh, knowing my mom would die with joy if she knew a teen honestly thought she was awesome.

"That's great," Leon says. "But we should really get inside before they actually notice our disappearance."

As we go in, I slip my hand in his and squeeze.

Leon and I keep tabs on each other, even when we're in separate areas of the party, talking with various astronauts and their families. It's a comfort that lasts me through the rest of the night.

— —— —

Since Mom went home early, I'm waiting for Dad to come out front so we can go home. The faint scent of tobacco drifts my way, and my eyes follow the smoke trail. Parked on the street, in front of the house, is the white van I recognize as the one StarWatch uses. Leaning against the car, alone, is the producer from the garden.

"Hey. Kiara, right?" I say.

"Good memory." Her cool demeanor clearly hasn't changed.

"How was your night, kid? Sounds like you and the Tucker kids were able to, uh, have some fun. Might want something to cover that champagne breath—here, hold on a sec."

She pulls me to the door of the van, hands me a piece of gum. After it's in my mouth, she says, "Close your eyes," and spritzes my face and neck with a soft vanilla-scented spray.

"This will last you until you get home." She smirks at my disbelief. "Not my first rodeo, kid."

"Thanks. How . . . did you know?"

"You're not the only reporter here, Cal." She gestures to herself. "And I heard you all chatting around back during my second smoke break out here, just before someone chucked a large glass bottle into the recycling. I made some educated guesses."

I laugh—if I wasn't a little buzzed, I might be more worried. But if she wanted to expose us, she wouldn't have told me. So I have to trust that there might be a modicum of dignity with *Shooting Stars*.

"Mind if I ask you something about StarWatch?" I say.

"Go for it."

"Do you . . . hate your job? I noticed you at the party, and your expressions only ranged from unenthused to enraged."

She shakes her head. "It's complicated. I think some of this is cool, but it's hard. We coasted for a few episodes on these parties just being fun and opulent and . . . champagne-fueled. But Josh has been breathing down my back lately to find a new story or get some drama. And let me tell you, these people are on their best behavior when a camera is on them.

We got some really good gossip early into the party, but Josh wants to save it for later."

"Isn't going to Mars dramatic enough?" I ask. "Maybe I'm naive, but there are so many people working on this project—especially outside of the twenty astronauts—that you could focus on."

She shakes her head. "I just do what they tell me. That's why I'm an *assistant* producer."

The Tuckers' front door swings open. Behind my dad stand Leon and his mom. Leon gives me a wave, and I return it weakly. My cheeks flush with heat. I break away from the van to go see my dad.

I turn back to Kiara. "Thanks for the . . . you know. Hope you find your story."

"I think I have." She smirks, and she slowly pans from me to Leon and back. "But we'll see how it plays out."

"Want to drive back?" Dad asks, confirming that he one-hundred-percent does not smell the champagne on my breath or see the blurriness that covers my eyes—I whisper a silent thanks to Kiara.

I shrug, then look up into the sky. The streetlights are dim, so it feels like you can see all the stars out here. Thousands upon thousands more than Brooklyn, that's for sure. Dad follows my gaze upward, to the sky, and releases a heavy sigh.

"Let's walk back," I say. "We can pick up the car later this weekend. Maybe you can remind me what all these constellations are, since I haven't seen them in a while."

He puts an arm around my shoulder, and I smell his

champagne breath. I know he's not that drunk—to be honest, I've never seen Dad super drunk. But he's feeling good, and so am I. Which reminds me to breathe downward, since I don't think he'd be too keen on me secretly drinking during my first week in Clear Lake, and a stick of gum can only do so much.

"Well, let's start easy. See those stars that look like a pan?"

"I know the Big Dipper, Dad," I say, laughing.

"What about that one? The five stars that look like a W?"

"Casio . . . something, right?"

He makes an affirmative grunt. "That's Cassiopeia, and there are a lot more stars than five in it. Can't really see most of them now, though. And if you look at that pentagon-looking one near it, that's her husband, Cepheus."

"Does Orpheus have a constellation?" I ask.

"Sort of." He looks down at me and smiles. "The constellation Lyra is around here. It's tiny, though, so I won't be able to spot it. It represents the story of Orpheus and Eurydice."

"And that is . . . ?"

"The brief version? Eurydice dies; Orpheus takes his magical lyre and travels to Hades to save her. He plays his lyre for Hades, who promises to return Eurydice under one condition: she would follow, but if he turned to look at her, she'd be gone forever."

"How'd that turn out?" I ask.

"Not well." He shakes his head. "But it gave us a good name for the project. Orpheus, son of Apollo. A story about trust, and moving forward. It's clever, I think."

We continue walking as Dad points out all the constellations he knows. He even acknowledges his star-mapping skills are rusty. But it's nice to have this moment.

"The astronauts are all really welcoming," he says. "The NASA administrators were too. They kept asking questions about you, since they saw your update. Josh Farrow, though, *whoo boy*, he was so salty."

"Look, I'm really sorry about that. I didn't think—"

"Don't be. *NASA* loved it. They want this stuff to go viral any way it can, especially to kids your age. They want you to keep doing it, since it's better than us olds forcing it on them."

My cheeks flush, and not because of the champagne this time. "Really? I don't even know if I want to cover all this. That's your thing; it seems . . . weird. Also, don't say 'olds' ever, please."

I'm expecting a weight to be lifted off my chest—I didn't get us all in trouble—but it's like the weight got swapped with an even larger one. NASA wants me to cover the missions, even though StarWatch is furious about it?

Anxious energy rattles around in my chest. On one hand, I don't give a shit about that trashy network or any of its shows, so making them angry kind of sounds fun. But on the other hand, having my content controlled by NASA?

"Donna said you could tour the facilities anytime you want. See the shuttles. Maybe I can take you to work with me one day. Oh, here."

I feel the pressure start to compound when he hands me her business card. When I moved here, I thought I'd only have to manage a new school, keep my head down for a year, and find a way to get back to New York to live with Deb. Within one week, I've got a new crush to deal with (and whatever baggage he's hiding), a pissed-off best friend (and whatever baggage she's hiding), and now the pressure from NASA along with the wrath of StarWatch (and whatever baggage they're collectively hiding).

I don't want my content controlled by anyone, but a part of me wants to help them. To really shove it in StarWatch's face. This *is* the most newsworthy thing going on in America right now, and I have a front-row seat. Now that my BuzzFeed internship imploded, and I have no plan, I feel the need to do *something* that gives me back the control I had over my life.

Having this card in my hand feels like an opportunity. One I won't be wasting.

CHAPTER 10

I wake to the sounds of chirping birds, and even without lifting the covers from my face, I take in the Texas sun with my other senses. The summer heat crawls through the room, pushing back the air-conditioning, and I feel its warmth spread over my bed. The window's shut, but I can still smell the cut grass and the damp humidity.

After an uneventful weekend of unpacking, delivered meals, and me overanalyzing every text from Leon, it's Monday morning. It's Dad's first day of work. And I can tell by his frenzied back-and-forth pacing, he's stressed.

"Oh good, you're up," he says as I step outside my room. "Could you get the car this morning? We shouldn't have left it over at the Tuckers' all weekend. Mom's on a work call, I have to fill out the new hire paperwork this morning and be in by noon, and I'm having a slow start. I can't be late on my first day."

I agree, and he leaves, so I jump in the shower and get ready for the day. Unease swims in my blood, in a way that I can't shake off. And I wonder if I'm starting to act like Mom in new situations.

There's something calming about my morning routine. Wake, water, social. A shower so hot it kind of burns my skin even though, yes, that's not good for my skin, I get it, this is my cross to bear. Next comes the face scrub, oil-free moisturizer—with SPF, because my pale skin can't even compete with the sun on cloudy days—then just enough hair paste to keep it all in place.

I'm not obsessed with my looks, which are fine—stubby nose, fanged teeth I wish I could trim down—but I like the process. Taking my time to get ready makes me feel better about myself. Yes, I notice more pimples this way, but I also feel my skin moisturizing, and I get to flip my bangs up in the front. It's my signature.

And this is what tethers me to Brooklyn, to home. It's the same process. The same steps. Sure, I'm doing this in a bigger house, thousands of miles away, but for now, I feel okay. Only okay, but that's okay.

Okay.

I still don't pull out my John Mayer hat. It's a kind of pork-pie hat with a brim so wide you could wear it to a Southern Baptist church. My style is flamboyant enough as it is, but one day, Texas will be ready.

I wear a tight white tank top with thin blue horizontal stripes, and jean shorts rolled up a couple of inches higher than they were meant to be. I opt for my strapped sandals. No, not clunky Tevas, but ones with thin leather straps that crawl their way up my leg.

After I actually settle on an outfit, I'm out the door and down the street, taking in the warming heat before it gets too unbearable. As I approach the house, I feel a little flutter in my stomach, and I remember leaning in to kiss Leon, how much I wanted to be there for him, but I didn't know how. I also knew it was something beyond me, and I wondered if he was seeing a therapist or taking medication or therapy or Reiki or whatever it is that could help him.

When I get to the car, I wave to Kat, who's sitting on the porch. She puts down the book she's reading and runs over to where I'm standing.

"Hey!" she says. I take in her spirit and try to make it my own. I'm not sure how she can pull off being so perky when it's this early. "I wanted to, well, thank you for getting to know Leon."

The sentence strikes me off guard. "I like him a lot. But why do you think you have to thank me?"

"I know he's my older brother, so it's weird for me to be saying this. But he doesn't . . . make friends that easily. He was so into gymnastics for years, and he had friends on the team, but he just kind of lost interest before the move. Dad's been trying to force him to keep training, to try to get back on course. But it's like he hasn't liked anything or anyone in a long time. Maybe he just needs to get back to the gym or something."

"I'm not sure what I can do to help." I gesture to my scrawny physique and outfit and say plainly, "I am not athletic."

My mind drifts to NASA's invitation to tour the facility and do a post from there. It's Monday, and I usually do a start-of-the-week video. Since my initial rebellion, I've been itching to create new content.

"Do you want to say hi to Leon? I think he might be up."

"I do, but I have to get back home so Dad can get to work," I say as I take out the business card from my wallet. "It's okay—we'll talk later."

I dial the number on the card and wait for the NASA social media woman to pick up the phone. I let each ring sound out, even though it's well into the normal workday at eleven in the morning, and she is most likely busy and wouldn't want to talk to a guy like—

"Donna Szleifer, NASA social."

"Donna, hi. It's Cal Junior. The FlashFame guy."

I hear a little gasp on her end. "Oh, hi, Cal. I'm so glad you called. I thought you'd be debating my proposition from Friday's party, and I didn't even get to talk to you about everything we have planned and what you could help with."

"That's what I'm calling about, actually. I wondered if, maybe I could come up sometime this week and shoot a video?"

"Not to rush you, but could you do it today? The astronauts are busy all day and we have some social posts scheduled and whatnot, but we could really use the boost of your followers right now. I know StarWatch is doing what they can, but bless them, they can't get any traction on that FlashFame app, and everyone seems really thirsty for info after your last vid."

"Oh. Well, I was going to do a weekly post today anyway, and I guess it would be cool to do it from the space center."

There's a pause on her end. "Perfect. Just perfect. You get your butt down here, and if I have to go put out first-day-of-school fires over here, you can just wander around. I'll get you a visitor's pass ready."

I look to the front of the house and see that Kat's long gone, but in her place is a sleepy guy who's so cute I could literally melt right here, leaving nothing but my hipster tank and unraveled sandals on the hot pavement.

"Can I bring Leon Tucker?" I ask quickly. "I need someone to film me."

"Two passes, then! Come along with your dad, and I'll get you guys."

I can't help but admire Leon, all lanky and tall, with a lazy smile and his wrinkled T-shirt and gym shorts like he just got out of bed. I walk up to him, smile briefly, and take in the discrepancy of our outfits. A smirk forms on my face, just before he leans in and gives me a hug. I feel his arms wrap around me, and I'm so caught off guard by it that I almost gasp.

Yes, this is how some people say hello, but that's not exactly what we do in Brooklyn, so I'm a bit alarmed by it. And comforted by it. And kind of never want it to stop.

But, unfortunately, it stops.

"Hey, Cal."

There's a slight drawl in how he says my name, and I almost die at the sweetness. This crush is strong. This crush is too powerful. This crush will be the end of me.

Or maybe I'm just being dramatic.

"I'm going to the space center to record a Flash vid. They said I could bring you. Want to come?"

"They?"

"Yeah, the social media woman I met at the party."

There's a weird silence in how he sizes me up just now. His eyes narrow, and he shakes his head almost imperceptibly, but in a flash, he drops all the tightness in his body. He relaxes, and offers a genuine smile, and nods.

"Yeah, I'll go. Let me get changed."

"Okay, be quick. I have to pick up Dad so I can take him to work."

He's very quick. Like, he literally just changed his shirt and threw on some shorts and called it a day. He didn't shower. Which, I guess, is fine. He doesn't smell bad or anything. And his shirt is actually cute—it's a plain T-shirt, but it's a pale, soft blue. The kind you see on the crayons that get used up first in a huge box. The color pops in contrast to his dark brown skin.

I get the urge to kiss him again. He's not low right now, and nowhere in my perverse mind do I think he needs this kiss to fix him. I want him, and I want to do it for me. And for humanity, even. I want the world to be that much better because of our lips touching and his hand in my hair and . . .

My heart is racing. Thudding against my rib cage and shaking my body. I've never been able to go back and forth between

126

being so perfectly content and so perfectly lustful of someone so quick. It's like a switch. And I want it to keep flipping on and off. On and off.

I stop outside the house and call Dad, who comes out dressed in a sharp suit and tie. He's carrying this boxy briefcase I've never seen before. It's all somewhat adorable, and this must be what parents feel like taking their anxious and/or excited children to their first day of school.

Swap the briefcase for a carry-on bag, and it's not too far off from his Delta days. But he definitely carries himself straighter now. His smile comes easily, and his giddiness takes over the car the moment he steps in.

"Thanks, Cal. And good morning, Mr. Tucker."

Leon gives an uncomfortable laugh at the formal title. I make eye contact with Dad in the rearview as he buckles up in the back seat.

I look up directions on my phone, and see that Deb's sent me a ton of listings for studios all over Brooklyn, from Lefferts Gardens to Bay Ridge and everywhere in between, so she can't be that angry with me for how self-centered I was acting when we last spoke.

Brooklyn is where I'll live; Manhattan is where I'll work and go to school. Texas simply doesn't fit into the equation. But I can't hide the fact that, even though I so recently fell into this opulent and bizarre world, the thought of leaving makes my chest ache with regret.

— — —

We pull up to the gate, and I pass Dad's ID to the guard. He lets us in, and I wonder if Dad feels embarrassed now, having his kid drive him to his first day of work, in one of the most respected professions in the world.

But if he feels that way, he doesn't say it . . . and he is the type of person who would say it.

Dad leads us in through the main gate and shows us around the various labs and the gift shop and points us to the section where they have a pop-up Mercury and Apollo museum with pieces of the old spacecraft that he got to touch on his last interview.

"Cal!"

Both Dad and I turn—sharing my name with Dad is the bane of my existence—to see Donna running toward us, iPhone flailing precariously in her loose-wristed grip. She smiles at the three of us and clarifies:

"Cal Junior, that is."

Dad looks deflated, but he smiles anyway, and gives me a quick nod to instruct me to follow her out. I want to stay and make sure he knows that she didn't mean anything by it, that he matters to this mission one bajillion times more than I do. But I don't.

And I know I've hurt him. Just by existing. By being needed in the one place where it should have been him. For the second time, I've stolen his thunder.

Leon and I join Donna as she talks to us about the tour she'll take us on and points out about fifty "really special" places for video shots. Leon's participation in the conversation dwindles to nonexistence, so when she turns a sharp corner and we're momentarily alone, I place a hand softly on his shoulder and squeeze.

"This is overwhelming, huh?" I say. "I don't think she's taken a breath since we left the lobby."

He laughs. "Yeah, she's . . . something."

"Hmm," I say after a bit of hesitation. "We could shake her and do some exploring. Find some 'really special' places of our own."

He side-eyes me, so I laugh and break into a jog to catch up to Donna, who's still chattering. Even as I find my niche, and I start to fit in around here . . . as I start to feel a little happy, a little positive or hopeful or whatever it is, I think of my dad. His smile faltering, while Donna made a show of taking me around. It's not fair to him.

But something in me wants to hold tightly to this. With BuzzFeed out of the picture, it's all I have.

I can't give it up. Even if it hurts my dad.

CHAPTER 11

Luckily for us, Donna had to be yanked away for a social media emergency—her term, not mine—and nearly pushed us into the elevators with directions for how to get back to the lobby.

In the elevator, it's strikingly clear we're alone. When I was dating Deb, all we had was alone time, but here it feels unusual, rare to be in such a small space with him. With no distractions. And I get the very, *very* real urge to kiss him now.

Before we get to our intended stop on the second floor, he punches the number six and the elevator slows to an early stop. He grabs my wrist and leads me out.

"Where are you taking me?"

He responds with a sleek all-teeth smile, and I feel myself growing weak. I'd follow him anywhere, I realize. My brain tries to talk me out of this feeling. It can't be smart to feel like this for someone in a town where you see no real future, where you have cameras on you whenever you're in public.

I follow him through winding halls, passing nothing particularly fascinating. The rooms are bland and identical; the only thing to differentiate them is a small plaque with increasing numbers.

The tiles beneath my feet are a sterile white, and everything looks, feels, and smells fresh and new. The tang of citrus cleaner hits my nose. This is the NASA I can get behind. The practical one that doesn't care about flair and isn't clinging to some weird retro reality.

We stand in front of a cracked door. The placard out front says Launch Demo Room IV, and I can feel excitement radiating from Leon's body. He stands on the balls of his feet as he raps his knuckles on the door. His attitude is infectious, and I feel my heart rate increase, my breaths shorten in depth and length.

A woman opens the door and beams when she sees Leon. She's in a bright green collared shirt with solid black pants, and the way she moves is art. She sways from left foot to right, sliding her curves in line confidently.

"Carmela!" Leon says. "How are you?"

"My boy! I haven't seen you since the holiday party. I miss you, son. I tell your mom to tell you hello every single time I see her, twice a week. I hope she's been telling you."

He laughs. "She has, she has."

We shake hands as she looks me up and down. "Oh, Leon, who's your fashionable friend? I like him."

"Cal. My dad's the new astronaut."

"Oh, right. Nice to meet you, darling. I'll be seeing a lot of your dad. Come in, come in!"

She waves us in like she's inviting us to her home, which in a way she is. Behind the door is a surprisingly large space, adorned with a couple of thin metal tables with MacBooks strewn about. Beyond the tables sits a large cockpit encased in glass.

"Whoa," I say. "What is this?"

"It's a simulation room," she explains. "An identical re-creation of the spacecraft's sensors and cockpit. I program the simulation to fail in some way, like taking out an engine or giving their monitors a bad reading, and the astronauts find a way to keep everyone alive. We practice successful missions too, but that's not as fun for me. You boys want to check it out? There's space for two."

Leon turns to me hopefully, and my answer is obviously yes, but I pause a few seconds to look at the reflection of the fluorescent lights in his eyes before I respond.

"Just don't press any buttons," she says. "It takes ages to reset everything, and your mom and his dad are coming in at three to do an introduction."

At the other side of the warehouse-like space is an open cockpit. There are two seats, one on each side, with a mess of panels and buttons from the ceiling to the floor. When we walk through the glass door that separates the two rooms and shut it, it feels like we're on hallowed ground.

The buzz of machines and the rustling of office activity are replaced with a very clear silence. It's only my breaths. His breaths. Our footsteps, coming closer together.

We're alone.

"Is this what you wanted to show me?" I ask.

"Yeah. I love it here. It really makes you feel like this is something special. Something huge."

"I thought you didn't really like this stuff," I say.

"It's not that. It's . . . I don't know what it is. I hate having the world watching us, waiting for us to entertain them."

I take a seat in the right side of the cockpit, and I imagine my dad in here, running tests and logic scenarios. Could he really be this badass? Could he save a broken ship and bring the crew back to safety?

Could he really be capable of all this?

"Which side of the tests would you want to be on?" I ask him. "Carmela's, or your mom's?"

He pauses for a second, and from his light smile, I can tell he's thought about this before and he's picturing it now.

"I'd want to be Carmela. I want to create these logic puzzles, throw them curveballs. I want to take a situation, list a thousand ways it could go wrong, and prepare the astronauts to fix each potential problem." He pauses. Deflates. "I don't know. I just like math and logic."

"I get that," I say. "Want to know who I'd be?"

He shakes his head. "Don't need to. I know which one you'd be. You'd want to be the one in control—solving the problem, saving lives, getting the glory."

I nod. "I'm that predictable, huh?"

His hands grace the buttons between our seats. The energy pulsates through my body. My breaths are shallow, and I'm not getting enough air. I can't focus, I can't wait anymore.

Lightly, but with purpose, I grab his hand, and he gasps at my touch. He rotates his hand so his thumb touches my palm. It sends shivers up my back and over my shoulders, into my chest. My breaths are nonexistent now. Air smoothly flows in and out of my lungs without the dramatic pull of breathing. We should wait. I should be smarter about this. But I can't— Carmela is turned away. We're alone, and I want to make it count.

I lean in, more than halfway to him, and he considers me for a moment. I can tell he's panicked, but that he wants this. But I can't do it all. I can't go all the way in—but god, I want to so badly. He has to meet me here, in the in-between.

And after three excruciating seconds, he does.

His lips are soft and perfect and tug at mine like he's been waiting for this moment forever. Like he's been waiting for more than just a week to be with me like this. In seconds, our mouths are on each other and his hand is behind my neck. And my heart's about to beat out of my chest.

It's too fast and not nearly enough. And it's over.

Our foreheads touch, and I breathe, and I breathe, and I breathe. My lips sting. Then he pulls away from me, and I can't read his expression. His eyes are wide, but his gaze is on my lips. Was this too much for him? His hunger felt insatiable when he pulled my lips into his; the bite of his teeth kept me connected to him.

He breaks eye contact. His gaze falls to his lap.

"I shouldn't have done that," he says. "Sorry."

"Oh, right. Why wouldn't you immediately regret that?

Right. Great." I gesture to the cockpit. "Thanks for a lovely flight."

I don't know what to do, and he doesn't either. I know I'm probably making it worse, but I can't handle this awkwardness. So I stand up and start for the door, shielding my face from Carmela's blank stare as I walk by her.

Shooting Stars
Season 2; Online Content

LIVE UPDATE: Tune in live at 12:30 p.m. (CST) as we check in with Donna Szleifer, head of social media for NASA, on how the new astronauts are getting along on their first day.

"Sorry, just let me fix my hair—oh Lord Jesus, we're already live, aren't we? Oh well, at least we can give the viewers an authentic look into the fabulous life of a social media director."

"Good afternoon, *Shooting Stars* viewers. I am your host, Josh Farrow, and that was Donna Szleifer, head of social media for NASA—although, as you can tell, she's a bit disheveled today, on the first day the Orpheus team has been assembled in full. So tell us, how are the astronauts getting along?"

"Great question. You know, first days aren't quite as glamorous as you'd think. It's mostly paperwork and orientation—yes, even astronauts have to sit through that too. We've got Calvin and a few of the other newbies off to get fitted for their gear right now, but as the twenty astronauts all came together this morning, there was something very special in the air. We were thrilled to start their journey with a short ceremony, which you can find on our Twitter, Facebook, and Instagram. We unveiled a new patch and logo for Project Orpheus, and in the style of the Mercury Seven, we're dubbing this team the Orpheus Twenty."

"Ah, what a perfect honorific title. The Mercury Seven were, of course, the original seven astronauts selected by NASA to see if humans could survive spaceflight. In that respect, the Orpheus Twenty have big shoes to fill, wouldn't you say?"

"To say the least!"

"Okay, as this is a live bonus segment, we're going to start with a few questions submitted by our viewers. First off—oh, interesting. Regarding Calvin Lewis Jr., what is NASA's official response to the allegations that he broke the clause in NASA's contract?"

"Oh, what an interesting and . . . specific question. Going right for the jugular, are we? Ha ha—no, that's fine. I get it. But we've looked into this, and he is technically not in breach of any StarWatch or NASA policies. The contract signed by the astronauts cannot apply to their families, and our lawyers see no reason why his content cannot coexist with that of *Shooting Stars*. We will encourage him to keep up the great work, and we're looking into ways to partner with him on some very exciting content. It's actually great news for all of us, don't you think?"

"Hmm, okay. Our second question—"

"You know, Josh, I think I'm going to cut this conversation short. It's a big day, and all your viewers are more than welcome to reach out to us on all our social channels if they're interested in the Orpheus project. If they're still curious about Cal Junior, I suspect they can find out more at his channel too. In the meantime, like we here at NASA say, keep your eye on the sky, folks!"

CHAPTER 12

"Cal, wait!" Leon shouts down the hall.

My muscles are tight; my entire body curls up to protect myself. To protect my chest, my heart right now.

He catches up to me as I'm about to call for an elevator. When he grabs my shoulder, I flip back toward him. The movement stuns him, and I observe his shocked face as he takes in my hurt.

"I'm sorry," he says. "I don't . . . I don't know what happened."

"We kissed. You thought it was a mistake. I panicked. Look, if you're still figuring things out and kissing another boy is such a shattering hyper big deal to you, call me later. I wish you luck, but I can't deal with that. Or, if you just don't actually like me, and I'm not the person you'd like to be kissing, let me know. Preferably not right after a makeout session, but I'd love a heads-up."

"Cal, no. I mean, it's more complicated than that."

"I don't want someone who's half in, half out. Don't get me wrong—I don't need a ring or a relationship or any commitment. But I can't help you accept me. I can't help you accept yourself."

He grips both of my shoulders. "What's wrong?"

And that shuts me up.

"Cal, I'm sorry. Talk to me."

"I've done it before, and it broke me," I said. "I dumped my ex-girlfriend because I kissed this guy I was really into. But I saw regret in his eyes every single time we kissed. I can't deal with that again."

He considers me for a moment. And he leans in and plants a kiss on my lips. Everything feels instantly better, and I hate myself and him for the reaction. I push him off me softly, gently, and ignore the tears coming to my eyes.

"If I don't get to kiss you when you're sad, you can't do it to me."

"I'm not kissing you because you're sad. I'm kissing you to show you that I like you. See? No regret. It takes me a while to process my feelings, sure, but please, trust me."

We kiss again, and I nearly push him into the wall. Even in Brooklyn, I've never been so public with my feelings. They've never been this intense.

My chest is raw with panic. And the reason I stormed out settles with me.

"You scare me." I consider my words. "I scare myself, I mean. These feelings aren't normal. It's too fast. This is not normal for me."

"You're right. It's so fast, it's not normal. But there's also a part of me that likes this new version of normal."

I feel the same way. I don't say it out loud, because I hate how the words feel, boiling in my stomach. My face is flushed. And I'm supposed to go back to normal now, to find some nerds to interview and cab home like everything is totally average, but I don't know how.

We walk in silence to the elevator, down to the second floor, and through the halls to find our first interviewee. We follow Donna's instructions—which came in the form of a rushed, typo-laden text—and approach Brendan, the guy who helped us move into our new house.

"Hey, man," he says. "Nice to see you again. Are you all settled in the new place?"

"More or less. So, did Donna brief you on what I'm here to do?" I ask.

He chuckles. "Per usual, that scatterbrain barely gave me any info, so I had to look up your FlashFame. I watched some of your videos, and I think I get what you want. But . . . are you sure anyone will care?"

I'm not sure of anything, I think, but that's never stopped me before.

"We won't know until we try."

I take some deep breaths to get the oxygen in my blood. I crack my neck, stretch my arms, and out of the corner of my eye, I see Leon's smile widen. When I make eye contact, he clamps his mouth shut.

He bursts out in laughter. "You really have a process, don't you?"

"Just . . . let me do my thing," I say, rolling my eyes. "Brendan, get ready, I'm going live. Leon, I'll hand the phone off to you after my intro. Ready? And . . . we're go."

Tagging the video as being hosted live from the NASA Johnson Space Center made the viewer count spike, counting up from three- to four- to five-digit numbers.

"Heya," I say into the camera. "Today, we're going to have a special interview with a scientist here at the space center, Brendan Stein. I'm passing my phone off to the very famous Leon Tucker." I reverse the phone's camera. "Say hi!"

He ducks out of the frame immediately, causing Brendan to laugh. As I hand over my phone to a bitter Leon, I whisper, "That's what you get for making fun of my *process.*"

He smirks, and sizes us up in the frame. We're both sitting on stools, with the bright white of the NASA research lab at our backs.

"So, we spoke earlier," I say, "and you were saying you play in the dirt for a living?"

"Ha, you could say that," he says with a shrug. "If all goes to plan, one day we'll be running tests on different types of Martian soil, right here in the room behind me. Actually, here." He jumps up, and I follow him to a table with a thin, sealed glass cylinder. "Okay, Leon, can you zoom in on this? So you see here, one of our geoscientists is working on a sample from Earth. This tube of sediment was drilled and taken from six to six and a half feet underground. As you can see, the bedrock is a marbled red color all the way through, except for this inch-long solid gray line that runs right through it."

As the camera focuses on the sediment, I lean back to see how many people are watching live. I blink hard, just to make sure I'm reading it right—but it's right there, over seventy-five thousand people are watching Brendan talk, and that number's only growing.

And he thought no one cared about dirt?

"This is a layer of ash from a volcanic eruption about seven thousand years ago, and where the sediment gets darker and more compact, this line down here, implies there was some sort of extended flooding. If we can get a few samples from Mars, there's so much more we can learn about the planet's past, present, and future."

His eyes brighten at the camera, and a feeling stirs inside me. The same sort of passion that swept through me during Mark Bannon's speech. It's what drives me, and it's why I want to be—why I *am*—a journalist.

I join Brendan again. "And all these tests are in preparation for soil that we won't get for years?"

"By the time Martian soil enters our atmosphere, we want to know exactly how we're testing it. We'll jump right in, and we'll start to know right away what Mars is truly capable of." He laughs. "I know it sounds strange, but Mars could be an integral part of Earth's future, one way or another."

He takes us on the tour of the lab, stopping at other similar stations and pointing out infrared tests, pH testing, and more. At each station is a MacBook and a notepad, all of which seem to contain the exact steps to test the soil. Before I know it, thirty minutes have passed and my channel has found a few thousand new followers.

I gesture for Brendan to wrap it up. There's no doubt my fans would let him talk for an hour if he wanted, but I always like to leave them wanting more. Not so much they feel like I'm teasing them, but just enough to keep them on the hook.

"Looks like we're out of time." He laughs and winks at the phone. "And just as I was about to show you the *really* cool equipment."

"That was wild," I say to Brendan after we sign off. "I thought it'd be a five- or ten-minute thing, but we had about three hundred thousand people watching live the whole time. Barely anyone dropped off! Just leave me a comment if you want me to tag you in the video."

"Thanks. God, that felt good. I know it was just me talking to an iPhone, but it really felt like someone was listening to us. The media folks keep batting down our press releases. I don't want to blame StarWatch, but . . ."

"Maybe we could change that," Leon says, and the three of us share a silent nod.

"But anyway," Brendan continues, "I'll share your video with my colleagues, and I'll download the app and see if I can figure it out. God, I'm twenty-five and I already can't keep up with technology."

As Brendan takes us to the cafeteria to meet back up with Donna, I ask him, "Do you think you'd ever post more videos? If NASA's batting down your announcements, why don't you just put them out on your own?"

"If you asked me yesterday, I'd have laughed in your face, but that was fun . . . I think I might try. How do you even build a following, though?"

I shrug. "Just have to keep putting content out there that your followers like. I'll tag you and tell people to go to your page for more updates. Let's see if that does anything."

"Well, this is where we say our goodbyes," he says as he passes us back to Donna.

We pace away, and I notice Donna's a little more erratic than normal. She seems frazzled, her face flushed and hair disheveled.

"Sorry, kids. I just had . . . a hard interview, let's just call it that."

Once she calms down, she talks to us about their social media campaigns. I'm somewhat interested, because it seems like a cool job, but I'm too zapped of energy from the interview to respond much.

"The fact of the matter is, we're funded by Congress. If we don't have public interest, we don't have a program. But *StarWatch* thinks people only care about drama, reality TV, that stuff. And then you came along. I've said this the whole time, Cal, but I think you're going to do wonders for this program. Keep doing these videos." She grabs my wrist, and our eyes meet. "Show everyone what this program is really about."

———

When the cab gets to my house, I squeeze Leon's hand before leaving.

"Thank you for, you know." I pull in a shallow breath to still the butterflies in my chest. "It was really . . . nice."

He lifts my chin and looks into my eyes. "See you soon?"

I lean in and plant a kiss on his lips. (In a cab. In Texas!) There's something gratifying about kissing someone goodbye. Just having someone to kiss goodbye is special, and I hope I never take him for granted.

When our lips pull apart, he smiles, and I taste his breath one last time before I get out of the car.

The steps I take to my new home are lighter somehow. And I feel the city life peeling off me like cicada skin.

When I get into the house, I see Mom curled up on the couch with a too-thick blanket and her Nintendo DS. The air-conditioning is on full blast, but she'd spend her whole life under a blanket if she could. I know better than to mess up her postwork self-care ritual, so I give her a quick "hey" and slide into my room.

Mom's anxiety has always been present, even with her therapy appointments and an assortment of low-dosage medication. She'll leave parties early, and traveling and traffic give her a bit of panic, but she manages.

One hour of quiet time each day is her goal. Time for her. Even Dad respects that, regardless of the fights they might get in and the yelling that probably counteracts all her meditation.

No sooner do I have my headphones on and a new tape in when Mom peeks in my room. From this far away, she seems at peace. She stares at me, pleasantly, from across the room, so I return an awkward smile.

"Want to grab dinner tonight? I don't feel like cooking, and there's nothing in the house. Plus, your dad won't be back until late tonight—they're starting flight tests, or something like that."

"Just like that? On the first day?"

I'm used to Dad not being home some nights, or getting home incredibly late. He was an airline pilot, after all. But being late because he's stuck in Colorado because of a blizzard makes a lot more sense than this.

She shrugs. "We should probably get used to it. You know your father won't say no to anything, especially not so soon. It'll be worse if he gets put on that mission, god forbid."

I agree to dinner and suggest a Tex-Mex place Leon told me about while we were chugging champagne. She smiles at that and bounds out of the room. If she's happy, and Dad's happy, and I can still do my videos . . .

Maybe Clear Lake won't be so bad.

Shooting Stars
Season 2; Episode 7

In this episode of *Shooting Stars*, astronaut Mark Bannon sits down with host Josh Farrow to discuss the new candidates, as well as his future in the Orpheus missions. (New episode airs 6/17/2020)

"My man Josh, how are you?"

"Astronaut Mark Bannon. We're so glad to have you with us again. For those of you just joining, welcome to *Shooting Stars*. We've got an exclusive with Mark Bannon tonight. Last time we had a one-on-one was . . . I think it was back in Florida, last season."

"Ah, right. The Orpheus IV launch. Thinking back, did I come off as nervous? Because I was a wreck that whole week. You know, if IV wasn't such a clear success, I don't think we'd have Orpheus V on the horizon at all. It was the Apollo 7 to our Apollo 11—one mistake and we'd all be unemployed right about now."

"That's true, Mark. Last season had such a different tone, don't you think? This was just after Grace Tucker was brought on, just before the Senate pushed through funding to, presumably, get us to Mars. But back then, we simply didn't know if the people were going to want to invest in the future of spaceflight."

"You know, you're right. It's good to look back on some of those old interviews. You really came in and ramped up "interest in the program, Josh. I don't know where we'd be without you."

"We found it to be a really interesting opportunity, if you don't mind my honesty. We saw it as a way to bring the country together. To rekindle that patriotism we've been missing in the past few years. Our viewers might not know; it was one of the first truly bipartisan issues since the midterms—one that a very polarized Congress didn't know how to act on, with the party lines looking jagged."

"Indeed. So they turned to the voters, who called in droves, demanding the funds be set aside to complete the Orpheus project. And that's why we of the Orpheus Twenty are able to get us closer and closer to Mars every day."

"So let's talk about the new recruits. You've been working with them for a full week now—any stars among the pack?"

"Do you know how many thousands of applicants they get? They're all stars."

"Then let me ask the more devious question, Mark, but the one that's most asked by our faithful viewers. We've been going back and forth on whether you or Grace Tucker would be taking the lead on Orpheus V. Well, now we've got another jet pilot in the ranks. Could Calvin Lewis Sr. be a threat?"

"We've been in flight tests all week, and I'm not lying when I say I'm proud to work with such brilliant pilots. But let me set one thing straight. This isn't a competition. There aren't threats. This isn't 1968. Orpheus V will most likely go to me or Grace because we know the ship the best, but that has nothing to do with skill. We *all* have the skill. Think of Orpheus VI. Orpheus VII.

Those endeavors will need pilots too, and NASA's going to match up the best person for each job, just like they carefully select every other scientist. Look, I'll level with you: I think you guys at StarWatch do a whole lot of good, I'll be the first one to say it, but this isn't a reality competition. The stakes are high enough—it doesn't get any more *real* than life or death. We're all just glad to do our part."

"I understand. Hopefully our viewers do too."

CHAPTER 13

It takes about thirty seconds for me to realize something's wrong. My mom's stomping around outside my door, and the house shakes with her every step. A look at the clock confirms what I already know: It's way too early. Or late.

Settling into this new environment has made the days stretch longer than the ones I had in New York. It's been three long weeks since we moved here, but every time I wake up, I get that momentary disorientation. Where am I? Who replaced my exposed brick wall with this awful stucco mess? *Why is my bed so huge?*

I sit up and slide my legs off the bed. I check the clock—one thirty. Dad should have landed in Florida by now to tour the launchpad with the other astronauts. I stretch out my toes on the carpet and crack my neck before locating a pair of shorts to throw on. I step out of my room just as the tail of Mom's nightgown flutters around the corner into the living room.

"Well, what *can* you tell me?" she demands.

"Mom?" I ask, then gasp at the sight of her. Her bloodshot, watery eyes dart away from me, while her chest rises and falls at too quick a rate to be healthy. A deep unease settles in my chest, making my own breaths more shallow.

"You don't get to withhold information like this," she shouts into the phone. When she looks up and finally notices me, her anger drops. More tears well in her eyes as she grips me in a tight hug. "Can you go back to your room, Cal?"

I want to question her, but I don't. Though I spend a majority of my day talking back to my parents, when something feels wrong, when something deeply unsettling happens, I somehow revert to an obedient kid.

I slip back into my room, and once I shed initial panic, I sprint to my phone. I check it, but I don't have any texts. I need answers, so I start opening apps.

When I open the FlashFame app, I see my feed is getting a startling amount of traffic, even though I didn't stream or post anything today. I check the reactions and comments and try to piece together what's going on.

A wreck . . . a jet just off Cape Canaveral . . . a private jet carrying five unnamed NASA employees. Three expected to be astronauts. One was pronounced dead on the scene; two were rushed to the hospital. It's all hearsay on my page, though. I click through a few local news links that confirm the story and look up to see my mother in the hallway.

"What's going on, Mom?"

One dead.

I shudder, and fear rushes back into my body. It burrows in my bones and tells me how nothing will ever be okay again, how the one death is sure to be Dad, how his dream is over. How futile all this would be if he was going to die in his first month of work.

"Dad was in an accident," Mom replies. "But he is okay. We will have more details when NASA deems it *appropriate* to tell us."

I sigh and feel the immediate release of the tension throughout my body. "It said there was a wreck with three astronauts on board."

"Yes, all I know is Mark and Grace were on that jet."

"I found out more information, though." I gulp, hoping the words are a lie. "One's dead, Mom."

Fire pours into my lungs and burns up my insides. Restlessness claws up my leg and into my shaking body. I need to get out of here. I need to know if it was Grace. I can't imagine a space program without her.

The realization that Leon's down the street having this same conversation with his family hits me. Or, he could be having a very different conversation right now.

"Dad's okay, though? You know that?" I ask.

"Yes. He's at the hospital under watch, but is fine. I'm not allowed to fucki—sorry, I mean . . . You know what, I mean fucking. Those NASA people won't let me know a single thing about where he's at or when I can talk to him."

She's holding the phone between her ear and shoulder

while she wrings her hands together. There's an antsy vibe about her that's contagious, and I feel my own stress levels compounding.

"He's okay. At least we know that," I repeat. "But I have to go check on Leon. I need to make sure Grace is okay too."

Mom looks at the clock, and I see the uneasy expression take over her face.

"It's just down the block. This isn't Brooklyn; I won't even pass another human on the way there. It's safe, please."

"Can't you just call him?"

"I'm going to call him on the way. But, I mean, what if it's her?"

Understanding washes over my mother as she sees this desperate, smitten side of me for the first time. She nods and gives me a soft smile.

"Oh, honey, I didn't realize you two were . . . go, go," she says. "I'm fine. I'd rather you not be here when I curse out that NASA rep, anyway, if they ever take me off hold."

I slip into my running shoes, grab my phone, and dash through the front door.

The wet Houston night sticks to my face just as heavily as the day does. It's pitch black, save for the scant street or porch light, and I'm already sweating—but to be fair, half of it is from panic. My feet squeak in my running shoes, and I wince with each step. I probably should've paused to put on socks.

One of the astronauts is dead. It's a possibility that had lingered in the back of my mind. Of course astronauts have died—jet crashes during training, the Apollo 1 fire, the *Challenger* disaster. Deaths have, at times, marred the history of American spaceflight.

I never thought it could be someone I knew.

I never thought it could happen so soon.

As I sprint down the sidewalk, the air courses through my shirt and hair, and I feel a different kind of moisture sliding down my face. A tear. Then, another. I'm getting closer to his house, and my sobbing starts, so I have to stop. I don't know what's causing it. Fear, mostly? Panic?

At least I'm alone here. And I can cry without worrying about anyone seeing me. To wake up in the middle of the night, discover that your dad might be dead, then to know that your relief means someone else you care about might really be hurting.

Please, let Grace be safe.

And then I'm not alone. Footsteps are coming toward me, quickly, and I try to put myself together, even though I'm panting and holding myself up from my knees. I'm a mess, and the streetlight overhead amplifies the messiness.

Maybe they'll go around me. Maybe . . .

"Cal?" Leon's voice rings out. It pierces through the night, and I suddenly catch my breath. That, or I stop caring about oxygen altogether. "Cal, no, was it your dad?"

He runs up to me and envelops me in a hug. I pull him into me and feel his warm body close to mine. His ear is next to my mouth, so I whisper—it's all I can manage—that Dad's okay.

"I was scared it was . . ." I stop. We're panting in unison, so

I pull back to take wider breaths. "I thought it was your mom, and I was worried about you."

"That's why I'm out here too."

The dim light around us seems to gather and amplify in his eyes. I see the panic there, where I didn't notice it before. He blinks twice and my body shudders. This time, it's not for fear. It's for . . . something else. I don't know what it is, but I know I've never felt it before. My chest physically aches, and I actually feel that yearning for him, even though I have him right here.

"You look beautiful tonight." A chuckle escapes his lips as he wipes the tears from his face. "I've never seen you like this—you're usually so dressed up, even that time you helped with the community garden."

"I didn't have any time," I say. I pull my tee down awkwardly and try not to let him know how embarrassed I am to only be wearing something like this in front of the boy I like. He grabs me by the shirt, and I let him bring me to him once again.

Our noses touch.

"It's Bannon. The NASA people slipped and told Dad an astronaut died, so it's got to be him." His brows furrow as the uncomfortable truth sinks in. "God, that's so sad. Mara. His family is going to be . . . Is this going to change things?"

I shrug. "You're asking me? I just got here."

He shakes his head like he's trying to knock a memory out of there.

"You've read the stories, right? Mom was rumored to be lead pilot for the Mars mission, Bannon her alternate."

I pause and think for a moment. "Do you think my dad will replace him? Do you think he could actually become an alternate for this mission?"

In the resounding silence, I think I have my answer. Dad's chances of being a part of Orpheus V just skyrocketed.

"I have to go and see if Mom has any more info," I say. "I'm so glad your mom is okay."

"Likewise with your dad. But before you go . . ."

He pulls me into a kiss. This one isn't as passionate, it isn't as hungry, but it makes my insides jump the same way. There's a caring force in the tug of his lips, and in his bite, I lose control of my body and feel light-headed.

"I like you," I say. It's such a four-year-old thing to say, but no other words will come to my lips.

He laughs and pulls me into his chest. His deodorant's long worn off, but I take in his scent. Warm and tart, it envelops me and brings me closer into him. "I like you too."

StarWatch News
Breaking News: Live Report

"This is Josh Farrow with StarWatch with some breaking news. If you're just tuning in, here's what we know so far. A jet carrying astronauts Mark Bannon, Grace Tucker, and Calvin Lewis Sr.—along with two other NASA scientists—was bound for Kennedy Space Center at Cape Canaveral early this morning. Mark Bannon, who piloted the jet, noticed panel outages as the craft came in for landing. A related mechanical malfunction caused both the right and left engines to go out shortly after, along with all the lights.

"Radio signal cuts out completely at this point, so we don't know exactly what happened next. But what we do know is the jet's landing gear never came down. Coasting at a dangerously high speed, Mark diverted the plane toward the ocean for an emergency water landing.

"We've just received word that Mark Bannon, an integral part of the Orpheus project, died upon impact. But thanks to quick thinking on his part, the other four lives were saved. Grace Tucker and Calvin Lewis Sr. remain in the hospital under close supervision, though both are reportedly in stable condition. We've reached out to NASA for comment and will update when we have their official response.

"Tomorrow night, we are replacing our previously scheduled episode with a tribute to Mark Bannon. We expect to have more answers at that time."

CHAPTER 14

"Honey, you need to get up," Mom says.

It's not even six the next morning, so there's a part of me that goes right back into terror mode, thinking Dad was more hurt than they let on, thinking that everything is crumbling around me, but then Mom puts a hand on my shoulder and smiles. I relax. I breathe.

"It's five forty. Why are . . . why?" I groan, and flop back on my bed.

"Sorry, honey. StarWatch people are on their way to Grace's place to talk about the accident, and we have to be there too."

"But Grace is in Florida."

"Yes, but her husband and the kids are there."

I groan, because this doesn't mean I have to just open my eyes. I have to get up. Shower. Get dressed. Show up and put on the proud yet pensive face while I talk about the death, how grateful I am that Dad is alive and unharmed.

I am feeling all those things, of course. But I don't need the public to see them.

I didn't sign up for this.

But when I think about Leon, my insides untangle, and it becomes clear how much I want to see him again. It's only been a few hours since we last met, kissed, but I want his lips on mine again. I want to pull his body into me. I want to . . . god, there's so much I want to do. Probably nothing the Star-Watch people should see, though.

When I check my phone, I see two emoji on the screen in a text from Leon: the heart and the rocket ship. I laugh and release a heavy sigh.

That's what gets me out of bed, after this no-sleep night and the panic that still writhes through my bones. Someone I've met has died. Someone the country knew and had hopes for has died.

Somewhere around four a.m., I got to talk with Dad, which settled my nerves a bit. He's "banged up," but nothing's broken. Which means, while he's okay, the country will be mourning, and I have to play my part. All while StarWatch wraps it up in a neat little bow for their tribute to Mark Bannon.

So I jump into the shower, then get ready as quickly as I can. When I step out of my room, the smell of eggs and veggie sausage hits my nose. I inhale as much of it as I can, realizing how hungry I am after such a weird night.

"Breakfast casserole?" I ask, knowing the answer is yes.

"The NASA comms person said I should bring something."

"Well, this is your specialty." I laugh, even if the message isn't untrue.

She pulls the casserole dish out of the oven, and it takes all I have not to grab a fork and go to town. It's a simple recipe, but oh my god it's so good. The ultimate comfort food. We pack the car and make the short journey to Leon's house. I think Mom secretly likes the convenience, but in my mind, getting into the car for a three-minute drive does not compute.

We park, but before I get out of the car, Mom grabs my hand.

"What is it?" I ask. But I've seen this before. Her body visibly tenses, and I don't understand how she can be so animated sometimes—in fights with Dad, or when she's talking about the video games we both like—yet be scared stiff when it comes to social interaction.

"He never asked me if I could do this," she says. "I mean, he knows how much stuff like this affects me. I can't be on *television*."

"You'll do fine, Mom. StarWatch makes this shitty for all of us," I say, though I'm at least used to performing in front of a camera. "But yeah, I see how it'd be probably harder for you."

She shakes her head. "I'll be fine. I'll live. I just hate this. And I haven't found a good therapist, and the old one I used to use online is a bit too judgy for my tastes, and—and you don't care about all this." She laughs.

"Well, in the meantime, you can talk to me. Or maybe Grace can give you some pointers—she's really nice."

"It's funny," she says, "well, not actually funny, but growing up I'd always talk to Tori about this. I felt like she was the only one who really understood what I was going through."

I smile. Aunt Tori had a no-nonsense attitude and a loud, boisterous personality. She was the opposite of Mom in so many ways—she'd walk into a grocery store, talk to everyone she passed, forget half the items on her grocery list, but come out with five new friends.

"You know those weird bushes she helped plant in Prospect Park?"

"Of course," I say. "She took me there all the time. They were so ugly."

Mom laughs. "She loved those twisted, thorny, bizarre bushes. But I used to go back there while you were at school and Dad was . . . up in the air somewhere. Even though we were in one of the biggest parks in Brooklyn, I was always by myself there. It was my own private space to be with Tori."

Even though Aunt Tori died of pancreatic cancer a few years ago, it still feels raw sometimes. Brooklyn was full of memories of her: grabbing a slice at her favorite pizza place, her haggling with street vendors (with remarkable success) to get all her Christmas gifts.

Mom looks down to her hands, which are folded in her lap. "I always felt a connection to her there. I would prune the bushes and talk to her."

"Oh," I say. "Is that why you got so mad at Dad about all of this?"

"Part of it." She shrugs. "He just doesn't think about it. We can come to the same conclusion, but he gets there in thirty seconds and is ready to change our lives, and it takes me a little longer. I'd already said goodbye to Tori once. I didn't think I'd have to do it again."

We get out of the car and walk slowly to the door. Aunt Tori's death was slow and fast all at the same time, but if Dad died in that crash, this would have been sudden and nearly impossible to handle.

For both of us.

As we approach the front door of Leon's house, I take the casserole dish from her, because I know what's coming. I look up at her, and I realize she's completely unprepared for what's about to happen, especially in the sentimental, vulnerable state she's in. She goes to knock, and I say, "The cameras will be on us immediately. They'll follow us. Just look sad but relieved."

My stomach churns as the door opens, and the bright light of the camera flashes in my face. I have an even look on, and I can't check how Mom's doing, so she's going to have to hold on a bit longer. I take the lead, though.

I step in and greet Tony, and nod to Kat and Leon in the living room. There's a tension in the air. There's always some tension when StarWatch is in the room, but this is something darker. Different.

"You've got their intro, right?" Josh Farrow says to Kiara,

who's holding a camera like I'd hold a newborn. Uncomfortable, hesitant.

"Got it," she says, and the flash of the light is gone from my eyes.

I blink a few times, but when my vision returns, I see Kat's face. I've never seen her like this, I realize. Subdued, almost broken. She wrings her hands in front of her, pulling at her dress at random intervals. A nervous tic, I guess.

Leon just stares toward the floor, frozen.

It doesn't take me long to see why. Sitting there—in the middle of the floor—is a woman I know. Someone I should have known would be here: Mara Bannon.

"Oh god," Mom says. "Mara, honey. I'm so sorry."

While Mom instinctively crouches next to her, I place the casserole on the counter and immediately turn to the Tuckers.

"What's going on?" I ask.

"StarWatch asked her to come over," Kat says. "She didn't want to be alone."

"It was fine before the cameras got here." Tony shifts uncomfortably in his chair. "They started asking her very pointed questions about . . . the accident. She held it together as long as she could."

"We need to get them out of here." Leon's voice is low, almost a growl. "Can't we just tell them to go?"

His dad covers his tired face with his palm. "That's up to Mara. And she wants them to stay."

"Wait, what?" Rage starts to burn in my chest. Maybe it's the lack of sleep, or the general panic of the room, but I can't accept that answer. "She lost her husband *hours* ago. They're manipulating her, doesn't she see that? I don't even think *I* should be here, let alone these cameras."

Mara Bannon starts weeping loudly, which cuts off our conversation. I grab two mugs from the table and pour coffee for me and my mom. When I turn, I see my mother's soft but concerned face as she consoles Mara.

Kiara finds the best angle for the camera to capture both of their faces, and it makes me feel a little sick. Sure, she seemed pretty apathetic before, but this is just heartless.

"All right, that was a great moment, Becca," Josh Farrow says to my mom. "Why don't you join Tony and start talking like worried spouses. Mara, do you think you're up for a few more questions?"

It's like the room flinches. The soft burning rage inside me bursts into flame. Seething, I step toward Mara. Screw Star-Watch. If Tony doesn't have the guts to kick them out, I will—

"Mara," I say.

"Oh, Cal." She sees the look in my eyes. "No, no. I, um, I think I can finish the interview. It's what Mark would want."

"You tell me the moment that changes," Tony says.

She nods, and more tears leak out of her eyes. Someone puts a palm on my back and leads me away from the living room. It's Kiara.

"Calm down, kid. She wants this, and we're on a tight deadline."

I laugh mockingly. "That didn't sound like it. It looks like she feels obligated to do this. You're telling me, in all honesty, she wants to grieve for her husband in front of the whole country?"

She flinches, and I get my answer.

"Okay," she says. "I'll level with you. Mara's uncomfortable. I can tell she wants to go, and I feel icky. But the Bannons were always big fans of what Josh did for the program. I think she just wants to see this interview through in his honor."

"You think, or you *know*?"

"I don't *know* anything." She shakes her head, then drops her voice to a conspiratorial whisper. "Like Tony said, it's complicated. There's no clear right or wrong."

Mara and Tony sit next to each other now, and Josh is talking them through the next recording session as if it were a scene in a movie and they were the actors. Mara's expression turns hollow, and her face is seared in my mind. I see it even when I look away.

It's then I realize I disagree with Kiara. There may be no clear "right," but what StarWatch is doing? This is clearly wrong.

"Well, if you don't mind," Kiara continues, "I need to go back to filming a grieving lady for money, before I inevitably go to hell."

At this, I chuckle. The delirium from the lack of sleep juxtaposed with her straightforward humor makes my shoulders ease and my neck loosen from its spasm. I'm starting to think clearly. I know what I can do.

Mark liked StarWatch, and was on *Shooting Stars* more than any other astronaut, true, but in his last interview, he showed a lot of aggravation toward Josh. *". . . this isn't a reality competition. The stakes are high enough . . ."*

This *is* a reality show. One that profits off others' pain.

I take a deep breath, and I've made up my mind.

Kiara turns, but I grab her shoulder before she leaves the room. "I'm going to stream this. I need to expose this story."

"I don't think there's really a story here, champ."

"Don't call me champ, *sport*. And I think there might be." I nod in the direction of the living room. "Maybe my followers would like a behind-the-scenes look at this whole operation?"

She laughs. "You take down StarWatch, you take down NASA. Even you know what we did to spark interest in the program. I don't think that's a smart move."

"I don't want to take down StarWatch. I want to . . . put the focus on something important. You sparked interest in the program by showing Mark Bannon in training simulations and getting people politically active." I throw my hands in the air. "I mean, I posted a thirty-minute video of Brendan talking about Mars dirt, and it got two hundred thousand views in one day. It's still one of my most popular recordings. People care about *the program*, don't you see that? They don't care about StarWatch. At least, what it's become."

"To tell the truth, I don't like StarWatch either. But it's my job to make things more dramatic. Our ratings are slipping, and it's freaking the great Josh Farrow out, which he then takes out on *me*. I hate my job, but I do like *having* one . . ."

I pause to think. "Can you get Josh to really shine once I

start streaming? I think I can keep you out of it, and 'the face of *Shooting Stars*' will never know what hit him."

Hesitation crosses over her face, showing a rare moment of vulnerability from her. Within seconds, she snaps back, smiling.

"I can do that."

Kiara and I return to the room, and Mom gives me a confused, slightly concerned look. I just smile and shake my head. She'll know soon enough. Everyone will know.

CHAPTER 15

I pull out my phone and give it a light kiss. I've never done something like this before. I'm changing how the world sees this space launch. NASA is touting the sixties as this perfect era, but it *wasn't*. Dad always talked furiously about one interview from the midsixties. When astronaut Gordon Cooper was asked about the possibility of adding women astronauts, he referenced the first test flights NASA did with chimpanzees, saying they could have sent a woman up instead.

The sixties are bright and shiny and *white*, and NASA actually thinks people liked these families because they were fabulous and perfect. These families reinforced the chauvinism and racism that marred the entire decade, with little exception.

The record player plays a sad, soulful song—one that must've been picked by StarWatch to set the mood and reference the era. I scoff.

Nostalgia is a blindfold.

Those families were fabulous and perfect because the six-ties media demanded that of them. The astronauts were loved because they were brave explorers. Behind all that, though, they brought our country together with a unified goal—one rooted in science and innovation. That's what the Orpheus project is missing.

This isn't the first time NASA's turned this into a reality show, but if I have it my way, it'll be the last.

— — —

I hesitate before hitting the LIVE button. From behind the screen, I see Leon and Kat, looking altogether uncomfortable. Mrs. Bannon has moved back up to a chair, off from the wallowing spot on the floor where she started. My mother sips her coffee slowly and methodically. She sits poised and polished. You can see from each of their faces how sad they are, and how much they don't want to be here, while Josh rambles about what the next "scene" is going to be. He gives us talking points, but tells us to keep it natural. People just want to see everyone bonding together.

"I'll be asking questions throughout that were submitted by our viewers," he says. "Just answer honestly, but keep your tone even."

And it starts to make sense: Grace's concerned expression in every interview, Mark Bannon's irritation at being pitted against Dad and Grace, the strain that they all carried in their interviews. It's about how StarWatch treats them and their mission.

"Fuck. That last shot's blurry," Kiara says dramatically. "The whole clip is ruined."

That's my cue. After a deep breath, I start the live stream.

"We can't go live without that shot," Josh snaps. "That's the teaser. How did this happen?"

"*Probably* because you made me take over videography after our videographer quit," Kiara says, but I keep her face out of the video. "I have no idea what I'm doing with this thing."

"Any of you watch StarWatch's coverage?" I whisper to the camera. "Because you're about to see what's really behind that mask."

The tension in the room is palpable. I scan the room to see Kat gripping Leon's arm. Mom presses a hand to her chest. Adrenaline surges through my body, making it hard to keep my phone's camera from shaking. I need this to go right.

"We have to do it again," he says. "The whole thing— Mara, I know this is a very hard time for you, but can you get back on the floor and grieve for a few minutes?"

It's silent. Kat eyes her dad wearily, and I lock gazes with Leon.

"You . . . you want me to *what*?" Mara says.

"I know, I know. But we only need a few minutes of video. This is going to be a really special episode—we're even dedicating it to Mark. His memory. That's why I need you to show that emotion for the cameras again. Don't you think you sort of owe it to Mark?"

Silence descends on us like a wet blanket. The hairs on the

back of my neck prick up at the audacity. And in some sad part of my heart, I'm not even surprised.

"It's time for you to leave," Tony says. His voice is cool and even, but the heat behind his stare says otherwise. "You've taken advantage of three shaken, grieving families today."

"Excuse me," Josh says in an unusually polite tone. "But we've got the right to film in your houses, and the *people* want to see this. I have a list of questions here from our viewers. This is like a journey for all of th—"

"Stop." Tony clears his throat. "Isn't it strange that every time you have a pointed, insulting, or otherwise nasty question for us, you make sure to mention it's 'from our viewers'? I am taking away your right to invade our homes like this. And you might want to watch how you respond—you're the one being recorded this time."

Tony nods my way, and something in Josh snaps. He storms over to me, and I raise the camera to his face. He's young too, and I feel momentarily bad for throwing a wrench into his career so soon after he was given his own show to host, but I stand strong. I'm not afraid of him.

"You're going to blackmail us? You think we won't hesitate to sue you the moment that video goes live? Without us, without *me*, there is no NASA."

"See, Tony actually meant to say *streaming*, not recording." I look at the screen and get overwhelmed by the numbers, so early on a Thursday morning. "Eighty-five thousand, and climbing."

"And how long does it take to go viral?" Tony chimes in.

I roll my eyes briefly, wondering if anyone over the age of thirty actually understands how things go viral and what that word even means. "Not long," I say to appease him, then flip my screen to the front-facing camera. "I'm cutting this video short, for obvious reasons. Our families are going to be with one another in this challenging time. StarWatch doesn't get to be here anymore, so my job is done."

Kiara and I high-five in the hallway before she takes her packed-up camera and leaves the house.

— —— —

After they're gone, a silence falls over the room. Then, as if we rehearsed it, everyone but Mara jumps into action. Leon and Kat bring out an assortment of juices, Tony grabs Mara's coffee mug to refill it, and Mom starts cutting up the casserole.

StarWatch's control starts to unravel in front of me. Crystal juice glasses are put back on their shelves. They're replaced with plain drinking glasses, while paper plates are swapped for the retro china. The record player stops.

While everyone's busy cozying up the home, making this a warmer environment to grieve in, I take a seat next to Mara. Guilt gnaws at me, and I worry I've made a mistake. Her posture has fallen, but her expression is unreadable.

"I'm sorry," I say. "Did I . . . go too far?"

"We've done so much for StarWatch, Cal." She shakes her head. "Did you know that before NASA signed them on for *Shooting Stars*, they were almost forced to go online-only?"

I shake my head, and she continues. "When I was growing

up, I remember watching StarWatch for *all* the celebrity news and gossip. They made Hollywood life seem so glamorous. But over the years, they switched programming so many times—reality shows, fashion shows, celebrity cooking shows—it became more of a scramble for ratings than anything. I think they lost sight of the . . . aspirational aspect of the show. At least, that was the part that I loved."

The others have joined us in the family room again, the smell of casserole permeates the air, and everyone's leaning in to hear her story. Except Tony, who walks out of the room to take a call.

"Once we started working with them, though"—a smile crosses her face—"I would watch myself on the show, drinking out of those fancy champagne flutes or leading the community garden, and it brought back all those feelings I had as a kid."

"It seemed like Mark loved them too, for a while," Kat says with a laugh. "He was always in front of a camera."

Mara sniffles and presses a tissue to her nose. "He never liked their gossipy flair, but he loved being the center of attention."

My insides start churning, and I wonder if we could have found some other way to bring StarWatch back to their wits.

"I shouldn't have done that," I say, reaching for Mara's shoulder. "I didn't realize—"

Her strained laugh interrupts me. "Oh, Cal, honey, no. Someone needed to knock them down a peg, and I'm glad you were there. I was about to get on the floor. I really was."

Tony reenters the room, and something about his presence makes us all look up at him.

"Well, that was fast," Tony says. "That was Donna Szleifer, and she is furious. They've banned StarWatch indefinitely from entering any of our homes, and she says NASA is considering terminating their contract entirely."

Leon takes the empty space on the couch next to me and pulls me in to a side hug. "You did it, babe," he whispers in my ear.

A wave of uncomfortable sadness washes over me as I imagine Kiara losing her job and NASA losing StarWatch. But I know she's not guiltless here. I think of all the interviews Leon's been forced into, and how she keeps asking him questions about his gymnastics career. I think of the pointed questions directed at my dad, at Donna, at anyone attached to this mission.

Viewers—at least, *my* viewers—are smarter. They care. They're invested in this mission, and they're invested in making this country the best it can be. But they can't do that without *real* information.

America deserves better.

But one thing trips me up: Josh's expression as he left, pure fury and disgust, plays over and over in my mind, and the terrifying consequence hits me all at once.

What if StarWatch turns on NASA?

CHAPTER 16

Because leaning against my dresser became too much of a hassle, I've moved my cassette deck to its new home on my bedside table, and I lament the fact that I haven't gotten any new cassettes since moving here. It's all I can do to distract myself from a hellish week: a funeral, a hospital visit, and roughly a thousand troll comments to clear off my increasingly viral video. But, hey, my cassette collection can get me through anything.

I inherited all of Aunt Tori's cassettes when she passed away. Meaning, they didn't really *have* anything to give me, and Dad wanted to throw them away like they didn't mean a hell of a lot to her.

Sure, I started with her massive collection of Dolly Parton and REO Speedwagon, but that was merely the beginning. I'd stumble upon them weekly in Brooklyn, from stoop sales and street markets. Within months, I fell right in with cassette culture—which is totally a thing.

But today, it isn't helping.

I'm restless. My leg shakes without my brain giving it the command. I feel an itch in my chest, and I almost can't handle it. It's seven thirty, and I'm already in bed. I think of Leon. We barely saw each other all week, unless you count a stolen kiss between funeral activities.

I think of his lips, his taste, his . . .

I've got to see him. I shoot over a text without giving my mind a chance to talk me out of it.

"You up?"

"It's only 7:35," he responds. *"How much sleep you think I need?"*

A smile tugs at the corner of my lips. Again, my mind broadcasts that I've got to see him. So I ask if he wants to take a drive.

Within minutes, and with a little bit of convincing from me to my mom, I'm in my dad's Corolla. I pull out of the driveway and roll the windows down all the way. My arm turns into an airplane wing, cutting through the night sky so quickly, I could almost see the wind bend around it.

But since we live so close, that feeling only lasts a second.

"Hey," I say when Leon gets into the car.

"Cal." The way he says my name is the way I've always wanted someone to say it. Packed with emotion, warm and syrupy.

I turn back onto the road and drive through the Houston

suburbs. Stars punch through the night sky, and I'm left with a pit in my stomach, homesick for a world I've never had.

"How many views is your StarWatch video up to now?" he asks. "Millions? Bajillions? I've seen it linked *everywhere*."

"It's gone so viral, I can barely keep up with it anymore. But honestly? I don't want to talk about that right now."

"Okay. What should we talk about?"

"Can you tell me more about Indiana? Were you raised in the suburbs?" I ask. "Like this, with stars and huge lawns?"

He laughs. "Sort of. Indiana suburbs are a little different. Bigger yards, boring brick houses. Same amount of Olive Gardens, though."

One of the only Olive Gardens near me is the one in Times Square that boasts four-hundred-dollar meals on New Year's Eve. But I don't tell him that.

"Sounds relaxing, I guess," I say. "I'm still not used to sleeping at night without strangers shouting outside my window or cars beeping relentlessly."

"New York's that cliché?"

"Brooklyn is amazing and awful, all at the same time. You can get killer vegan Chinese food delivery at midnight, but you can barely see the stars at night. Nothing stops in Brooklyn. Manhattan's even worse."

He places a hand on my leg, and sparks fly. I can't catch my breath, but I keep talking.

"I can't wait to go back. Maybe try for another BuzzFeed internship? First, I thought I wanted to study journalism, but some of the university programs seem kind of dusty and out of touch, so I'm not positive on that one. And I'd have to take out a hell of a loan, or I could try to monetize my channel to pay for it." A pause. "The future is hard, eh?"

His grip tightens on my leg. "Not so hard if you refuse to think about it. I have no idea what I want to do with my life. Is that bad?"

"No!" I say, but it's too forced and quick to feel honest. The truth is, how do you *not* know what you want to do by now? "I mean, there are so many options. What do you like to do? Any jobs sound cool? Will you be going back into gymnastics? Can you make that a career? Have you looked at colleges yet?"

"Whoa, whoa, slow down, babe. I don't know. Any of that. I kind of think it'll hit me when I realize what I want to do."

I sense that I should let it go. But I get an itching in my skin—a need to put him on the right track before it's too late. *We're about to be seniors!* I breathe. I can let it go.

"But what if it doesn't?" I ask, apparently not letting it go.

I know I can help him.

"You don't have to worry about me," he says, like he's reading my mind. "I'm not lost, just indecisive."

"Well, let's think about it logically. What about your gymnastics? You still go to open gyms from time to time, right? Even if you don't want to compete, there are plenty of scholarships out there, I'm sure, and I assume colleges have gymnastics teams, right? Like, that must be a thing."

"That's definitely a thing. Just . . . not a thing I'm really into."

"You know, I watched the videos of your last competition before you came here. You were incredible."

"I was, I guess." He sighs. "It's like one day I woke up, like *really* woke up. And realized I'd given thirteen years of my life to gymnastics. Time I can never get back. And it hit me really hard: it didn't make me happy anymore. I . . . faked being sick that day and canceled my practice."

"Is this related to your depression? I mean, there's so much my mom avoids because of her anxiety, and I wonder if it's something like that."

"Your guess is as good as mine," he says with a shrug. "I must have liked it at some point, you know? But even now, I can't think of a meet where I was actually happy. Not since I was a little kid, when they'd just let you do somersaults all day."

The thought makes me chuckle. "Oooh, look at my athlete. You'll have to show me your somersault someday."

"Oh, so I'm *your* athlete now?"

My face flushes with heat, and I reach for the air-conditioning. As I direct all vents toward me, he leans forward, slowly, and plants a soft kiss on my cheek.

"I like the sound of that," he says. "Being yours."

"Really, it's kind of an antiquated way of looking at relationships, if you think about it. Me being possessive over you? That's toxic, right?"

"Hey, Cal?" He laughs. "Maybe spend less time on social media."

— — —

We pull onto Jordan Road, a silent, dusty road with no lights. All is still. And the tension inside my shoulders eases.

I should be alive with sparks and fire and romance, but I'm a little more focused on the point of our conversation. I feel so obnoxious—*Why does someone else's lack of career ambitions make* me *this anxious?* I wonder as I stop the car on the shoulder of the road.

Leon lets out a fake gasp. "Is this where you murder me?"

"It *is* a deserted road," I observe. "Left my weapons at home, though, so I guess we should just make out?"

Instead of leaning in and kissing me, like I made it very clear he should do, he gets out of the car. It's pitch black now that I've turned the car off, and there's nothing to hear but the crickets shouting. It's like a weird sensory deprivation tank.

I step out of the car, and a cool breeze hits my leg. Well, cool for Texas. I take a deep breath and release it, blowing out all the bad feelings from the past week.

Leon leads me to the middle of the road—it's not like many cars actually drive down here—and I survey the area around me. As my eyes adjust to the blackness of night, I see a few old wooden fences, keeping in acres upon acres of land on both sides. Cattle farms, I assume, since it doesn't seem like they're growing much else out this way.

"What about this—is *this* like Indiana? Just with different farms?" I ask.

"No, it's different," he goes. "It just *feels* different, you know? Like, we would be flanked by giant cornfields, or rows and rows of soy. The wind moves everything there. Giant trees, the farm crops. Everything's moving, and alive. Here everything feels so . . ."

"Dead?" I assume. He doesn't respond, so I guess he feels it too. "I get that. New York's alive in a very different way, but here it feels so plain. Simple, I guess. I don't hate it, though."

I let my gaze wander. The only source of light out here is a large building and complex about half a mile away. The glow of the space center looks eerie from here, looming. Like it's the one thing that can disrupt this calm and perfect moment.

My mind starts to process something I've been ignoring until just now. How quickly Bannon was erased from our lives.

"Mara Bannon left this week," I observe, though it seems pointless to say.

Leon catches where I'm looking and grunts in assent. "It happens fast, I guess. Never know when we'll be going back home. I wonder who will take over NASA's community gardening days."

He takes a seat, cross-legged on the empty road, so I do the same. We're a foot apart, but I feel this magnetic pull into him.

I want to be closer than this, though we're basically touching.

I want to be more alone than this, though no one's around.

"I don't want to lose you," I say. "I don't . . . I don't like how quickly things change here."

"Things won't change," he says, and he leans in to kiss me.

But they kind of will. NASA's announcing the six Orpheus V astronauts and their backups any day now. They're dying to get some good publicity after Bannon—"dying" might have been a poor word choice considering the circumstances—and they want to restore some hope that was lost in the death.

"What if they don't pick my dad, for the mission or backup? He hasn't been around for long; why would they put him on this first flight?"

Leon looks uncomfortable, like biting his lip will help him hold back something. "I think he'll be on, as an alternate at least. I wouldn't worry about that."

His eyes glisten in the moonlight, and I sense a bit of turmoil in his expression. I should let it go, but I've never been good at letting anything go.

"What's wrong?" I ask.

The silence expands between us. I feel it in my muscles, in my chest. Anticipation drives my hand forward, and I place it lightly on his face.

"I can't stop these thoughts," he says. "It could have just as easily been my mom who didn't make it back from Florida, and I should be relieved, but I don't feel anything but . . . There's this heaviness that I can't shake."

He breaks eye contact, but I keep my head level with him. "I'm here to listen, if you think it would help. I won't even interrupt you."

His eyes greet mine.

". . . Much."

"That's what I thought," he says with a smirk.

"Is this something that you've dealt with before?"

"Since I can remember." He pulls back and leans against

the bumper of the car. "Sorry, I'm not ready to talk about it. I thought I was, but I'm not. It's weird—"

"Hey, it's fine. Just . . . know I'm here."

He smiles. "I know."

We sit like this for five, ten, twenty minutes. We talk about our upcoming school year together like there's no doubt we'll both be in Clear Lake, graduating from the same school next year. Like everything couldn't change immediately. And it's good to talk about the future. To have a future I can see here, in Houston of all places.

I look away, and my eyes fall on the space center again. The mission launches in the spring.

"This might be the last quiet week we'll ever get," I say.

Leon considers me smoothly. I feel my emotions all at once, bursting through my heart, but I don't know what he's feeling. He's calm, I'm frantic. He's pleasant, I'm panicked.

But I know I need him now.

This kiss is different. We start softly, growing in intensity. Exponentially. I press him into me, and he wraps his arms around my neck. I crawl closer to him, until our legs are entangled. His warm leg slides up mine, causing chills to take over my body. I shudder as I pull him into me.

We're pressed to each other, and there's nothing on my mind but his taste. His tongue slips into my mouth, and I press mine against his. I moan softly because it feels so right. So perfect.

I put my palm on his chest, and with a smile, I push him back against the road. He looks uneasy, so I don't make a move. I just keep kissing him. We keep celebrating our closeness in muffled moans and gasped breathing.

And then my phone starts buzzing.

Then Leon's phone starts buzzing.

We're forced to stop. We're out of breath, but the unusualness of these simultaneous calls shakes me to my core. Our parents know we're out, not necessarily that we're doing *this*. I look at the caller ID.

"It's my mom," I say.

"It's Kat," he says.

We answer, and simultaneously shout a "hey" into the speakers.

My chest tightens as my mom speaks. Her voice is laced with excitement, worry, panic, and she can barely get the words out. Her words all mush together, and she's not actually saying anything.

Kat's much more articulate, apparently, because Leon pulls the phone away from my ear.

"Mom's on the mission. Your dad's her alternate." He smiles weakly. "It's really happening."

CHAPTER 17

Streetlights fly by my car as we ease from the rural farms to suburban houses. The flat, straight roads start to bend and twist, and the space center fades away in my rearview mirror. I feel like I'm soaring, but a look at the speedometer explains that I'm actually driving under the speed limit. My body's forcing me to go slower, but everything feels fast. Everything feels tight. My hands are numb.

Leon's mom is going to Mars. My dad's her alternate. We're really, really in this together. Our families are tangled up in a fascinating, seemingly ancient tradition. A silent understanding of practicing the same job, both for the astronauts and for the families. In *Apollo 13*—the movie, and debatably in real life—Marilyn Lovell advised an overwhelmed Mary Haise to respond to the press with three words: Proud, Happy, Thrilled.

That's my life now, and I *am* having all those feelings.

I'm proud of my dad. Just six weeks ago, things felt settled. The only constant in my family life was the yelling that my parents did. But that's become rare in the past month. And he's become . . . useful? Driven.

I'm happy too, but part of that is because of Leon. The way he makes me feel when he sits next to me and strokes my hand is too much. I'm falling so hard for him, and I wish there was some way I could stay grounded and think logically about this. My dreams of going back to New York and living with Deb are fading quickly. He's my present. This is my present.

And that makes me thrilled.

But I'm also terrified. I've missed four calls from Deb this week to talk about the crash and what happened, but I can't face her. I can't explain my feelings to her on any of this, and if she's watched any of the news stories lately, she'll have seen me and Leon together. She'll know I'm kind of *with* someone, and she must know how that could jeopardize our plans of living together.

"I haven't told my parents about us," Leon says as we pull up to my house, where cars line the driveway.

I shrug. "I think Mom figured it out the night of the crash. We haven't talked about it, though."

A smile is plastered on his face, and I know mine must look the same. I park the car on the street and meet Leon on the sidewalk. We survey my house, where everything has changed in the past twenty minutes. Our families' fates dovetail at this moment in more ways than one, and I hope they stay on the same path for a while.

He takes my hand, and we walk into the house and hear the applause and cheering, and it's nice to imagine that it's for us.

Kat immediately finds us and nearly tackles us both with a hug. "Guys, oh my god I'm glad you're here. Everyone else is already getting drunk, and it was starting to get really awkward."

"Nice place," Leon says. "Less retro stuff than ours."

"Thankfully," I say.

We make our rounds. Dad gives me a hug that's too tight, but his eyes are still teary. Mom eyes the situation wearily, and I see anxiety setting in. But she still has a pleasant smile when I give her a kiss on the cheek.

"At least he's not going up there yet," she says. "I mean, he gets to be a part of everything, but he doesn't get to go up there."

I don't reply, just squeeze her in a hug. She shakes her head, like she's clearing out the bad thoughts. "Sorry, you know how I worry. It's just happening so fast. And now we all have to fly to Florida in a couple days to see that satellite launch. It's . . ."

I laugh. "Believe me, I get it. Let's just celebrate today."

I move around the room, dodging champagne glasses and drunk astronauts. There are about ten of them in my living room, and I find it fitting that they're here right now.

Through the Mercury, Gemini, and Apollo projects, the astronauts' alternates would take care of everything the first line didn't have time for—the parties, the press events. They'd do it all while waiting in the wings for their chance to really shine.

After Dad got back from the hospital, he was forced to take some time off as the rest of NASA scrambled to manage the disaster. He spent that time unpacking the boxes from storage. Among the mess was his collection of *Life* magazines— pretty much every one that covered the space race. He pulled out a model of Apollo 8 and a signed portrait of Jim Lovell, the commander of the near disaster that was Apollo 13. Needless to say, I learned a lot about the history of spaceflight in Dad's time off.

It was all here. A secret obsession, a secret dream.

I look up at him and smile, because he gets to live it.

I'm not sure where all the champagne came from. This time, they don't even have soda, or snacks, or anything else. This was a last-minute effort, and I imagine them clearing out the wine shop's champagne stock just before they closed. Or, maybe NASA just has a secret, endless stock somewhere.

When I make eye contact with Kat, she nods in the direction of my room. I excuse myself and follow her, with Leon not far behind. Once I shut the door, I realize that I've brought a boy to my room for the first time ever. That thought makes me sweat a bit.

I sit on the bed with Leon as Kat tears through my cassette collection.

"You are a weird egg," she says. "Who listens to Nirvana? Other than, like, Dad, if it accidentally comes on his alt nineties playlist."

Regardless, she takes the cassette out of its case and studies it closely. After a few wrong buttons, she opens the holder in my deck and slips it in upside down before getting it right. She sighs in frustration as she finally gets the cassette in place. She presses play and waits.

"Why is nothing happening?"

"There's a little bit of dead time before the cassette starts—hold on." As I say it, music starts pumping through the speakers. "See?"

"I don't get it," she says. "Any of this cassette business. Hey, Leo, why so quiet?"

When she says it, I turn to him. He's looking down at his shoes, which are pointed inward toward each other. He looks a little bothered, a little bummed, like he's slipping away again. I put my hand on his back and stop myself from asking if he's okay—he knows I'm here if he wants to talk.

"Honest question," he says. "Do you ever feel like you don't matter? I walked in that room, and I was actually happy because I was"—he pauses and shrinks away—"holding Cal's hand. And I realized that today, like every other day from here on out, no one would care. I wanted Dad to be taken aback or Mom to give me a big smile or something. I've never had a . . . whatever we are. And I know it's Mom's big day, but aren't all days Mom's big day here?"

"Don't you like that, though? No one gives a shit about us," I say, and pull his mouth to mine in a kiss. "We're kind of on our own."

Kat laughs. "I think y'all are lucky, if you ask me. I guess sixteen is still young enough to have them all up in my shit about books and the future and all that."

"But they never really cared about my future. I mean, they kind of gave up when I quit gymnastics."

Kat eyes me, then looks down. I wonder what she wants to say, but Leon cuts in, saying, "You can talk about it."

"I think since we found out about your depression, they haven't really wanted to pressure you." Kat paces the room, but her voice doesn't fade when she says the word. When Leon's eyebrows rise, I get the feeling she's the only one who doesn't hesitate around him. "I mean, have you heard the word 'gymnastics' in the past few months in this house? They're all afraid they pushed you too hard."

"Wait. They actually thought my gymnastics career gave me depression?" Leon's got this incredulous look on his face. "They can't actually think that's how it works."

"Maybe they thought they were making it worse," I say. My voice is quiet, because I don't want to defend them, but I don't want him to jump to conclusions.

"I think it was getting worse on its own. I couldn't stop it. It was just more obvious in gymnastics. I kept cutting down my trainings; I'd show up unprepared. God, on my off days last summer I couldn't even get out of bed, let alone make it to the gym."

"You seemed to like it when we went to the open gym last month," Kat says.

"I did," he says. "But I was just goofing off. My form was

awful, and I fell off the pommel horse twice before I could even spin around once. It was a mess."

"But you had fun," I said. "Just like those somersaults from when you were a kid. Maybe you should do gymnastics, but for fun this time. Find a team that does smaller competitions. Don't hire a trainer. Don't let the reporters call you a future Olympian anymore. Just do what feels right to you."

Kat takes a seat next to Leon, so he's sandwiched between us. We're both hesitant, but respectful of his boundaries. Our shoulders touch.

"The moment I step into the gym, the cameras are on me. StarWatch thinks that's the only interesting thing about me to report on, and if I make it clear my sights aren't set on national competitions . . . I'll just be letting everyone down."

Leon groans and stretches out on the bed, *my bed*, and there's a rapidly growing piece of me that wonders if I could ask him to stay the night. Then I silently scold myself as this is one-hundred-percent not an appropriate thought to have at a time like this.

"But it's not like I could ever pick it back up like I did before. Could you imagine what my life would be like? Training for national competitions seven days a week with the weight of the world on your back?"

Again, I feel the urge to hold him until it's better. But I think of what he told me the first time I saw his lows. I can't help this urge I have to try to make it better, to insert myself into this when it's not my place.

I don't know how to be with him in the way he needs. If he needs space, I'll respect that. If he needs time, I'll give it to him. The tug in my chest illustrates my struggle, my compulsion to fix things and make it better.

That's what makes our relationship so different from any other I've had. That's what makes it so special. I'm learning, not fixing. For once, I'm listening—or at least, I'm trying to.

"Why don't you just tell your parents what you told us?" I ask. "That you just want to do it for fun."

"Don't see the point." He looks to Kat. "I'm just the side attraction here. Mom's going to Mars, and nothing's going to be *about us* anymore."

As soon as the words leave his lips, a smile comes over Kat's face, and she almost shouts:

"Well, screw those guys. Let's make this party about you, then. Here"—she motions us to sit even closer together, and she pulls out her phone—"do you have any pictures together yet? Let's get some good ones to celebrate your relati— or . . . whatevership."

Our eyes meet.

"Relationship?" I ask.

He smiles back. "Relationship."

Between smiles and light kisses, we pose in a few pensive, straight-faced poses, then a few happy beaming ones.

"You can have one kissing picture. Because that's all the cuteness I can handle right now. Make it count."

We make it count.

CHAPTER 18

Over the course of the next few days, we made it count . . . a lot. Our families were so busy that slipping out was easy, not that we were even hiding anything. I woke up every day with the sting of his stubble on my lips and a vibrant buzz pulsing through my veins.

Fun fact: Did you know that astronaut families fly coach to Florida while the astronauts themselves fly via jet and sidestep the lines? I'm not looking for handouts here, but that does seem a bit unfair, seeing as my father is a *True American Hero*!

Yes, I know that's a stretch. No, that didn't stop me from using that line when I didn't want to take my fashion boots off at the TSA check.

As I lie across three airport waiting area chairs, I review the emails I sent Leon last night. There were four, and they were all links to vaguely condescending quizzes like "What should I be when I grow up?" Alongside some real resources for figuring out your career.

As for his school selection, I dug up four very promising universities that all have competing gymnastics teams. That said, from their Instagram accounts or from the YouTube videos I found, it was clear they all focused a little more on having fun than winning competitions.

I also slipped in a Hogwarts House quiz, because when I told him I was Slytherin, he said, and I quote, "That's the bad one, right?"

In my mind, it's pretty simple: He feels lost now, but that's just because he doesn't have any direction. Any career goals. I don't expect anyone to be operating at my level of preparation, but there's only so much I can do.

But he hasn't responded yet, to any of them. How do you help someone who doesn't want to be helped?

"Hey, kiddo."

I smile when I see it's Kiara. She's in black tights and brown boots, with an infinity scarf and beanie. It's like Brooklyn style transcends the oppressive early summer heat, even in Texas. Her bright pink phone sticks out of a chest pocket on her denim jacket, the only pop of color she apparently allows herself.

God, I miss Brooklyn hipster style so goddamn much here at Polo Shirt Headquarters.

Her piercing eyes look through me, and she tilts her head sweetly.

"Looks like someone's having, let me guess . . . boy problems?"

I laugh. "Ten p.m. problems. I need my beauty sleep."

She's got her carry-on bag with her, which seems to be filled with only camera equipment for StarWatch.

"You know, the great Josh Farrow almost got *fired* because of your video? NASA almost terminated our contract, but we got off with a warning." She flashes a quick smile. "I think we're going a bit nicer now. It's part of our new image."

"I'm sure." I roll my eyes. "Thanks for helping, though."

"It was worth it to see Josh so flustered. I think all the— and I use this word very lightly—*fame* got to his head. Plus, it's been nice not being on call. We haven't had much access to the astronauts since your incident went viral. We've resorted to sharing some of your videos as part of our coverage." She smirks. "Actually, anything we say about you gets us a ton of attention, so that was a fun discovery."

"No one asked me for permission," I say. "I mean, I would've given it—even to StarWatch—but why didn't anyone ask? How am I a more responsible journo than you all? No offense."

"None taken, and I wouldn't call us real journalists. Our name is StarWatch. The TV show is called *Shooting Stars*. We're not exactly an A-list cable news network."

I laugh, trying to shrug off the annoyance. But it bites at me. *Do your job. Say you want to use my footage. Have some integrity, even if you are a glorified gossip show.*

"Don't get all caught up in the details," she says. "I'm looking out for you."

"Oh, yeah? How so?"

"I've been in talks with some big ad companies. Do you know how much they'd be willing to give you for a sponsored post on your feed?"

"I've been approached by a ton of ad companies. I mean, I could probably charge five thousand per sponsored video—these people are very loose with their money, and my followers are more active than ever, since I have an inside look at the Orpheus project." My expression drops. "But I can't do that to my followers. I'm sure some wouldn't mind, but what about the ones who have been there all along? I've seen so many Flash accounts grow into ad machines, and I can't become one of them."

"So . . . what's your end goal? I'm sure I can help either way. I've got contacts in New York, and they're all fascinated by you and your big following. I went back last weekend, and my friends and I had a long conversation about your career over brunch. *New York* magazine, *Teen Vogue*, the *Today* show. Potential internships were discussed."

"You could get me an internship at *Teen Vogue*?"

"If you wanted," she says. "My friend at Condé Nast has been following you for a while. They're expanding their live video reporting. Unless you're too cozy here to move back."

"Of course I'm going back to Brooklyn," I say. "But I'm seventeen, I can't just . . . go. Believe me, I want out of here. As soon as I can."

Preferably, out of here with Leon by my side. But I don't say that, because she's weirdly invested in my life as it is.

Kiara takes my contact details to forward along to her

Condé Nast friend, before we finally board the plane. Once I'm settled in my window seat, I put on an audiobook. I have to rewind four or five times before we take off because I'm so distracted. When that doesn't work, I close my eyes and fall asleep.

— —— —

Okay, I know I complained about Texas humidity, and I apologize profusely, because Florida is a literal swamp. Even this late at night. I feel the nearby cape more than I see it or hear it.

After a short ride in a black car, we're sent off to our hotel rooms to get whatever sleep we can before our early morning wake-up call. I wonder if all launches—for satellites or shuttles—are this early. I think about covering the launch tomorrow, but don't feel the need. We'll have the cameras all over us anyway, as the little, but important, antenna gets shot up into the sky.

"See, the antenna will make it to Mars a few months before we do, and enter the orbit. We'll intercept it when we get up there, and it'll help us triangulate our touchdown."

Now that we've reunited with him, Dad is explaining this in great detail to Mom, and my attention is fading in and out. It's interesting, so I make a note to track down the people who worked on the satellite and see if any of them want to have an interview with me.

The hotel on the premises has a kind of military feel that I can't put my finger on. The rooms are suites, with a tiny working kitchen and two separated bedrooms with a living room in between. Everything is brick. The exterior, the interior. I claim my room at random, my parents take the other, and I fall flat on the comfy bed.

I love the privacy of this suite. I have a door that locks, and I'm separated from my parents by an entire living room. I imagine sharing this king bed with Leon, feeling his body against mine all night. The idea thrills me but scares me too.

There's a chance we could get away with it. Leon wouldn't want to share with Kat anyway, and his parents are going to be too distracted in their own room to notice. My breaths fall short as the idea rushes through my head.

It's too risky.

Or . . . is it? None of our parents seem to notice us even when we're not sneaking around.

Before I can talk myself out of it, I leave the suite. Kat's in the hall, holding a bucket of ice.

"Have a good flight?" I ask.

They took the earlier flight because NASA couldn't fit all the families on one passenger plane. Most of the alternate families were on ours, while the lead crew families were on hers.

Kat's hair is a damn mess, and I don't need her to say a word to know she is ready for bed. The launch is obnoxiously early tomorrow, after all.

"It was okay. They're all asleep already—I just went to the ice machine because I need my water cold. You probably don't care about my ice needs, sorry, just not looking forward to tonight."

"You sharing a bed with Leon?"

She groans. "He takes up the entire bed. And it's a king. I'm about to just sleep on the couch."

"What if I told you I had an . . . alternate solution?"

Her eyes widen, and a smirk comes over her face. Her gaze darts between me and the door of her hotel room. I see her mind work through it. Will *she* get in trouble?

"Right now I'd do anything to have that bed to myself. I'll make it work. You clear the path to sneak into your room."

My spirits lift, but I don't get ahead of myself. I don't know if this is what he even wants. If he wants to wait to share a bed, or if he doesn't think it's worth the risk. And in the anticipation, it's clear to me:

It's what *I* want, so freaking badly. I grab her arm before she goes back to her hotel room.

"Just, let him know he doesn't have to. And don't pressure him. Okay?"

"I don't think it'll be a problem." She winks.

Now that I'm alone, I pace between our two doors. My heart pounds in my chest, and I feel the ache spread across my shoulders and down my arms and legs. I'm panicked. He could say no. Or worse, what if he says yes out of obligation? Or what if I sneak him in there and we get caught and the Star-Watch cameras come in and he leaves me forever and—

The door opens.

I forget how to breathe.

Until his smile lights up the damn hall.

"Hi." I pull him into a firm kiss. "You okay with this?"

"Are you kidding? I'd do this every night if I could."

My heart plummets to my feet, and I dizzily walk to my door. I slip the keycard into the slot and hold a finger out to Leon to wait. No one's in the main room, and all is quiet, save for my panting breaths. I creep in and see my door open and room empty. I signal Leon to go in there, and he dashes past me. My blood pressure spikes as I shut the door and pray for no one to enter.

He makes it.

I walk over to my parents' room and hear them chatting on the other side. It's a level, quiet conversation. I haven't heard them fight since the accident, now that I think about it. Between the boy in my bed and the peace in the house, maybe this astronaut thing was exactly what our family needed.

I knock on the door and tell them good night. I hear them call back a good night, love you, and all the other obligatory parent stuff, and I cross the floor to my room.

"Hey," I say.

He's sitting on my bed, a little awkwardly with his inward-pointed feet and slouched shoulders. I sit next to him and lean in for a kiss. He tastes like mint—he must have brushed his teeth before he came out. I turn the lights off, and we slip under the covers.

"I've been thinking about what you told Kat. And how you don't feel like you matter. Around your parents, I mean." I can't form the words right, because all I'm thinking is, *I'm in bed with Leon*, but we haven't had any alone time since and I have to get this out.

"Yeah?" he says, and his intense gaze pushes into me.

"Okay, so I'll just say it. Have you been with a person who made you feel worse? More alone? I just don't want to be that guy, and I want to learn, but I'm inherently bad at doing the right thing when it comes to you and—"

He puts a finger to my lips, and I melt.

"There's been no one else. I kind of dated someone in sixth grade, but that doesn't really count. I've kissed a few people, some girls, some guys. But nothing real. Nothing like this."

"Oh."

It's all I can say.

The news surprises me. I could write a novel about how attractive he is, how good he smells, how fucking sweet he is when you really get to know him. But I'm the first person he's found datable.

"It's funny," he says. "Well, maybe not, but in Indiana, Katherine always had a boyfriend. Like, always. Dad would have to run her around on dates, it was wild. She's had two boyfriends since we moved here. But I haven't had any, until now."

"But you're so . . ." I try to think of the right word, and fail miserably. "Hot."

His smile is perfect. "Am I, now?"

On that cue, we pull off our shirts, and I press his body into mine. His breath hits my neck as our legs hook around each other. We're a mash of tongue and teeth and warmth, and when I pull away to look into his eyes in the dim light, my heart stops. I'm all in with this guy. I never want to stop kissing him.

There's nothing that can prepare you for something like this. The fire and heat pulsing off another body in your bed. How no matter how close you are, how much you squeeze each other tightly, it's never enough. It's been a month since we first kissed, and already, my relationship morphed into a need that can't be satiated.

"I think I might love you," he says.

I press my lips onto his and don't let go.

Shooting Stars
Season 2; Episode 11

EXCLUSIVE INTERVIEW: On this episode of *Shooting Stars*, NASA prepares to launch a satellite into space. In advance of next week's season finale, we take this time to look back on another year at NASA's headquarters, and we've brought in a new expert. (New episode airs 7/15/2020)

"Hello, and welcome to *Shooting Stars*. I'm Josh Farrow, and sitting opposite from me is a new guest to the show. Ariana Rogers, CEO and founder of the privately funded space program JET-EX, welcome to the studio."

"Lovely to be here, Josh. I feel like I'm breaking some unspoken rule by appearing on your show—not that we don't work closely with NASA, of course. But you've been in their back pocket for a couple years now, right?"

"Ms. Rogers, with all due respect, I think they've been in *our* back pockets. We're simply fans of the Mars mission and the fascinating astronauts who bring this mission to life. The angle we haven't explored at all is privately funded space exploration. If you don't mind, I'll jump right in to our viewer questions. For many years, privatized spaceflight groups like JET-EX were seen to be adversaries of NASA. Why do you think that is?"

"It's a good question. In the end, we reach into the same pool of astronaut candidates, engineers, and other scientists. I understand the perception, but I think we truly haven't seen this kind of enthusiasm from within since the early decades of spaceflight."

"Is it that competitive nature that drives this enthusiasm? Obviously in the sixties, Americans were focused on beating the Russians to the moon. Now the dream may be more nebulous, but there is still a great deal of competition. And it looks like you might be getting beat to Mars."

"Ha, Josh. No need to be brash about this. We're supportive of NASA's mission, but the one thing we have that they don't is secure funding. After Mark Bannon's passing, there was a moment I legitimately thought the government would pull funding from the Orpheus missions. I mean, you lose one of your most famous astronauts and injure two others? It's the kind of thing that makes lawmakers put a screeching halt to it."

"Whereas you have the resources, being privately funded?"

"Yes. We take calculated risks, like anyone else, and we could always have shareholders pulling out, but there's a lot more faith in us. Even from NASA—we're actually building and testing a few pieces that will be a part of the Orpheus V launch. Either way, it's not a competition. We've offered to help with the planning for Orpheus VI and are looking for other ways to collaborate in the future."

"That is, if NASA *has* a future."

CHAPTER 19

When I wake, I feel the chill of the air-conditioning creep around my half-naked body. Through squinted eyes, I see Leon's silhouette beside me, next to the bed. He pulls the covers over my shoulders and plants a soft kiss on my forehead.

He leaves the room, and I stay awake just long enough to hear the outside door click, to make sure he got out without being seen or heard. A sigh escapes my chest, and I feel remarkably great all over. I pull his pillow into my arms and breathe in his scent, steal the last of his warmth from the empty bed, and fall back asleep.

It's still dark when my alarm sounds. It's nothing short of magic that I'm not only ready to get up, but excited for this. I'm ready for my first of many launches over the foreseeable future. This satellite may be small, but it plays an important role in the whole mission—without it, they wouldn't be able to land part of the ship on the Martian surface. Triangulation. Or something. I should have paid more attention to Dad when he explained it, but to be fair, dads can make anything sound boring.

I check my notifications, which are flooded by followers who are excited for the launch. Everyone expects me to cover it, but for once, I don't want to cover this story. I only want to share this moment with Leon.

My body feels light with energy. I'm excited to be with him again. I want to be with him all the time.

I never responded to his maybe confession of love, but I might be feeling it too. I've never felt this. I can't control it, and that scares me. He left my room maybe thirty minutes ago, but I miss him. I actually miss him. An emptiness eats away at my chest, and all that's left is the soft burning, yearning, wanting.

I finally leave my room, shower, and before I know it, I'm standing in the waiting area with my family. Our departure time was seven thirty, but I didn't think to ask when Leon was supposed to get here. I only see a few families left. We're all civil toward one another, and I'm stuck being more formally introduced to a few scientists I've met while doing video interviews for my followers. I don't see him, which makes my chest ache all the more.

We file into a black car, and we join a caravan of similar cars that must last a quarter mile. This part of Florida is . . . sparse. It's wet and swampy out there, but the dirt still seems dry. I could count the trees we've passed in this drive.

I realize this is the longest I've been with both of my parents in a long time. It brings back a nagging question that's been on my mind for a while.

"Dad," I say, "can I ask you something about StarWatch? About the jet crash, and Mark?"

He sits up straight.

"Um . . . sure?" Dad replies. I worry that what I'm going to ask is too much, and maybe that he doesn't want to think about them, but he turns to me in an open way.

So I take a breath and ask.

"Did it ever feel to you like StarWatch was *looking* for a catastrophe? I keep trying to figure out if they're really on our side or not. I don't think they even know."

"Well, whether they're on our side," he says with a chuckle, "I think we can safely say no. They care about themselves; they care about ratings. But I don't think they'd wish someone's death over it."

"But something doesn't add up," I interject. "They were so supportive at the beginning. They influenced the bill that secured funding through the rest of the Orpheus program or whatever. That teaser video with Mr. Bannon . . . they did everything they could to make Bannon and this whole program look like a safe bet. They got attention for being NASA's biggest supporter. And now, they're treating it like NASA is on the verge of collapse and focusing on—"

I'm cut off by his sigh. "Man, I don't know. Those first videos were kind of tacky. They played both sides—the bill was bipartisan, but people were *bipartisanly* against it too. Yes, I made that word up.

"Anyway," he continues, "for the Republicans, they hated that we'd be pulling from the military's budget. Democrats worried that once this money dried up, NASA would take funds from education and social programs. Why should we explore space when we could fix our broken health-care system?"

There's a wave of silence that passes through the car. That's a good point.

"Can this be just between us? Not on your show or even to your friends?" Dad asks, and I nod. "The late sixties were not great times in America. We were in an endless, pointless war that took so many lives. Kennedy's promise was the one thing all sides of the political spectrum could agree on: that we'd get a man on the moon by the end of the decade. StarWatch thought that fervor could work for them. They thought they could replicate it in our current political climate. NASA just wrote the checks."

"So that's where the sixties decor comes from? StarWatch did this?"

"That's what Mark told me at least. That's why we're in these fancy houses with midcentury furniture and record players. And that's where StarWatch's video, painting him as Mark Bannon, a True American—someone who could unite the country after the disaster of the past few years—came into play."

It dawns on me. "They got too much power?"

"I think that's why they've been treating your father so poorly," Mom cuts in. "They thought Bannon was the best fit to head the first mission."

"StarWatch was trying to pull strings, which is why things have been . . . weird with all of us. Your streaming that didn't help them. But I think it put us in NASA's good graces."

We get out of the car, and we're ushered into a fenced-in area beyond the launch zone of the satellite. It's pretty small for a launch. I knew we were sending up a vaguely human-sized satellite inside a giant metal tube, but I couldn't stop my mind from imagining big shuttles and massive launches.

To my right, behind the crowd, StarWatch is setting up. They're finding the right angles to shoot us in the rising sun, and I imagine StarWatch meetings where the producers wonder why people don't tune in anymore and decide the answer is to twist the knife and cast a dark cloud over the program. It's all nonsense.

After we walk out into the viewing area, they shut the door beyond the fence. I scan the crowd and look out past the barbed wire.

I take in the scene and realize I'm standing around with some of the most impressive minds in the country.

And for the first time, I include my dad in that. To see him here, respected by his peers, even respected by his country, makes me smile. Everything I thought from before—the families accepting us, the country being bored by us—was wrong.

I separate from my parents and slide past kids and spouses and dressed-up astronauts. Out of the corner of my eye, I see Grace shaking hands with a guy in a suit. Leon must be close.

They've started the countdown, but I want to get to him first. I push past people, and my chest burns with anticipation.

Finally, I catch his eye and he smiles at me. As I glance to the right, I spy Kiara as she sets up her camera behind him. She nods to me, and I know what they want.

Their new angle.

It's the perfect picture. The perfect thing to revitalize the waning interest in the launch. Young love and a shuttle launch. I stand next to him, our backs exposed to the camera. Faces pointed upward. As the satellite lifts off, I slide my fingers between his and squeeze.

It's beautiful, and perfect, until the satellite explodes in the sky.

CHAPTER 20

For a moment, it's peaceful. We're barely knocked back by the blast, like a strong but very warm gust of wind blew through us, and then the multibillion-dollar antenna becomes nothing but some smoking ash in the field beyond the barbed wire.

After the shock registers, Leon lets go of my hand and rushes up to get to his mom. People shout orders at me, to get back, to move toward the door, to do . . . something. I can't concentrate, and everyone's moving in different directions.

"This is the nail in the coffin for NASA," I hear one of the astronauts say, loud enough for too many people to hear.

Could this really be such a big setback?

I can't find my parents, and I can't find Leon anymore because I've been brought back into the building. Concerned murmurs flood the small office space, and some scientists sprint back and forth.

I don't want to be alone right now. But everyone's left me. Or I left them.

So I do the only thing that will calm me down, make me feel like I'm in control. I get out my phone and start streaming.

"Okay, so, here's what I know. It's, um, eight fifty in the morning. We've just had the launch of the antenna that would help direct Orpheus V to a safe landing on Mars. That launch saw disaster, as it exploded a couple miles after it blasted off from the ground." I pause to breathe. It becomes a pant. "All the astronauts appear to be concerned, and some have even hinted at an indefinite delay of the program. I'll track down someone who can speak to why the explosion happened."

I look off the camera and think I see my mom in a corner.

"I've got to go," I say. "I have to find my family."

I cut the connection and sprint across the tiled floor, dashing around still-scurrying scientists, until I meet my mom on a bench. She looks at me, and I see the panic across her face. It's still fresh; she'll need some time to really wrap her head around what just happened.

"We're okay," I say. "At least we're all okay."

"I can't go through this anymore." She shakes her head. "I mean, your father almost dies in a jet crash, and the first launch I've ever seen turns into an explosion? How are any of us supposed to handle this?"

I can fix this. I can fix this.

"Let's go back to the hotel. Is Dad here?"

"He had to go. All the astronauts did."

The caravan of black cars is stalled outside the building, so we get in one and I give the hotel name to our driver. Mom's calmed down some, and I think removing her from the situation must have helped. But that doesn't stop the panic from settling in my body.

Something feels wrong. Everything feels wrong.

When we get back to the hotel, there's nothing I want to do more than get in bed and breathe Leon in some more. Mom goes to take a shower, so I walk next door and knock a few times. No response. I knock harder.

The door opens, and Kat steps out.

"Hey, everyone okay?" I ask.

Her face tells me the answer before she says it. "No, not really."

"Can I see Leon? I mean, if that's okay with him?"

"No, well, yeah. He's just really wigged out by the whole thing."

I don't really say anything, but she lets me in anyway. I make my way to their bedroom. He's facing away from me, sitting on the bed and holding his knees.

"Is there anything I can do?" I ask. "I know you're super upset, but are you . . . worried about future flights, or angry at NASA? Or—"

"I'm sad," he says. And the way he says it makes me sad. "Like, I know that sounds juvenile, but I'm so sad. It feels hopeless, like there's this big gaping hole in my chest, and it's slowly eating me from the inside. It's like this anytime something bad happens, but also when good things happen too. Last night"—he lowers his voice—"was so amazing, but even when I was with you, holding you, it was like this . . . haze was over me. You were so close to me, and I'm fucking in love with you, but that doesn't fix it. Nothing does."

I sit on the bed, a reasonable distance away from him. His jaw is set in a hard line. His brows are furrowed.

"I'll help you, however I can. I swear. I'll do anything. You want me to help you find a new therapist? My mom just found one online who she likes, but there have to be physical offices around here. I know I tried to kiss you that first time you were upset, but I want to be here for you in whatever way actually works."

I stop myself from telling him I love him too. Even if I do mean it. Because, fuck, I do love him. I love him so much—but I can't tell him now. I can't tell him this in an attempt to try to patch him up, pull him together. He deserves so much more than that.

I kiss him on the knee.

"What was that for?" he asks, laughing.

"Well, I can't kiss you on the lips because that's probably insensitive, but I can't *not* kiss you right now, so I figured knee kisses were the most unromantic thing I could possibly do, so it wouldn't be seen as me making a move to make you feel better."

He leans forward to his knees and gives me a kiss on the lips.

"At the risk of sounding incredibly cliché," Kat says, "could you two get a room that is preferably not mine?"

I turn my head toward her and roll my eyes. "Fine, I'll go."

Leon rubs the back of my neck. "Not to bring things down, but you know things could be changing, right?"

"What do you mean?" Kat asks.

"They might cancel the whole mission. Either of our parents could get laid off. Anything could happen, and then we'd be gone."

"I'm not leaving you," I say, even though I know the possibilities. "We don't have enough information to freak about this. Let's just . . . enjoy what we have. Trust me."

"I trust you." He keeps looking down, so I sigh, then stand.

When I go to squeeze through the door, Kat gives me a quick hug before jumping into the spot next to her brother.

Shooting Stars
Season 2; Online Content

LIVE UPDATE: Tune in live at 11:00 a.m. (CST) as Grace Tucker joins us by phone from Cape Canaveral, Florida, about the recent explosion that could shutter NASA for good.

"Grace, dear, I want to start by saying how heartbreaking it is that the Orpheus Twenty—I'm sorry, the Orpheus Nineteen—have to deal with the fallout from this. Can you walk us through the incident?"

"Well, Josh, we're keeping a positive outlook. The satellite was necessary for launch, but I'm being told we're already planning the launch of a secondary satellite that will work as well, just not give us all the readings we were expecting. And that's okay. The important thing is that we figure out the issue that caused the explosion, and we keep everyone safe."

"Do you mind if I ask a bold question?"

"I've never stopped you before."

"Ha! Fair. Our viewers always appreciate your openness, Grace. Does NASA have the funding to build and launch another satellite? Last we heard, the program was strapped for funding as it was."

"We can keep Orpheus V funded, but we need to make sure the government doesn't back out on its promise to fund the full project. We're not going to Mars just to say we did it. We need more resources to build a flexible base on the planet, where we can continue to do research. In the future, we could find a way to make Mars habitable, sure, but more important, we could learn more about how Mars became what it is today, and mitigate that process on Earth. The first step on Mars will be a huge moment, but what comes next will change our entire future for the better."

"If you don't mind, I have a few more viewer questions about funding. First—"

"If you want to talk funding, why don't you have your JET-EX friends come on again? Thank you for the opportunity to talk, but I have to go. To all the viewers, I hope you know how much your support really means to all the astronauts, scientists, engineers, and every other person on our team, from Houston to Florida. We all sincerely thank you for your interest over the years. And, Josh? We will *always* be the Orpheus Twenty. Remember that."

"Well, there you have it. Stay tuned for the season finale of StarWatch's most watched show, *Shooting Stars*. You won't want to miss this."

CHAPTER 21

Since I returned to the house, my life has been devoid of conversation. Leon hasn't felt like talking to me, or anyone, apparently. Mom's still recovering from the explosion, and the fact that we haven't seen or talked to Dad in three days is alarming to all of us. But she can throw herself into her coding. Kat's been coming over for more lessons lately. Anything to distract them, where they can zone out, stare at screens, and wait for time to pass.

I don't have that luxury.

NASA's panicking, that much is clear. Last we heard, Dad was still in Florida, in meetings all day to see what could be salvaged from the wreck. He and Grace, along with a team of engineers, are tasked with figuring out how to land without the antenna, if NASA can't solidify the funds to build a new one.

StarWatch has promised everyone a revitalizing special tonight—one that will reportedly be extremely interesting to their viewers.

I check my phone, watching a few likes and comments trickle in. Most of them are from my postexplosion video, which is nearing a million views. There aren't many videos out there of the immediate aftermath, and mine's the easiest to embed in a news story or pick up for a live report.

I went from streaming four or five times a week to abruptly posting nothing for three days, but I don't have much to say. It's all fucked. We're all fucked.

When the phone rings, I momentarily get excited, thinking it's Leon. But it's not—it's Deb. I feel a nostalgic relief wash through my body, and I pick up the phone.

"Hey, what's up?" I say.

"Finally answering your phone? I was just going to leave you a voice mail"—she pauses—"with my new address."

My stomach lurches. "Your what?"

"Yep. My family got evicted, so I packed a suitcase and left. Don't have the credit or savings to get a real place, but my cousin lives out in Rockaway and he had an empty couch. Once his roommate moves out in a couple months, I'm going to take it over. Thought you should know."

Panic floods my body. She was my backup plan. If things got too bad, she was supposed to be there when I moved back to Brooklyn.

"But did you hear about the explosion? With that and the

jet crash, we might be coming back sooner than I thought. Did you not still want to live together?"

There's a heavy silence. "Dude, my parents don't have a home anymore. You left me for Texas, then implied you might never come back. Not to mention that we haven't actually spoken in two weeks. Don't make everything about you, just this once."

Another pause, then, "You know what, never mind. I'll text you the address. I'll see you around."

Silence.

As the line gets cut, I let out a groan. I had a plan. Even if it was a backup plan, it was a plan. And now that plan is gone.

A pang of guilt hits my chest. Once my mind detangles from my panic, I realize what I've done. What an ass I just was. I go to apologize via text, but that feels cheap, so I call her back.

After three rings, her voice mail kicks in.

I call again, and it goes straight to voice mail.

So, I sulk. I sit on my bed, music pumping through my headphones, drowning out the rest of the world. Deb and I have gotten through worse fights than this, and I know I'll be able to apologize once she cools down. I pull out my phone to make sure she hasn't texted, and when I see she hasn't, I message Leon to see if he and Kat want to watch the overly hyped *Shooting Stars* finale together. Within a few seconds, I get a reply:

Hey, sorry. Mom's home so we have family time tonight. We can text through it tho.

I'm initially disappointed, then suddenly concerned. Grace is back from Florida, but we haven't even heard from Dad. I leave the room and go to find my mom, who's simultaneously stirring a soup she made for lunch and playing her DS.

"Have you heard from Dad?" I ask.

She eyes me wearily, and I get the feeling that she has heard from him. And it's not good.

"He's just been busy," she offers. She's closed off again, frustrated. It reminds me of before.

"What do you mean? Leon's mom is already home; why would they keep Dad longer?"

She considers this and shakes her head. "Honey, I really don't know. But he doesn't have time to explain anything. He's under a ton of pressure."

I realize that either Mom is keeping something from me or she's been too worried about pushing the point in case they start fighting again.

Either way, this situation is messed up.

I go back to my room and call Dad. Straight to voice mail. I call Leon next.

"Have you talked to your mom much this week?" I ask in place of hello.

"I mean, a little? Kind of normal stuff, though."

"My dad hasn't come back yet, and Mom's acting really weird. Wasn't sure if he was especially stressed or what."

"I mean, everyone is stressed about it, but they can't do anything else right now. NASA needs to figure out if they can postpone the launch or if they can keep it on schedule, and based on the next week or so, if the people still like us and stuff." A pause. "Are you okay?"

My pause is longer. But I recover quickly. "Me, yeah, sure. Don't worry about it." I keep out the burning fear that he can hear the weakness in my voice, the worry in my cracking inflections. I'm the one who does the fixing. I'm unfazed, unbothered. My resolve is a freaking rock.

But the rock is breaking. It's cracked and worn, and I know it. But if Dad comes home and things get okay again, I can handle it.

"Calvin?" he asks, and a gasp escapes my lips. I feel the tears welling up, and I don't even know why. Everything is fine. Everything is fine. So I say it.

"Everything is fine."

He believes me, or stops pressing the issue. Either way, I'm relieved. I say goodbye and end the call, and beg the tension in my body to release its hold on my chest.

Headphones on, I fix myself so I can go back to fixing the world.

— —— —

It's eight at night. Dad's still missing in action, though Mom doesn't seem to be worried—does she think he's still in Florida? Could he really still be there?

My mom and I sit on the couch with the television tuned to *Shooting Stars*. She is cuddled up with a knit blanket, and I'm just staring at my phone, reading comments.

When I look back up, Josh Farrow takes over the show.

He's in a sleek blue suit, a little more dressed up than usual. I see something familiar in his glare; the mischievous glint is back in his eyes. It's the polar opposite of when I last saw him, rushing out of the Tuckers' home, full of shame and rage.

"A devastating explosion, teenage love, a shocking twist: your astronaut update starts tonight."

He begins with the basics, showing us a few stills of the satellite before the launch, and briefly explains its purpose. But he rushes through this section and generally keeps his tone flat. It's like he's forcing his listeners to be bored by this.

"He thinks no one cares about this stuff," I say. "It's kind of insulting, to everyone."

"I think your dad has always liked both sides. The drama, also the science."

"Everything in moderation, I guess."

Josh narrates the launch in full detail alongside video footage, and suddenly I see Leon and me. Our hands clasped together. I smile and look over to my mom for her reaction.

"Did you know they were filming you?" she asks.

"I saw them," I say. "Kiara said they were changing their image—looking for a happy story. I thought it would help ratings and interest in the project."

"And Leon knew?"

I swallow, hard. Her eyes on me make it seem like this wasn't something obviously good. But she doesn't know how he felt. How he was never the center of attention in his family, in his life.

Here he is—not his mother, not his family, *him*.

"I think so?" I say, and my phone buzzes as the explosion rocks the video.

I read Leon's text: *"uhhhhh"*

Immediately, the feed cuts out. Josh Farrow steps forward and briefly explains the explosion, really dumbing it down for the viewers.

They replay the explosion three, four, five times. They play it in slow motion.

Then they show the aftermath. Astronauts, families, reporters run around in chaos, and the camera zooms in on me. I have my phone up, and I'm giving my update to my Flash following.

"After the explosion, social media superstar Cal Lewis checked in with his followers on FlashFame. Yes, you may have noticed by now, this is a theme for the young Mr. Lewis, whose reach has increased from five hundred thousand to *one-point-two million* followers since he started covering the NASA missions and interviewing a laundry list of scientists and astronauts."

"What does that have to do with anything?" I ask, looking to Mom. She just stares at the screen in confusion.

"From the moment Cal stepped into the great city of Clear Lake, it appears he's been manipulating many of his interviewers, not to mention his followers. As astronaut Mark Bannon once said, 'The Orpheus V mission to Mars is a beautiful but challenging journey.' And we at StarWatch have always focused on showing the challenges—both technical and interpersonal—within this mission."

Josh's face looks grim, and it feels like my heart's stopped beating. It's such a one-sided argument, and it makes no sense. Sure, I'm always looking for ways to increase my following, but I do that by telling the stories people care about.

"Our guest tonight is our very own Kiara Samuel, assistant producer for *Shooting Stars*. Kiara, why don't you fill us in on what you've been looking into the past few weeks."

She clears her throat and looks through the camera; her gaze pierces my composure.

"When you think of Cal's reporting," Kiara says, "you think of his authenticity. But as I've come to know him, I've seen a side of him that is troubling, to say the least. For example, at Mara Bannon's last gardening day—we didn't know it was her last at that point, of course—he complained to me extensively about how awful it was, even saying he would pretend to be sick the next time. But as soon as the camera turned on, his entire demeanor changed. I chalked it up to the hot weather, but the dishonesty stuck with me a bit."

I gasp as a chill hits my core. The glint in Kiara's eyes, the confidence and bravado of this whole program. Josh is settling a score, and Kiara's right there with him.

"And if I might cut in, Kiara, some journalists tend to, let's say, play with the truth—it's a big challenge in our industry and something we at StarWatch have always tried our best to avoid. Sometimes we fall short," he says while looking into the camera and chuckling, "but we try. That said, I want to know more about why Cal is doing this to the space program. To what end?"

"Well, we have a clip that will answer that very question."

"I've been approached by a ton of ad companies. I mean, I could probably charge five thousand per sponsored video—these people are very loose with their money, and my followers are more active than ever, since I have an inside look at the Orpheus project."

I remember, back at the airport, the phone tucked into her shirt pocket was the only pop of color in her entire ensemble. What I didn't know—what I *couldn't* know—is that the camera was running.

Josh chimes in. "I hear he might not have that inside look for long, though, is that correct?"

"Right again, Josh."

My mother slides over to put her arm around me. She reaches for the remote, but I pull her hand back slightly. I need to see this.

StarWatch plays one clip after another.

"You could get me an internship at Teen Vogue*?"*

"Of course I'm going back to Brooklyn. As soon as I can."

"Cal hasn't yet commented on whether he'll be continuing his FlashFame reporting, or whether he's in a deal to sell it out to Condé Nast. Either way, it looks like Cal Lewis has gotten all he can out of these missions: viral streams, new followers, influencer deals, and maybe even a career."

"That's . . . not how the conversation went," I say.

It wasn't so cut-and-dried. Of course I want to go back to Brooklyn, someday. But the viewers don't know what's keeping me here or what draws me back.

My followers will think I'm trying to jump ship and monetize the channel with ads, or worse—BuzzFeed wanted to enhance my coverage, but a larger media company like Condé Nast *buying* my account? Josh's lie is almost plausible.

Leon, Kat . . . they'll think I'm trying to bail on them as soon as possible. Even though they're two of the biggest reasons why I want to stay.

"That's a lot to take in, Kiara," Josh continues, "but I think it's worth mentioning: this is the same guy who threw us under the bus as we prepared for the Mark Bannon tribute episode, which never did air."

What Kiara told me at the airport echoes in my mind: *"Anything we say about you gets us a ton of attention."* Well, they're getting their attention. And their narrative is crafted perfectly. I'm the villain. StarWatch has been around for decades; their fan base is large and loyal. I just started streaming a couple of years ago.

A sinking feeling hits my gut, and I think I might puke. Not only did Kiara get up there and attack me, but she'd also been using me for weeks, and for what? To scare me away from StarWatch's turf? To get in Josh Farrow's good graces?

She was a breath of fresh air—a Brooklynite like me trapped in the middle of Texas. But she turned out to be nothing like me. Tears rush to my eyes, but I won't let them drop.

After watching the horror unfold in front of me, I'm given relief in the form of a commercial break. I try to call Leon right away. Straight to voice mail. I stand and pace, and that is all I can convince my body to do.

"Honey, these gossip shows do this," Mom says. "They haven't been fair to our family this whole time. It's going to be okay. Do you want me to call one of the other astronauts? Or maybe you should talk to Leon? I bet they all have stories like this."

Her rambling isn't helping, and I feel bad for tuning her out, but this could be very, *very* bad. The fallout could be so bad, StarWatch's report could be the first thing that comes up when you google my name. It could ruin me forever.

But I can't lose control.

The rock hardens again. I'm fine. I'm okay.

There's the noise of a key getting forced into a lock, and for a brief moment, I thaw when I see my dad. Something's unusually comforting about having your parents around when your life devolves into a disaster. But there's a glazed look in his eyes, and I wonder if he's been crying. I wonder if he ever cries. He storms away.

Looking back at my phone, I see notifications start to pile up on my FlashFame app—I know what they'll say. I can't check them, and I can't form a coherent response fast enough. I look up at Mom with a panic-stricken face.

She's torn between me and Dad. She's deciding which one to console and which to leave alone to deal with his emotions. I know who she'll choose. It won't be me, because I'm always okay. Put together. In control of my temper, my emotions.

But I want to yell out and for once say that I need her. That I'm *not* okay. That my rock is all broken and I am falling apart, but I won't do that. My chest tightens. I can't do that.

I refresh my expression. Breathe. Nod. And she follows him into the bedroom.

The show comes back on, and I'm in such a daze I almost forget to pay attention. *Please let them drop the topic*, I beg.

Logically speaking, I can explain everything to Leon and make sure he knows I don't have one foot out the door. It's not unfixable. He'll understand my quotes were taken out of context. I know he'll believe me over a jerk like Josh Farrow—he *has* to.

Then, I think of my followers, the ones I've had since my very first news reports. I'm sure I was awkward and the video quality was shit then, but they stuck around. They'll know it's not as simple as me wanting to break "into the biz" like Star-Watch said. I can balance my career with my content—*unpaid* content—and they'll support me every step of the way. Won't they?

I can fix this.

I can fix this.

"Now for the big dish."

I groan. Josh's personality causes me physical pain.

"We've got a leaked clip straight from the mouth of Todd Collins from NASA's public affairs team."

The video is blurry, but it's unmistakably from that first party. The one where I met Donna Szleifer, Mark Bannon. The first night I really got to know Leon. Actually, the footage appears to be intentionally blurred, to make it seem more intriguing and secretive.

"We're very pleased to have Calvin on board," Todd says. "He's going to be a great addition to the team."

I squint my eyes, not really understanding what it means. He said something nice about my dad. A lot of people did that night. He's having this conversation with Mark Bannon, and by the sparse crowd, this happened long before we got to the party.

"He's a good pilot, from what I've heard," Mark says kindly.

Todd laughs. "No, no. I didn't mean that Calvin—okay, well, him too. But Donna and I were the ones who got him the interview. He had good experience, but he wasn't a standout. But Donna recognized the name immediately. We knew all about his son's FlashFame videos, and we were looking for a way to get younger people interested in us. So we begged them to give him a chance, bring Cal Junior on, and bring all his followers to our side. It's already boosted a lot of our social accounts."

There's silence as the anchor lets the message sink in.

"How's that for some drama?" Josh asks the camera, poison dripping from his smile. "How many more qualified candidates were turned away just because this guy's son was good at social media?"

Kiara shakes her head. "And who would have thought that while Cal was sucking NASA dry to build his brand, NASA was using him too. Either way, it's troubling news, and it's a story I intend to closely monitor."

Mara and Kiara both hinted at it, but I never listened: when StarWatch's ratings are down, they ramp up the drama. And it's clear what the purpose of this whole show is. They want it to look like everyone's abandoning the project, that it was flawed to begin with. That no one can be trusted.

They want NASA to crumble, and they want to cover it all.

CHAPTER 22

I wait for the yelling to start, but it never does. An eerie silence fills the house, so I rush to my tape deck and listen to whatever cassette's in right now.

Dolly's vocals pump through my headphones, but it doesn't work. Nothing's going to get my mind off the events of the past hour. I used to be able to distract myself by being annoyed at my parents and their constant yelling, but this is so bad, no fight could possibly solve it.

I imagine my parents sitting in bed, staring at the wall, in disbelief at what NASA just revealed.

They led my dad on this whole time, and it's my fault.

I feel stuck. I wish I could do something to help, but I don't even know where to start. It seems impossible. I take off my headphones and let the silence sour my stomach. None of the tracks feel right. None of this is right.

What I really need is to hear Leon's voice. But he won't hear me out, as evidenced by the ten ignored calls on his phone. I picture him sad or angry or a little of both, and my heart aches.

I pick up my phone, hoping the eleventh time is a charm.

"Cal."

Leon's warm, comforting voice is gone, and my chest nearly explodes with tension. I've wanted to hear his voice so badly. But not like this.

"I need to talk to you," I say. "I need to explain."

"Do you?" And I hear it now. The coldness, the pain in his voice. "It was pretty clear from the start—this was temporary. You were always going back to New York."

I sigh. "I don't know if that's true."

"But you said it."

"Fine," I say. "I wanted to go back. From the moment I got here, I wanted to leave. But once I thought of this as a temporary home, I realized it wasn't so bad. And then I got to know you and Kat, and all the other families. And I thought I could help NASA with some of my videos, and . . . yes, I thought it would build my portfolio, but—"

"You said it yourself, when we first . . ."—he hesitates— "kissed. You couldn't be with someone who was half in, but even then, you weren't all in."

"With you, I was always, *always* all in." My voice is rough and low. I need him to understand this, if he takes nothing else away from this convo. "I'm torn, okay. She said she could get me a dream opportunity. She could get me back home. She clearly lied to get some shitty sound bites from me. But I have so much here that I wanted to stay for."

"Then take some time to figure it out." He sighs. "I love you, but when I heard you say those words, it kind of paralyzed me—the thought of you up and leaving me, leaving Clear Lake terrifies me. Like, I couldn't even answer your calls, because I thought you would tell me this was goodbye."

"I'm sorry," I say. It's all I can say.

"I can't expect you to make me your number-one priority. But being everyone's number two or three or four priority is really hard for me." His breaths come through the phone in ragged bursts. "Could you give me, *us*, some time?"

His words send a chill through my body. *Some* time? How long, exactly? Can I still text, or is he cutting off communication for good? How will I know when I can speak to him again?

Will I ever be able to speak to him again?

"I . . ." I can't get the words out. The tears are building, and I don't think I can stop them. "Okay. Whatever you need."

After we hang up, I sprawl out on the carpet in my room, because the move is just melodramatic enough to show how sorry I feel for myself. I know that Leon isn't perfect. I know that I'm way not perfect.

But in some weird way, it feels like we're perfect together. And of course I don't want to leave him.

I nearly jump when I get a text, in hopes that it's him, but it's only Deb texting me her new address.

When did Deb become *only* Deb? She was my world; we'd spend every day on the fire escape planning our future and cursing our annoying parents.

She was hurt by my leaving, I realize that now. And that only reminds me of all the others I've hurt. All the shit that's my fault. So many broken people I care about, and I can't fix any of them. I can't help Mom with her grief and anxiety or tell Dad I'm sorry that I'm the only reason his dreams have come—temporarily—true. Tell Leon that I won't disappear, that I won't be like his parents, who make him feel so lonely. Tell Deb how great she's always been to me, and show up to tell her how I never really left her. How we can go back to normal and everything will be all right.

I sit up straight, accidentally slamming my shoulder into the dresser.

"I could do that," I say aloud.

I google her new address, and map it out. Twenty-four hours. It's a huge gesture, but it would work. I'd sleep in the car, and I can leave a message on Mom's phone so she doesn't worry. I'd catch a ton of shit from Dad, but he barely uses the car anyway, since he's been carpooling with Grace to work.

I'm unsettled, and a queasy feeling creeps into my stomach. I know it's a bad idea. But if I could just show one person that I'm there for them. If I could just . . . fix something. I think I can keep going.

I slip out of my room and grab the car keys hanging by the door. I turn off the lights and release myself into the hot

Houston air. It's sixty-five in Brooklyn right now. If it holds up, I'll be nice and cool when I get there in a day or so. Maybe I should've brought a sweater.

Behind the wheel, I feel a little bit of power come back to my life. I plug the directions into my phone, and I'm off. The farther I get away from that god-awful town, the more relaxed I feel. My grip on the wheel loosens. I can finally, finally breathe.

But the breaths get heavier, more ragged.

I'm nearly alone on this road, even though it's a separated highway. But the good thing about driving in middle-of-nowhere, twenty-miles-to-Beaumont, Texas is there's plenty of room for me to pull over. Since I can barely see through all the tears that cloud my vision, I do just that.

My chest heaves, so I press my forehead to the steering wheel. I turn off the music and beg the silent night to keep me calm. My shoulders tense so hard, I start to shake. Haphazardly, at first, then steadier. It's like being outside in a snowstorm, or jumping into a freezing lake. The chill creeps through my body, though it couldn't be less than seventy-five in the car.

Three things become abundantly clear: I can't fix anyone. I don't want to leave Houston, now or ever. And I really fucking love him.

Sobs come fast and hard, and I unbuckle my seat belt so I can hold my stomach. I'd feel so embarrassed if I wasn't completely broken right now. The hole in my chest grows larger, and it physically hurts. I can't breathe, I can't exist. I can't keep this up.

This isn't a way to make things better. This is me running away.

For the next twenty minutes, I curl up into a ball in the driver's seat and alternate between heavy panting and light sobbing. I can't control myself. I don't even know the last time I cried. Like, really cried.

When I finally calm down, sort of, I take a step out of the car to get rid of the smell of tears. I look up to the stars and feel a refreshing breeze blow through me. I want to enjoy it, but I can't. Not now. I need to get back. I can't run away.

CHAPTER 23

When I wake up, I spend twenty minutes just staring at the ceiling of my room. It's a tacky off-white spongy paint design that makes me want to look anywhere else, but I don't have the energy. I can't make it through this. And then I wonder if I'm being too dramatic, so I summon all my strength and roll over on my side.

I grab my phone.

Not surprisingly, my notifications center is blank. No one has reached out to me. Leon hasn't spoken to me since that call. I check my comments, and they're flooded with people asking about the StarWatch exposé. Seriously, they keep calling it an exposé, like I'm someone worth having an exposé on.

A lot of them think I'm a sellout.

Some of them think I'm "using that guy" to get more famous.

But all of them are vindicated by my silence. My follower count still goes up, despite the many comments with people saying they're unfollowing. I want to text Leon and just say how much I love him. But I can't do that.

There's a knock on the door.

"Come in," I say. My voice cracks.

It's my dad. "I suppose you saw."

"I did."

We were never much for conversation, even if that had changed recently.

"Look," I say. "I don't buy it. Who'd consult their social media people to make a hire for something this important? I think they're a little full of themselves, even though their media campaigns are awful."

"Doesn't really matter anymore," he says. And I think he might actually mean it. "I don't think we'll be here long. They're making big cuts, and I don't even think your . . . celebrity will help me make it."

"But the launch!"

He shakes his head and looks down. He almost doesn't even need to say it. "They're canceling it. They called each of us this morning—don't tell your app friends or whoever. It's not official. But they're not going to want a pilot if they don't have any ships to fly."

"Sorry, Dad."

"Don't be sorry." He steps out of the room. "It was fun for a while, and I don't regret any of it. I'm proud of you, you know that? You did a lot for NASA. I just wish we'd have gotten the chance to see this mission through."

The door shuts, and I imagine packing all this up again.

Going back was all I wanted, but I need to stay. For NASA. For Leon.

For me.

In a month (hell, in a week) Leon and I could be hundreds of miles apart. And I know that, either way, I *have* to see him again. I give him a call, and it goes right to voice mail. I call Kat next, and she picks up right away.

"Hey, Cal." She pauses. "Are you okay?"

I cycle through my automatic responses in my head. I'm fine. I'm okay. Don't worry about me. But . . . I'm not. So, for once, I'm honest about it.

"No. Not really. How's Leon? I really need to talk to him."

"He's . . . not really okay either. But I can see if he wants to talk to you."

"Just tell him that I'm coming by in a few minutes, and we can take a walk and talk. If he doesn't come out, I'll understand. And tell him . . ." *I love him*, I finish in my head. But I don't say it. "Never mind. Just tell him that, okay?"

"Will do. I hope he goes with you."

I smile. "Me too."

Standing in front of my closet, I feel a rush of excitement flood my veins for the first time in days. I try to keep it simple, but I also want to look good. But also not like I'm trying so hard . . . so definitely not the John Mayer hat. Houston's still not ready.

I end up wearing my gray jeans with brown chukkas, and I throw on a red plaid shirt. Looking in the mirror, I see the smile grow on my face. God, I missed my own smile.

I start down the street. With every house I pass, my breaths get heavier. My chest hurts. When I pass the lamppost where we met after Bannon died, the tears come back.

The heat and my tears tag team to suck all the moisture from my body. I feel light-headed. Weak. I decide to be as cliché as possible and sit on the curb by the gutter.

I'm suddenly not alone anymore. I look up, hoping to see Leon, hoping he could fix me and put me back together.

But it's Kat.

"Hey," she says.

"Um, hi. Sorry."

I apologize for my weakness, but no apology could ever express everything I was truly sorry for.

"I'm on my way to your mom's for another coding lesson." She crouches next to me and puts her arm around my shoulder.

My eyes narrow. "A coding lesson? Mom's not even here—I think she took a walk to the park or something. Things have been a bit stressful."

"Okay, fine. I came to check on you, because you're my friend." She reaches out to me. "Come on, let's walk."

By some miracle, I find the energy to stand. She slips her arm in mine, and we fall in step.

"I'm not going to leave him," I finally say. "At least, not if I can help it."

"I know. And I think he does too. He wanted me to say he wasn't ready yet, whatever that means. But he loves you."

I sniffle. "Did he tell you to say that part too?"

She shakes her head. So I squeeze my eyes shut, begging the tears not to come.

"He didn't, but it's obvious. Look, I'm not sure what all I should say here, but his therapist has been teaching him to be self-sufficient, like, not depending on others to determine when he's happy or sad. And I think you might need to figure out the same thing before you see him again."

"I don't—" But I stop myself, because I know: that's exactly what I do. I'm angry when my parents are angry. I'm happy when Leon's happy. I take everyone else's burden.

"I think that's easier said than done," I say. I smile, and she does too. "See?"

We laugh, and I sit on the curb outside my house. I pat the spot next to me a couple of times in an awkward fashion.

"I love him too," I say. "I mean, I haven't told him that and I don't want you to say anything, but . . . it's true."

"Good! Then I hope y'all figure this shit out soon so we can get back to being close."

"Kind of a moot point if we all get kicked out of here."

"If NASA wouldn't have treated this like a reality show, they wouldn't have blown it." She clenches her fists. "Fucking StarWatch."

"Fucking StarWatch." I pause as the realization hits me. I stand and help Kat up. A jolt of electricity shoots through me as it all clicks. "Actually, I have an idea."

Shooting Stars
Season 2; Online Content

LIVE UPDATE: Tune in live at 1:15 p.m. (CST) as we interview US Representative Halima Ali, who will discuss her new legislation to halt the government funding of the Orpheus project.

"Good afternoon. I'm *Shooting Stars* host Josh Farrow, and it's my honor to welcome US Representative Halima Ali from Maryland. You may remember her as the most outspoken opponent of the government's allocation of funds toward NASA. Congresswoman Ali, it's good to have you with us today."

"Thank you for having me. I admit, I was a bit surprised Josh Farrow, of all people, wanted me to come down for this interview."

"We like to have all sides of the story, and one side of this NASA journey we haven't touched on much is back in the news. Everyone wants to know, Do you think the government will be pulling funding for the Orpheus project?"

"I certainly hope so. And I don't mean to be rude—I understand the repercussions of this, but the funds can be put toward so many more important projects."

"Congresswoman, do you think that space travel is important?"

"I think all forms of exploration are deeply important. It's gotten us to where we are today. But my constituents don't have the faith in NASA to use the funding wisely. They've shown this over and over again. I worry—excuse me for saying this, but I think sending six of America's brightest humans to Mars can only end in disaster."

"We've also been speaking with JET-EX, as you might have seen. What do you think of privately funded space projects? Does that bother you less?"

"I'm always going to think this money could be going somewhere more important. The infrastructure in America is crumbling, and we're trying to build a base on Mars? Education is severely underfunded; our courts are underfunded. And I swear this isn't a personal vendetta, but someone has to play devil's advocate here. Someone has to challenge these rich idealists to make sure they're not doing it for fame or attention. But can we get back to government funding for a second?"

"Of course."

"As you have no doubt heard, I'm cosponsoring a bill that would remove a large portion of funding from this project, and the preliminary vote is tomorrow. NASA would still be able to operate, but we won't be taking such a risk."

"Interesting—and if that bill passes?"

"It has a good chance of getting through the Senate. I believe that this is our time to put an end to this and leave the exploration to JET-EX or whoever wants to fill their shoes. This wouldn't result in any large layoffs, and NASA could refocus on things that are affecting our citizens now: climate issues, for example."

"Well, I want to thank you for coming all the way here on

such short notice. This has been a refreshing conversation, and we at StarWatch will closely monitor the situation. If I may be honest . . . the way it's looking, season three of *Shooting Stars* might be taking place at JET-EX headquarters."

CHAPTER 24

"Dad?" I ask when walking into the house. "Dad!"

It feels weird being the one yelling in the house. I bust into my parents' bedroom—the door was open, don't worry—and find him taking a nap in the bed. "Dad!" I shout. "I need your help."

I briefly explain the situation to him. It takes a few seconds for my plea to register, but something must make sense, because he jumps out of bed and waves me out of the room while dashing to his closet.

Once he's properly dressed, we get in the car. I roll down the windows, and we fly down the country roads that lead to the space center. When I pass the spot where Leon and I kissed, I feel a pang of guilt in my chest.

We pull into the almost deserted parking lot after Dad flashes his ID. Soon after we park, we break into a sprint.

"I need one person who worked on the satellite," I say to Dad. "Also, one of the lead astronauts who StarWatch would find too boring to cover, and I'm going to find Brendan to talk about the mission and what happens to their team if it gets canceled."

Dad flashes a thumbs-up. "On it!"

We break apart, and I bring up Flash's scheduled video function. I prefer the live, impulsive act of recording something that's not overrehearsed. But this has to be right.

My first stop is the lab where Brendan works. I call his name, and he looks up to me with goggles dangling from his neck.

"Oh, hey," he says. "I've been watching your reports and doing some videos of my own. Still don't know how to use the app much, but I have a few followers."

"Want a few more?" I ask.

I tell him how when I go live with his video, I can promote his page and the followers who like it can start following him. He smiles, too eagerly, and I remind him not to get too cocky. As evidenced by all the harassing comments I've dealt with since the StarWatch story broke, the internet is a cesspool, and he'll be lucky if he doesn't go viral.

"Okay, start by telling us what you're working on now. Then I'll have you transition into what losing this mission would mean for your team, and for the country."

He starts off hesitant, like he's still not used to the camera, but when he delves into the new project his team is working on—one that'll help transport the soil samples and rock samples with minimal exposure to our atmosphere—he shines. He's not a smooth talker, he's not a natural behind the camera, but he's real. And he really cares.

That's what America loved about him the first time, and that's why they'll love him now.

I thank him and set the five-minute video to go live at 9:05 p.m., just after my live intro. As I enter the hallway, I spot Carmela running toward me. "Your dad told me what's going on! Come, we can show your online friends the shuttle test room."

A smile tugs at my lips. She cares so much. Everyone does.

Upon entering the room, she waves me over to her station. I point the camera at her.

"Oh no, Little Cal. Not this woman."

"Come on," I say. "People want to see behind the scenes, and they love the employees here. They loved Brendan."

"Brendan's young!"

"Come on!" I plead, still laughing.

"Fine. You stay on this side of my face."

"Just give the viewers a quick autobiography," I say, "and then you can show us around the test cockpit, okay? Act like all of America's watching. Three . . . two . . . one . . ."

"Hello to all of you! I'm Carmela, and I'm supposed to act like all of America's watching this. Well, you know what, I'm going to treat it that way." A self-satisfied look hits her face. She's found her platform, and the passion in her voice makes me lean in to hear her speak. "I live here in Texas—in *America*—because my parents risked everything to immigrate from Mexico just before I was born. One in every six Texans are immigrants, and I am proud to be a part of that statistic. My parents, who encouraged me to follow my dreams and supported me through my studies, would be proud to know not only what work I'm doing, but how much I love the work I do."

I hear the confidence propel her story forward. StarWatch rarely came in here, and when they did, they never gave her the space to speak. I'm reminded of when I covered the election. When I found a way to amplify my voice.

She transitions into a more instructional tone, detailing the tests she runs while pointing out all the features of the test cockpit. She gets inside and starts showing the viewers all the buttons.

"And don't tell anyone I told you, but there's no one as quick as Mr. Lewis on these trials. I throw him every problem I've designed, and he gets them almost always right. I've had to step up my game to throw him off."

My shoulders pull back, and I stand straighter. Confident. Even if nothing happens, and the mission gets scrapped, Dad will be able to see what people think of him. And even if he's frustrated right now, maybe he can learn that he was more than worthy for the job.

She goes on to detail some of the tests she does and why they'll help in the Mars mission. I ask her why it's so important not to delay it.

"Because I need a job, and they won't need me if there's no flight to prepare for." She smiles at the camera. "But seriously, Calvin, you should know this more than anyone else. It means a lot to these astronauts and to everyone on the team. It's something that no one's ever done before. But for me? I think Mars can be habitable someday. Maybe not in our generation, maybe not even in yours, but we'll never know if we don't take these first steps."

A text lights up my phone screen, from my dad: *"Come to 4501 when you're done upstairs. Satellite guy here really loves talking about antennas?"*

I end the recording with Carmela and set it for 9:15 tonight. I make a mental map of this show. If I spread them out, and if I bookend them with an intro and an exit, it'll take up about an hour with minimal downtime. The barrage of short videos might be taken as spamming my followers, but it'll be worth it if just a few watch them, or share them, or if it gets covered by other online media.

But I don't get ahead of myself.

Within minutes, I'm on the fourth floor, scanning the rooms for 4501. I find it. I was expecting a large workshop area where half-broken machines lay around, but it's just an ordinary office. Wooden desk, drafting table, large Mac.

"Ah, Cal. This is Kyle; he designed the antenna."

"Sorry about the . . . you know." I make an explosion gesture with my hand and widen my eyes.

He shakes his head. "It's annoying. I've designed ten antennae before, and most of the launches have been canceled. This was finally built, and it was supposed to be my first one in space. And then, like you said . . ." He mimics my gesture. "Not to mention what it means for Orpheus V."

"Wait, could you explain that a bit more on camera? Star-Watch barely even explained what its purpose was, so you might want to get into that too."

"You sure?" He looks back and forth between us. "Usually when I do my antenna talk, people get bored."

I laugh. "I'll cut you off if you get boring, but I'm sure that won't be the case."

He goes, then, and I never cut him off.

I go from office space to office space. I talk with the propulsion technicians who worked out the cause for the explosion, take viewers on an early model of the Orpheus V shuttle, and interview a round table full of engineers.

"And now, you." I point the camera at my dad. "Go."

"What? You don't—"

"Dad, I already hit record."

He looks away, and his face gets all flustered and red, but I just smile. He may be a lightning-quick space pilot, but it's always a little funny to watch your dad shift uncomfortably when you put him on the spot.

"Right, so I'm Cal Lewis—Senior, that is—and I'm an alternate pilot for the Orpheus V mission. I was born in the eighties, but my mom hadn't really thrown out a magazine since the fifties, so I grew up reading old *Life* articles about the Mercury Seven, and the Gemini and Apollo missions. I saw the first designs for space suits that made you look like a giant teapot, and I'd flip past eight or nine cigarette ads to get to anything with an astronaut. I was obsessed, and I always felt like I belonged in that world somehow."

He talks about his career, his time as a pilot in the air force, and how he would have been content flying for Delta until he retired.

"But I saw the open call. I saw how NASA was trying to re-create the spirit and energy of the sixties. And here I am."

"Do you think NASA did that?" I ask. "Did they re-create it?"

He laughs and slowly shakes his head. I see the wheels turning in his head as he thinks of a way to answer this. "No, they really didn't. See, that spirit never left. No one ever woke up and was, like—hey, spaceships are boring. This NASA tried to shove it down America's throat by bringing back the drama of the sixties and the fakeness of the 'perfect' family." His gaze drifts above the camera to meet mine, and he smiles. "We *all* know there's no such thing as a perfect family. But when that didn't work, StarWatch bumped up the drama, and who could blame them? They just want viewers."

He pauses, and I briefly worry that he's going to end on that bleak note. But he looks away from the camera and takes a long breath.

"But there's a lot to care about outside the drama. We'll get to Mars. And not because we're competing with Russia this time—we're working together with Russia, with Canada, Japan, and so many countries in the European Space Agency. People always ask me what's the point, and I don't have that answer for you. But I think if you've listened to all the stories Calvin grabbed here, you'll learn that the point is different for every person, and they're all right, in their own way."

His cheeks flush when he realizes he's been pretty senti-mental. So he grabs the phone out of my hand and points it at me. But I know what I want to say. I've been thinking about it for a long time.

I smile at the camera, clear my throat, and go.

StarWatch News
Breaking News: Live Report

"This is Josh Farrow from *Shooting Stars*. I'm coming to you live from the StarWatch news desk with some breaking news from the Orpheus project.

"We've been told Cal Lewis Jr. has his own special planned this evening, covering the almost surely doomed Orpheus V mission. The video is expected to drop at nine p.m. CST, and we've got no clue what's up his sleeve. But from the comments on his page, we can tell you—his fans, though most appear not to be of voting age, are very intrigued.

"Our experts say there's little that can be done at this point. Tomorrow's House vote is all but decided, but let us know what you think in our online poll: Cut NASA or Keep NASA?

"Let's see what our viewers think."

CHAPTER 25

Dad stayed at NASA, so I take advantage of the calm that's come over me. One thing about driving that I actually like, when there's no traffic, is how automatic it feels. It's almost therapeutic as I process all that's happened to me. All that's to come.

I pull over near a picturesque cattle farm to host a live video from the middle of the street, telling all my followers to tune in at nine central time for an hour-long special on saving the Orpheus V mission. After I end the stream, I resume my drive and take in the scenery. In the daylight, there's something really beautiful about Texas. It's slower, quieter, and has more room to breathe than Brooklyn.

And god, how I miss Brooklyn, but I feel okay here. And okay is so much better than I thought it would be. My gut clenches when I think of Leon. About how his lips taste and the way his body makes me feel so perfectly safe and relaxed when I'm curled up against it.

Despite my plans, my endless organizing of outlines in my head, I don't know what tomorrow will bring. I don't know what the rest of the year will look like. Will I be here in the open sun or hiding on my fire escape in the shadow of my building? Will I be in his arms again, or will I find someone else . . . eventually? An unsettled feeling bubbles up, and I squeeze the steering wheel hard to keep myself in check.

I need to know how to be okay all the time. I need to be able to see the fifty ways my life can go and be perfectly content with each one. But there's only one path right now that looks good to me. The one that keeps me here, with Leon. And Kat, and the other astronauts, and the Orpheus V mission.

When I open the door to the house, Mom looks up to me from the couch.

"Oh, honey. Kat told me what you were doing. Sit down."

I do. "It's all I could do to help. I think it'll help."

She puts her arm on my back, and I tense up. I shake my head, still thinking of all the directions my life could go, and it makes me feel nervous and frantic. Breathing is a challenge, and I clench my teeth together so tightly my jaw starts to ache.

"I want everything to be better," I say. "I know I can't fix people. Even if I try really hard, I know I can't do it. And I think that's okay—but this, I might be able to really fix. I have the following; they care so much about the mission, I think. I just—"

"Calvin, stop. It's not your responsibility to worry about the mission, or Dad's job, or the people in your life who need fixing, as you say. No one's broken. Nothing is broken."

But that's not true: I'm broken. I'm here in pieces on this couch and everything is so hard.

"Don't aim to fix people. Fixing seems so permanent, so absolute. Like there's no room for error. Aim to make things better. Your videos might not change America's opinion of the mission, but it'll make it better. People will know the real story behind Orpheus V, whether or not it ever gets off the ground." She leans over to look into my eyes. "Celebrate that."

"Thanks," I say.

Her words stick in my mind, and the tension in my chest starts to ease. I don't know if that's really what matters, or how futile this will seem tomorrow if no one cares. But I take her sentiment to heart. It'll matter to me. It'll matter to a lot of people at NASA.

At least I'll have that.

When I stand, I notice a box of new gardening supplies open on the kitchen table.

"What's this?" I ask. "You're . . . gardening?"

"Don't laugh," she says, "but I've been going to the park with the gardens. The one we worked at after we first moved here."

Without thinking, I groan, remembering that sweaty mess of a day. "I hate that place."

"It's nice. The bushes aren't as twisted and strange as the ones Aunt Tori planted, but they still need some pruning." She wipes away a rogue tear. "Anyway, I met up with the lady who runs the food kitchen that uses the garden, and she said no one's taken over for Mara. So I volunteered."

"And that means . . ."

"You're going to be doing a lot of harvesting this fall. Your peppers are coming in nicely, by the way."

I finally make it to my room, and on my deck, I see a new cassette: *Heart*, by . . . Heart. I don't really know who this is, or why this is in my room, so I put it in and press play. When I hear "If Looks Could Kill," the powerful eighties rock voice pierces through my headphones, overtop power guitar chords and synthesizer. She's incredible. I turn it up louder, until the wailing guitar starts to hurt my head.

I open my eyes and see Mom leaning in my door. I pull off my headphones.

"Where'd you get this?" I ask.

"Hey, it wasn't me. Someone came over today to drop it off. He wasn't sure if it was good or anything. I told him Heart was fantastic, and he shouldn't forget it. But he apparently found it in his basement, and they don't have a deck." She smiles and starts to lean back out of the door. "He had a lot of excuses for why he was bringing it over, but I think there was only one reason: he wanted to make you feel a little better."

I listen to the rest of the album. And by the end of it, Mom's right—I'm not fixed, but I'm a little better. I feel recharged, and excited, and I've really been putting off the thought that he was here at my house, expecting to see me and give me a gift. Which means, maybe he's starting to really trust me, and trust what we have.

I still haven't texted him, because I don't know what to say other than "Thanks!" which just feels cheap. I have to see him.

I can do that. I'm going to see him tonight.

— —— —

At eight fifty, I ring the doorbell to the Tucker residence. After careful consideration, I'm wearing a simple V-neck shirt, acid wash jeans with tan slip-on shoes, and the hat. The John Mayer oversized safari hat that Houston is still not remotely ready for.

But I'm ready for it.

Kat opens the door and breaks into a giggle as she sees me.

"Stop," I say. "No hat jokes. This is fashion."

"I'm so happy you finally brought it out. I thought you might've left it in Brooklyn—it's in so many of your videos." She pauses. "Oh, and did your mom add the code to your app?"

"She did, and it looks perfect. I played around with it all afternoon—it's so easy to use."

She shrugs. "I just wanted to help."

"So . . . can I talk to Leon? That is, if he wants to see me."

"Cal." She puts her hands on my shoulders. "He made me stop at a garage sale to go cassette shopping. He wants to see you."

"I thought he found it in your basement."

"That was a lie, because saying he went garage sale shopping for you sounds a little pathetic."

I pull Kat in for a hug, and she leans away from my hat as I do it. With her thumb, she points behind her, at the sliding door I slid through when I first got to really talk to Leon alone. Perfect.

The grass crunches under my feet as I walk around to the side of the house. Leon's looking up at the stars and the sliver of moon that's viewable from the side. I reach into my bag and retrieve the bottle of champagne I swiped from the dozen or so my parents have on hand. When the bottle pops, his gaze meets mine.

"What are we celebrating?" he asks.

"Us," I reply with a smile. "Wait, that was way too cheesy. How about . . . the fact that I was able to cobble together a full hour of content with no notice in one day and lived to tell the tale?"

"Kat told me your plan." He gives me a half smile, and I take the seat next to him. "It's . . . really great. It's worth celebrating."

"Well, then. Cheers."

I pull the bottle to my mouth and take a sip of bitter foam.

"Oh, and thank you for the cassette," I say. "I had no idea your mom had such good taste in music."

He chuckles nervously. "Yeah, I mean, I don't know. I think she likes it, but she probably didn't even know we still had it. In the basement, that is."

I let his lie slide, for now. The moon's glow mixes with the porch light, and I feel momentarily blinded. I take a sip and pass the bottle to him.

"I think Kat's going to run interference for us," I say. "But I have something to show you."

After pulling out my phone, I open the app to find five hundred thousand people waiting for me to start. Literally half a million people staring at a blank screen. It's a good sign, but we'll see if they stay.

"Do you want to be in this?" I ask, and he almost falls out of his chair because he jerks away so quickly. "I was joking."

I turn the camera on me, and adrenaline floods my veins. I'm in control. If I'm not in control of anything else, I am in control of this. I suck in a breath and tap the LIVE button.

"I'm Cal, and I can't believe so many of you are on right now. If we keep this up, we'll probably beat the entire viewership of that StarWatch episode. Speaking of StarWatch, I wanted to start with an apology." I reposition myself in the chair so I can see Leon over my phone screen. "I'm really torn. My whole life was in Brooklyn, and I thought my whole future was in New York. I still want to come back, but I really love it here too. And one day, when I do get an internship or job or whatever, I'm not going to stop using FlashFame. I will never post ads. Some of you have been around from the very beginning, and I hope you won't let one mistake, in one out-of-context quote from an episode of *Shooting Stars* ruin that. I really am sorry.

"As you can probably tell, I was appalled by the coverage. We are at such a critical time in the Orpheus V mission—interest is waning; we've had two major setbacks after losing one of our astronauts in a jet crash and losing a critical satellite. We need real information to be spread, now more than ever. We need awareness.

"Over the next hour, you'll see interviews with a diverse selection of astronauts, scientists, engineers, and everyone in between. Talking about their jobs. Talking about why Orpheus V is so important. Why we can't give up on it now. I hope you'll listen, and I hope you'll share."

I take a full breath and blow out all the bad feelings. "Thank you for following," I say, and I make my final plea to America.

CHAPTER 26

"Hi, I'm Brendan. Y'all saw my last video on here when I talked about dirt. Actually, almost a million people have seen me talk about dirt. Now, it's something that's always been fascinating to me, but hey, I'm biased.

"I studied chemical engineering at the University of Dayton, and shortly after, I started working with NASA. And to me, it's hard to really explain why all this is important. It's like asking me, 'Hey, why's gravity important?' Its roots are in the history of other planets. Theirs and ours. We don't know what, if anything, lived on Mars, but we know liquid water flows on Mars as we speak. We know the planet is alive with organic matter. What did Mars do wrong; where and how did it turn into the wasteland it is now?

"I play a small piece in the overall puzzle. We have scientists here who have been studying the weather patterns on Mars, some who will figure out what plant life could grow in the soil. Biochemists who will test the air, and explorers who will gather the materials and give us the best photographs we've ever seen of the place."

"Anyway," Brendan continues, "I hope you share this. I lucked out and got my dream job, and I don't want to lose it. We have so much work to do."

As he continues, I look to Leon. His eyes shimmer as he watches the video, and a small smile perks up at the corner of his lips.

"Think this will work?" he asks between swigs of champagne. "Like, really work?"

"How could it?" I say. "It can't do much but give the people what they've been missing for so long, thanks to NASA and StarWatch."

— —— —

There's a few minutes of dead time after the show, and I watch the follower count dip slightly. We're at one-point-three million viewers live, thanks to a lot of early shares.

When Carmela fills the screen, I can't help but smile.

"I'm kind of jealous Mom gets to work with her all day."

"Same. I want her to have her own FlashFame show, I'm gonna be honest."

The light of my phone glows on his face, and I want to lean over and kiss him. The urge in my chest weighs me down, makes my arms ache so bad it gets hard to hold up the phone. Without meaning to, my arm lowers. Leon takes the phone from me and scoots his chair in closer, his eyes never leaving the screen.

I fold my hands in my lap, not knowing exactly what to do or how close I can get to him.

And then his shoulder touches mine. It's so small and insignificant, but I shudder. Chills travel all over my body, originating in that light shoulder touch. I press into him just slightly and savor the moment.

When the video switches, he leans back and holds the phone with one hand. His other one slips behind my back, so I curl into him as much as my comically huge hat will allow me. Suddenly his scent is in my nose again, and I'm curled up with him in that hotel room, his lips on my neck and my hand on his cheek.

"She's brilliant," he says. "Mom's always telling me about all the times she's ended up killing the crew by throwing in her sadistic curveballs."

"Well, she can't stump my dad, apparently." I roll my eyes and keep it light, but he looks at me.

"No, really. I heard Mom telling Dad she was worried NASA would consider swapping them—making your dad lead Orpheus V instead of Orpheus VI."

"Wait," I say, "Dad's not leading any missions."

"Cal, if we make it to Orpheus VI, your dad is going to Mars. There is no question about that."

I lean back and look up to the sky. There's a sliver of the moon showing, and I'm suddenly overwhelmed. Like pins are poking all over my body. Breaths come hard, and I feel so small and Mars is really far away. Really, really far away.

Fifty years ago, when we landed on the moon, there were dozens of astronauts, wives, and Astrokids sitting on these same lawns. Looking up at the same sky. The moon must have seemed so much farther away. Literally impossible. But we did it then, and we'll do it again.

"I, um, never thought about that. Are you worried about your mom going on the mission?"

"Not really. It'll be weird for her to be gone for two full years. Like, that's not a normal amount of time to be away from your family, and when she gets back I'll be . . . somewhere else, I guess. Doing something else."

After a few minutes of dead time, the antenna designer Kyle takes over the show. He talks at length about designing the antenna that exploded.

— — —

"What you don't hear much is that it was meant to be multi-use—it would've been helpful for the landing, as you know, but it also would've given us the clearest weather readouts to date. We would have had it join orbit with Mars about three to six months before the astronauts got there, and it would have given us a clearer view of the meteorological state of the planet."

— — —

I look to the bottom-right corner of the phone and slap Leon's arm when I see the number.

"Four million. And climbing." The rule of thumb is that if you get more views than you have followers, you're in a good place. Right now, I'm in a *really good place.*

The sliding door opens around the corner, so I hide the champagne under my seat. But it's just Kat. Her phone echoes Kyle's voice back to us, and her face beams an "oh my god" expression.

"*New York Times* shared your link on Facebook," she says. "It looks like CNN and a few others have too, but I can't even keep up with all the hits. Plus, the videos are so good."

"I get why you think that," Leon says. "And I get why Cal and I would think so, but why would the average American even care about this?"

"Dude, Leo—we've been in such a drought for real information that people are hungry for this." She smiles. "Star-Watch is entertaining, but no one ever liked NASA because it was entertaining. No one writes sci-fi stories for the gossip."

"People who are like Josh Farrow? They don't get it," I say. "They never did. My videos have always been no-bullshit information. I got most of my followers by covering the election, and most of them weren't old enough to vote. People care about this information, but it's hard to find it through all the clickbait and fake news." I take a second to look at Kat. "I just didn't want NASA to collapse because of it."

Kat takes a seat next to us. I hand her the bottle, and she takes an eager sip. She leans forward and wipes some of the champagne off her chin. We watch the rest of Kyle's talk, then sit in complete silence as the rocket technician provides some theories for the explosion and reasons why something like this couldn't happen on a crewed launch.

"I hope this is enough," I say after all the other videos play. No one responds, but they don't have to. They lean in closer as my face takes over the screen.

My expression still has the light smile and confident persona, but there's something more real about it. Less scripted—even if I never use a script. Less prepared, even.

Raw, emotional, and real.

— — —

"This is our plea," I say. "NASA is a great organization with a sometimes rocky history, we all know that, but thanks to Star-Watch and a few members of their communications team, they've turned us into a circus. Yeah, we have drama here. It's competitive, it's stressful, and there are so many types of people here, we're bound to have arguments at parties. But to disregard everything good about this mission to focus on the bad is irresponsible, and honestly un-American.

"If you care about this mission, you need to show it now. There's a link on my page with all the tools you need to make your voice heard. With the tap of a button, you can share these videos, contact NASA, or contact your representatives, all thanks to some brilliant and quick coding by Katherine Tucker. Speak up. Let anyone who will listen know that this mission cannot be defunded, and that you're invested in getting us to Mars. We're so close.

"Again, thanks for following, thanks for sharing, and have a good night."

— —— —

The video goes blank, and in its place are links to share or replay the video. I close my phone and look from Leon to Kat. Collectively, we take a deep breath in, and out. Kat grabs my hand, and I reach out for Leon's.

It's the last bit of peace we'll be able to enjoy for a long time.

"I'm going to head back, I guess," I say. "I'm too nervous to sit here anymore."

Kat leans over to give me a big hug. "Either way, what you're doing is really amazing. I'm going to share this with everyone I know. We're not going out without a fight."

Leon still doesn't say anything, but gives me a small smile. There's still so much between us we need to talk about. I've shown him all I can, but I need to give him time. I can't force him to feel better; I can't force him to make decisions about his life. I can't keep trying to fix things, especially when he's not broken.

But I lean in and press my lips to his, just lightly. He doesn't pull away, but he doesn't join in much. Our eyes close and I let them linger there. Long enough to bring back the fuzzy feeling in my chest, the flutter in my stomach.

And it gets a little better.

CHAPTER 27

I wake in the morning and check my phone right away. I actually did this on seven separate occasions through the night, almost once an hour. I can't keep up with the notifications. Comments, shares, likes, views, all these numbers and words fly by my screen.

Social media is a weird space, so insulated by the followers that you have. But I have comments from my normal followers, plus the old grandma Facebook market, the geeky high schooler market, the college engineers, a staggering number of trolls, and everyone in between. It's overwhelming, it's beautiful, it's . . . it's national news.

Getting shared on Facebook by the *New York Times* is one thing, but waking up to a *Times* online feature is another: "Astrokid Calls on Americans to Save NASA From Clickbait Demise."

I start to read the article, but my phone is taken over when

I get a call. I answer the phone, and her voice pierces my eardrum with her excited shouting.

"You are famous!" Deb says. "Like, REALLY famous this time."

"I don't think that's true. NASA is famous still; my account is just attached to the shares."

"It's not just your 'account'—your face is staring at me on *Page Six* right now. They're talking about your FlashFame account. It's everything you've ever wanted. Do you know how easy it is going to be to turn this into a real career?"

I laugh. "We'll see. I'd settle for getting my BuzzFeed internship back right now."

"They'll have to fight for you. God, Cal, if you save this mission—you could literally alter the course of history."

That sentence makes my body scramble up in bed. I'm a seventeen-year-old guy in bright yellow shorts and a Dolly Parton T-shirt with major bedhead. I don't think I'm capable of altering anything.

"Okay, Deb. This is overwhelming for me. Can we talk about something else?"

"SOMETHING ELSE?"

I want to bring up our last call and the fight that ended with her hanging up on me, the knot in my chest that never really resolved . . . but I don't. I was selfish and self-centered and made everything about me.

"Literally anything. Let's pretend I haven't just altered the course of humanity." So I talk about her. "How's living with your cousin?"

"Fine." She grunts in defeat. "It's not bad. My parents are still pissed that I split, but we've started talking on the phone every once in a while, so I guess not all is lost. My cousin's roommate moves out in a few weeks, and I'm trying to make sure I have the money to make rent. My job's been cutting my hours, but I'm still okay." She sighs. "Okay, better than okay."

An idea pops into my head, and I feel a rush of excitement pulse through me. It's the perfect way to give Deb a part of myself.

"Wait!" I say. "Why don't you have a FlashFame account? You could activate the donations tab or something; maybe you could make videos and that would help you make rent?"

"I'm not exactly a media personality like the great Calvin— oh, right, we're pretending you're a very ordinary human right now, sorry." She laughs. "Anyway, I actually do have an account. I just never use it."

"Well, let me know if you do. I know my NYC followers are annoyed that I don't ever have weekend updates anymore. And you helped me find a lot of that stuff anyway."

She hesitates, and I hear her giving this some real consideration, even though I know how averse she is to getting on camera. I know it's not because she's so desperate for money or attention, but maybe a part of her has changed with this big move.

"I almost drove up to see you," I admit. "Like, hijacked Dad's car and almost got out of Texas before I realized how incredibly stupid it was. I'm so sorry about how I acted earlier."

I hear her laugh filter through the phone. "I miss you too. But you don't have to worry about me. Things with us will always be good, whether your ridiculous plan to save the entire future of spaceflight works or fails spectacularly. Whether you stay in Texas forever or come back to Brooklyn where you belong and fit in."

"I fit in here too. Surprisingly."

There's a pause.

"Oh my god, you wore that giant hat out in public, didn't you?"

"No comment."

"Calvin, I swear. John Mayer couldn't pull it off, and neither can you."

"No comment."

"Wow. Okay, go back to your fame and saving of the country. I'm going to sit here and shake my head for a while."

"No comment." I pause for effect. "Love you, Deb."

"Yeah, yeah. Love you too."

We hang up, and I feel entirely normal for the first time in the past twenty-four hours. I listen to the Heart album again, and the thought of Leon and Kat arguing about stopping at a random yard sale to rummage for cassettes of bands he's never heard of makes me almost laugh out loud.

I keep the panic out of my chest by unplugging my headphones and walking around the room. My future is a question mark right now. And I think that's okay. But god, I want to stay. This is all the agony of final exams, election day, and a dentist's appointment wrapped into one.

I'm starting to get texts from numbers I don't know, and some I do—old family members who once criticized all the time I spent on my phone congratulating me on the mention in the *New York Times*. Requests from journalists have steadily been pouring into my inbox. I want to respond to them, but the sheer volume of everything is wigging me out.

I leave my bedroom and find my mom in the living room. Sitting down next to her, I take a deep breath and release it.

"I think I'm famous."

"I think you are too." She laughs. "Dad and I watched your show. I still don't really get FlashFame—or maybe the kids just call it Flash?—but it looked like a lot of people liked what you had to say."

"I'm overwhelmed. I have all these media inquiries that I should get back to, and all these acquaintances are coming out of the woodwork to congratulate me. My face is in *Page Six*, apparently? Why do people care about me so much?"

She puts down her game and pats my shin. "Honey, don't take this the wrong way, but it's not so much you they care about. It's everything you're fighting for. It's NASA, and exploration, and science. You're the face they can put to the cause, so you might as well let them. You're the mockingjay."

I nod along with her words. It kind of makes sense. It's not me, it's the mission. It's also kind of me, but maybe I can ignore that for now.

"And about your media inquiries, NASA has a whole team of communications people who would love to respond for you.

Why don't you ask them for help?" The ache in my chest gets a little more manageable.

"Did Dad get a ride with Grace today?"

"Yeah, do you need to use the car?"

I take my space center visitor's badge out of my wallet— the one that helped me build support for the Orpheus project and allowed so many brilliant scientists to finally have a voice. "I think it's time I drop in and see if NASA wants to fix their awful communications campaign."

People can't be fixed. But awful communications campaigns? I can fix that.

I jump in the shower, and then dress up for the occasion. Dark brown pants and boots, a muted green-and-brown-plaid shirt, with a bright orange knit tie. I leave the hat at home.

CHAPTER 28

I've spent the full fifteen-minute drive to NASA breathing in with my diaphragm, then hissing out the air until my lungs are depleted. The more I do it, the more in control I feel of this situation. The more I think—despite that I dragged NASA's public affairs team last night—I can help them carry the momentum forward.

I hand my visitor's badge over to the guard, and he lets me in after a long look at my face. He stares at me for an extra beat, but I'm out before I can read too much into it. I find a spot near the back. So many people are in the office today—I've never seen the lot so full.

As I'm walking in, I see a large news van at the entrance. Only, it's not the news. It's StarWatch.

The realization makes me stop in my tracks. I consider hiding in my car until they're gone, but maybe this needs to happen. Maybe I need to confront them for the last time, compare viewers, and chew Kiara out for secretly videotaping me and making my relationship seem like a ploy to get a leg up in this business.

As I'm about to go through the front doors, I see movement from behind the van. A swath of unnaturally black hair blows in the breeze as Kiara throws a heavy suitcase in the van. I give my legs the command to run toward her. To get this over with.

"Kiara." I stand a safe distance from the van, from the girl who's still leaning in the back.

She freezes there for a second, then smoothly lifts her shoulders. As always, I'm caught off guard by her style— oversized denim shirt over a sheer tee with a deep V-neck.

We make eye contact, and I feel nine hundred times less confident. Her smile is easy and calm, and I wonder how she can get off on being such an awful person and not be fazed by it. My fists clench, and I take the opportunity to speak first.

"You shouldn't have done that. I didn't know I was on camera."

"Babe, you're always on camera with me, so I'd be careful with what you say."

I laugh. "You can use all the sound bites you want of *this* conversation. Or is this enough drama for your show? Maybe you can manufacture more or make it seem like I'm trying to use it to boost my career."

"Welp," she says with a shrug. "Your career certainly looks bright now, mister eight-point-five million views. And don't worry, kid. You win. Believe me. My boss is up there getting taken off the Orpheus V mission as we speak, and we're trying to line up our next assignment."

"Flocking to JET-EX?" I ask.

"No, no. They're siding with NASA. They're even talking about helping fund a new satellite and launch. So we're out of a job."

"I'm trying to feel sorry for you," I say. "But it's really, really hard."

"You know, I graduated top of my class in college as a journo major. I had so much experience, such solid writing examples. I was naive, like you."

I stay silent, because I can't tell if she's trying to get a rise out of me or if she really means it.

"I get this feeling," Kiara says. "That you're too good for StarWatch, or gossip sites, or blogs, or whatever's going on in your mind right now. You'll understand someday."

She slams the side door and jumps into the driver's seat.

"Even if I end up working on a show like StarWatch," I shout over the rumbling of the engine, though I don't know if she can hear me, "I'll always treat the people I interview like *people*."

And I guess that's it.

My feet take me away from the van, and I hate how unresolved everything feels. But maybe that's what real life is like. Unlike when you're stuck with family or friends for so long you have to make amends. You can end working relationships on a dissonant chord, one that leaves you feeling gross and wrong all over.

I pass Josh Farrow when I go inside, and he doesn't even notice me. If this were a movie, he'd catch my eye as he walks down the hallway, and maybe he'd give me a knowing nod, or a sneering headshake. But he just looks down at his phone, with a long frown tugging at his lips. Probably already working out the details of his next project that will ruin peoples' lives.

When I walk into Donna Szleifer's office, everyone kind of freezes. Todd Collins, director of public affairs, is in there, and an empty seat is pulled out, where Josh must have just been sitting.

"Oh, Calvin," Donna says, a stunned look dawning on her face. "Come in, come in."

"We were, um, just talking about you." Todd shuts the door behind me, and they both look at me expectantly.

"Have you been tracking the press hits from my video series?" I ask.

"Yes, we have. We also got the Associated Press to distribute a press release we made."

"And . . . what does that mean?" I ask.

"Right, sorry," Todd says. "AP is a kind of service where local and national news orgs can either repurpose or post full stories. It's a good way to get a lot of local press, and AP was all over it. We have about six hundred local news networks with local stories, and we included video clips, so it's possible some of the broadcast stations will pick it up too."

"Socially," Donna cuts in, "you've got some of the world's most famous scientist personalities—we call them influencers—sharing the videos."

"Donna," I say with a laugh, "I know what influencers are."

She continues as if I've said nothing. "A lot of traffic is coming from news sites, especially sites for teens, who are obviously more familiar with the FlashFame platform."

"Is this going to save the mission?" I ask, and I expect them to laugh at me or treat me like a kid who doesn't get the complicated goings-on.

"Well, maybe." Todd scratches his head. "It's not so cut-and-dried. The House of Representatives already delayed the vote to this evening so they can sort through all the voice mails and emails that came pouring in last night. The timing is good, and we have a lot of people on board."

"That said," Donna says, "we have a board meeting tonight, where they could also shut down the Orpheus project. A lot of people think the risks are too high."

"Anything could happen," Todd replies.

I sigh. It seems to run counter to the very idea of NASA. Risk is exactly what spaceflight is about—or, hell, any exploration. But I nod along anyway, knowing that there are a lot of people who need to weigh a lot of variables, and I am not one of those people. I did my part.

Now I wait.

"When's your meeting?" I ask.

"Three hours."

"Okay, here's my suggestion: I have about seventy-five interview requests in my inbox now. I can take some of them if I need to, but I don't even know what half of these publications are. Can I send them to you? I can interview, but I think this is something NASA should handle. I don't want to be the story. The science is the story. It's *always* been the story."

Donna looks so pleased she could burst. Her hands are clasped together like she's in the middle of an intense prayer, and maybe she is—this is Texas, after all.

"Forward them on," she says. "I'll take all the blogs and social sites. Todd, have your team split up the others."

For the next hour, I'm passed back and forth between the press office and Donna's, tracking all the new hits and tracking sentiment. Donna shows me a ton of tools where she gets to see how many people saw the video, plus how many people loved it enough to send it on, plus a hundred other little pieces of data that make me a little nervous to be living in such a digital age, but thankful too. And I'm glad NASA has someone like Donna, who—though she's a frazzled mess most of the time—actually knows her stuff.

In the end, Donna and Todd have one killer slideshow, thirty top news stories to mention, and big grins on their faces. The charge and electricity of the first astronaut missions are back, flowing through everyone's veins.

I wave goodbye as I leave the office, and head out to the car. I turn in my visitor's badge to the security guard when I leave. I won't be needing it anymore, even if the mission stays on. I can finally focus on my own path, or rather, figure out what I want it to be.

CHAPTER 29

I'm a firm believer in not counting chickens before they hatch. So having to attend an astronaut party right now is not what I need.

I fully recognize that the families throw a party almost weekly for one reason or another, but a party tonight, of all nights, seems like a bad idea. The vote's still delayed; the board meeting is happening as we speak. Soon, we'll learn whether the Orpheus V mission has been shelved or saved, and we can only guess what will happen.

Questions spin around my mind as my parents and I walk into the party and pass a few snacks—a crudités platter and hummus dip—to Grace, who's hosting this party. The signature stock of two dozen plus bottles of champagne is as impressive as always. Grace leans over as I admire it and whispers: "I'll be keeping track of those bottles, so don't try anything."

I turn to meet her gaze and see she's smiling. She winks at me and walks away. A joke—one that shows she has no idea about the bottles we've stolen in the past. I don't see Leon around, or Kat, and before I can go find them, I'm thrust into conversations with everyone.

Mom and Dad want me to hang around, mostly because they can't answer any of the questions about my Flash profile, because they're old and have no idea what anything is.

But I allow it, just this once.

Someone places a firm grip on my shoulder, and I spin around to see Mara Bannon beaming down at me before bringing me into a bone-crushing hug. She looks at me in one of those ways perfect movie moms look at their kids. Head tilted, barely contained smile.

"Cal, your videos made me so happy I had to drive all the way back here and tell you myself. Do you know how long it had been since I smiled—really smiled? Seeing your hopeful, powerful message . . . Mark would have been absolutely crushed if the mission got canceled in part because of him. I thank you so much for helping."

"Thanks, Mrs. Bannon," I say, letting her give me another hug.

"Oh, and I was furious when I saw how StarWatch started treating you. I watched their coverage, and I swear—those two were just about the worst humans on the planet, if you ask me."

"Of course," I say. "And not like it matters or anything, but the one producer, the girl, wasn't all bad. She helped me expose Josh Farrow when he tried to make you, you know, get back on the floor."

I think of Kiara—both sides of Kiara—and hope the good side wins out in her. There's a way to be a journo, even for a gossip blog or show, and still be a good person. She may be jaded, and I may be naive, but it has to be true.

"Well, anyway," she says. "I shared your videos with all my friends, and they were so pleased to see something positive come out of NASA. It's all been trashy lately, but it'll only get better. That's what I keep telling them."

"I hope so," I say in agreement, and get a third bone-crushing hug before I can slip away.

I return to my mom and dad. Dad's deep into a conversation with one of the Orpheus V astronauts, and Mom's just standing by with a glass of champagne, smiling and listening in.

"Thanks for suggesting I go to NASA," I say. "They were really helpful. They followed up on all my media hits and took over the interviews and everything."

"Well, honey, that's their job. They're professionals at it. You're a professional at doing the reporting. Let everyone play to their own strengths."

"And thanks for helping Kat with that site. I don't know how you two did it, but so many senators and members of Congress officially announced their support of the mission today. Doesn't mean the House won't vote to cut funding, but at least we've shaken them up."

"Don't look at me." Mom shrugs. "It was almost all Kat."

I'm about to say something, but I completely forget what it

is. Because, standing in the doorway are Donna and Todd, and they look like they know something.

Every face slowly turns toward them.

It's time.

"Can I say it?" Donna asks Todd as Grace lifts the needle from the record player. Everything is frozen for a minute when he gives a slight nod and Donna clears her throat. "We've just come from the board meeting. Every director in attendance was in agreement, and each gave their own spiel for why Orpheus V should be kept on. We even showed clips from Cal's video, which just passed twenty-five million views in less than twenty-four hours."

She takes a deep, cleansing breath in and hisses it out. Just like I do when I'm meditating.

"And after hours of discussion and analysis, we're proud to say that the board's approved the continuation of the Orpheus project."

"Also," Todd cuts in, "we had a chat with House Rep Halima Ali, who's willing to work with us to make sure funds are used properly. She made it clear that her bill would not have the votes to pass, and that they've canceled the vote entirely. Which means . . ."

Donna interrupts him by shouting, "Orpheus V is, without a doubt, back on!"

I get lost in the cheers and the shouting and the splashes of champagne. Mom hands me her glass to take a celebratory sip, and I almost laugh at her cluelessness. But I drink it anyway, and I start to understand why people celebrate with champagne. It lifts me up, it celebrates my own energy, and soon enough, I'm shouting along with the other astronauts.

One thing I don't do is get out my phone. No one else gets to see this moment. It'll never be in a history book. It'll never be on the news, or in an issue of *Time* for future kids to point at and imagine what it was like to live in this moment, this time when—for one bright moment—everything was perfect.

Leon's gaze meets mine from across the room. Kat's squeezing her dad so tightly with joy I think he might pass out, but they're all jumping up and down. Grace has tears streaming down her face—I would be crying too if I just heard that I was, for sure, going to Mars. She clutches at her son's shirt and pulls him close. She presses her cheek into his, and my heart melts.

Mom comes to me and lets out a yelp of glee, and she pulls me and Dad into a close hug.

"I can't believe it," I say.

Mom pulls back to look at me and nudges Dad with her shoulder. "*We* can."

My eyes are back on Leon's, and our smiles just keep getting bigger, and I realize that there's one thing left. That things aren't quite perfect yet. That one little puzzle piece is missing, and I'm going to make it fit.

CHAPTER 30

The din of the celebration is muted when I make my way to him. My vision narrows, the crowd parts, and I narrowly escape being hit with the spray from a few popping bottles of champagne. But I don't care about any of that right now.

All I care about is him.

In the steps between us, I feel a warmth building in my stomach. My senses feel dampened, yet heightened all at the same time, and the surrealness of the situation makes me feel so perfectly all right that I march up to him, place my hand behind his neck, and pull him in for a light kiss.

It's the simplest feeling in the world. Two sets of lips, barely touching, but my body nearly convulses with chills. His hands wrap lightly around me and pull me closer. People are still shouting, talking loudly, the music is pumping, and I realize how very public this make-out session is, but I can't stop it.

Once the emotions die down in the room, and I'm able to

pry my face from his, I stare right into those beautiful brown eyes and physically restrain myself from letting my love for him take over.

"Can we talk?" I ask.

"Sure. Out back?"

I shake my head. "Let's take a walk."

We file through the crowd, and I lead him out the door, down the steps, and into the deserted street. The clouds are out tonight, giving the night a soft feel, a cool light that glazes over trees and houses. I lace my fingers through his and squeeze.

We head down a side road that leads to a dead end, with a few houses on either side obscured by bushes. There's only one streetlight on this road, but it's enough to cast its glow over the pavement. I take a cross-legged seat on the strip of yellow on the road, and he does the same.

"I'm sorry," I say. "I know I've been shitty to you."

"I'm sorry too. I was so freaked about you leaving that I made things worse. I was really down, and just kept thinking: I was in love with someone I couldn't ever end up with."

"But I mean, even if I moved to New York, we could have stayed together. I emailed you—"

"That's exactly it," he cuts in. "You wanted to stay together on *your* terms. I could go to New York for college. I could study one of your ten quote, unquote, "ideal" majors for me. It's so great that you have it all figured out, but I couldn't lock myself into that. I still can't."

"The thought of someone not knowing what they want to

do with their life makes my palms sweat. It literally gets hard to breathe when I think of you not knowing anything about your future, and not having any urge to find out. And I recognize that's so not chill, and probably not very enlightened," I say. "Okay, definitely not enlightened. But I'm a planner. Plans can change, I'm cool with that, but not having a plan at all? It terrifies me."

"I've been going back to the open gyms. Every week, sometimes twice a week. And for once, I'm doing what I want to do. I just kept thinking about what you said, how I needed to channel that kid doing somersaults, and I have."

"Leon, that's actually amazing."

"And I met a trainer there, who—"

I cut in. "But you just said you were only doing it for fun?"

". . . who offered me a job teaching their five- to seven-year-olds early gymnastics skills. And I realized that every day I work there would be somersault day. I'm sure I'll have to deal with the intense parents—like mine—but it's the perfect side job. And without StarWatch around, I feel like I can just be myself."

"I'm so happy for you." I throw my arms around him. "And . . . what about college?"

"Look, you have to trust that I'll figure it out," Leon says. "Maybe not today, maybe not when I graduate high school, but someday I will."

"Okay," I say, and I mean it. "I'll support you, in whatever you choose to do and whenever you choose to do it."

"I need you to support me *now*. I need you to be okay with

how I am now, and not think of me as someone who is broken."

I grab his hands and nod. Not to fix him, or to make him feel better, but to show him that I can support him. That I'm trying, and learning, and will do whatever I can to be there for him.

"I told my parents," he says. "How they made me feel. I tried to help them understand my depression, and they seemed to be listening. We talked about you a lot. They really like you, and . . . and us."

A smile comes over his face, and it's so perfect I subconsciously reach out and hold his cheek. My eyes scan his face—his chin, his hair, his ears. He looks so beautiful in this moment, and I never want to forget this. How he looks. How I feel.

"I love you," I say. Not because he needs to hear it, but because I need to say it. "I love you so much, Leon."

He leans in to kiss me so fast that suddenly my back is flat against the pavement. I pull him close, and we kiss. We kiss. We kiss like we never have before—an ebb and flow of tender and rough, heavy and light, deep and shallow. My hands are all over his body, and his mine, and there's a small part of me that never wants this to end, but an even larger part of me that can't wait for what comes next.

I, Calvin Lewis Jr., have no idea what is coming next. And I couldn't be happier.

CHAPTER 31

As it turns out, I should have kept my visitor's badge. NASA's doing their best to fix their mess of a communications and social media campaign, but they asked me to keep covering the launches and keep interviewing scientists. Sure, it'll give my résumé some credibility to be so connected to NASA, but I won't be doing this for long. It's time for me to chase new stories, and interview different people—find my voice again while sticking to my FlashFame roots.

Slowly but surely, Brendan's gaining the following that NASA can use to take my place after I'm gone. His daily check-ins and weekly updates with different scientists on the mission have started to get some massive views. At least I'm not leaving them high and dry.

I'm sitting on my dad's desk in the open work space the alternates share, and I've got my feet propped up on a chair. As I wait until they're ready for me to start the video, I scroll through my feed, smiling when Deb's video pops up. I click it and watch as she walks backward through the West Village.

"I'm Deb Meister—*the Debmeister*, if you will. You won't? Okay. Never mind. Anyway, welcome to my NYC update. I know what you're thinking: New York's all murders and Amber Alerts, and none of this shit is changing. WRONG. I'm here to show you ten fantastic, fun, and freaky things you could be doing with your Saturday, starting with number one—"

She makes me laugh so hard throughout her bastardized version of my update that I almost choke. I text her after and remind her that she has a lot of journalistic integrity to uphold, and she replies with a middle finger emoji. Nice. But she's on her way to ten thousand followers, and her updates are fantastic, fun, and, yes, they're freaky too. She's getting donations to help her make rent, and her parents have started sending her some money to fill in the gaps, to make up for all the money they had to take over the past year.

I couldn't imagine how painful it would be to take your kid's money, even if she was the only one with a steady income. But since her mom and dad are back on their feet, they don't let money ruin everything anymore.

She's really happy. I can see it in the videos, and I can hear it in her voice. And maybe one day we'll actually get to be roommates in a shitty Coney Island apartment, bitching about how long it takes to get to Manhattan. I comment, saying I love her videos almost as much as I love her—because I'm feeling extra cheesy right now—when my dad waves me over.

Carmela is directing Dad into the cockpit, and Grace has me

set up the camera somewhere where I can easily pan between the simulation chamber and the open desks. I hit record.

"This one's new," I say to her. "You've got two simulation chambers now?"

"This one's for six," she says.

I lower the camera. "What do you mean?"

"Orpheus VI. It comes after V, dear?"

A smile is plastered on my face as I watch my dad get into the cockpit. *His* cockpit. He tests out a few of the levers and buttons, probably noting the differences between the two spacecraft. Grace puts her hand on my shoulder and leans in.

"I think she's taking out one of the thrusters this time," she says. "Calvin will flip, just watch."

The simulation starts. It's a landing sim, where he's staring at a screen that resembles the patch of Martian soil Orpheus VI will land on. The site's been triangulated and is meant to have the perfect conditions for landing. Smooth, level, with firm dirt. It's clear that everyone in the room is waiting for something to go wrong in the simulation. But the ground is coming up closer and closer in the view.

I zoom in and catch a bead of sweat dripping down Dad's brow. He's jamming the control to the right, harder than the craft would normally take. His breaths become pants; his gaze becomes a laser. He's in a state of total concentration.

"We're pitching," he says. "Left thruster is dead, bringing up backup."

A few moments pass.

"Backup is dead—prepare for a rough landing."

His voice is calm and even, and he reaches for buttons I didn't even know existed. His motions are fluid.

And it really hits me, after all this time: my dad's a fucking astronaut.

Touchdown.

"We have a touchdown," Dad says. "How many oxen did I lose in the river?"

"Brilliant, Calvin, just brilliant. Your crew might have a few bumps on the head, but that's all. Bravo!" Carmela says. "See, what did I tell you? Your dad is impossible to stump. He's going to keep everyone very safe in a couple years."

"And you're going to keep trying to kill me until then."

"Sir, that is my job," she says, and we all laugh.

I end the video and watch it get shared and viewed thousands of times within minutes. News sites instantly pick up my videos now, and the hunger for information about the Orpheus program is insatiable. StarWatch is long gone, and everyone's trying to be the news source to replace it.

I spend the rest of the day taking video of more scientists and astronauts in their natural habitat, and I save those videos for later. My follower count is almost at real celebrity levels, but people have started to leave me alone. All my press inquiries go right to NASA, and on principle, I don't give any interviews. "I'm the interviewer," I usually say. "Not the other way around."

While Leon still hasn't made a decision about college or the real world—I'm really okay with it, really I am (really I'm not, but I am *trying*)—I've got a list of ten schools with programs to apply to. At the top of my list are New York University, obviously, Columbia University, and Ohio University. But I'll be applying to schools in Texas, California, and all over the East Coast. Leon's helping me be more impulsive, and it's making me keep my options open. I'm flexible. Cool and breezy.

Okay, maybe not.

Maybe I'll never be breezy, but that's just me. Most important, I'm starting to realize when it holds me back. To be so laser focused on one city, or one specific future, could hurt me in the end. So I'll leave the breeziness to someone else.

After we're done, around five thirty, Dad and I get into the car and he takes the country roads back. He hasn't gotten off this early in weeks, basically since NASA decided to keep the launch on schedule. I roll down the windows, and the cool air floods the cabin. Fall is just around the corner, and I'm mostly excited to be able to use my sweater collection. I've made peace with the fact that I'll never have to bring my peacoat out because of the ever-present heat, but it's almost sixty today, which in my book is cause for a celebratory sweater party.

"Cal," my dad says, "thanks for everything. I know I made a lot of this about me—I mean, I got overwhelmed with the new job and didn't really have time to think about how everyone was taking it. I didn't even ask if you would be willing to move down here."

"I would've said no if you gave me the choice. If you gave me any other option than coming here, I'd have taken it immediately." I scratch the back of my neck. "But it would've been the worst mistake I'd ever made."

CHAPTER 32

When we pull into the driveway outside our house, Dad motions for me to stay in the car. I pause with the seat belt in my hand, and I give him a confused look. He shakes his head in reply.

"Let's go out to dinner tonight," he says. "You know, we haven't actually gotten to just hang out and talk, the three of us, since everything went down. Actually, since we moved. I'm going to go see if Mom is okay with it."

"It's okay if she isn't," I say quickly. "Spontaneity isn't really her thing."

Mine either, I think.

"I know," he says. "If she doesn't want to, that's fine. We'll figure something else out."

That's what sits oddly with me. Not in a bad way, but more in a . . . peculiar way. Something as minor as this would have set off a fight back when we lived in Brooklyn. Is he starting to actually understand my mom?

While Dad's inside, I cross my legs in the car and start to text Leon, like I have been doing for basically any downtime in the past week. When you're an unemployed FlashFame star who is no longer trying to save humanity with his videos, turns out you have a lot of downtime.

"Want to come over tonight?" he asks. After literally no thought at all, I decide that I do very much want to come over tonight. We meet at his house more often, mostly because his bedroom's way bigger than mine. We have to keep the door open when we're in there—again, the obliviousness of his parents is nothing short of adorable—but I've barely talked to my parents about Leon, though they obviously know (they're not blind). To invite him over would mean having that talk. Would mean my mom being super awkward and inviting him to stay for dinner, where things would continue to be awkward until the end of time.

His place is much better. I text back: *"I'm having dinner with my parents, maybe? But I'll call after."*

There's something so pleasing in the mundane way that our conversations have gone lately. Something right about how easy things are now. Sure, when I see him, everything is fire and passion and kissing and touching, but there's an old grandma side of me that just loves hanging out with him and watching a movie, or whatever we end up doing.

Dad comes back, and I assume he'll just wave me inside

after a failed attempt to be spontaneous. But he keeps walking. And Mom follows him out and comes to the car. I get out and slide into the back seat, and we take a drive together for the first time since we moved here.

"Tex-Mex?" Dad asks.

We nod our assent, and within minutes we're at the nearest restaurant with a giant margarita in front of Dad and an equally large basket of chips in front of me.

"This is nice," Mom says for probably the fourth time.

I sit up straighter, and my gaze darts between my parents. "What's this about?" I ask warily.

"You know how I have that therapist who I meet online?" Mom asks. I nod. "Well, we, meaning me and Dad, found one who specifically works on . . . relationship issues."

"Oh. Um. What's wrong with your relationship?" I ask, though I kind of know the answer.

"I think you know," Dad says. "We're learning—about sixteen years later than we should've—how to deal with conflict between each other. See, your mom and I are different. We react to things differently, and we are trying to understand our differences, I guess."

"Yes," I say with a smile. "You two are very different."

"Very," Mom says before sneaking a sip of Dad's margarita. "And we started to realize how much this was affecting you. You were usually closed off in your room or downstairs with Deb, listening to music or posting Flash videos. We thought that you could ignore it."

"I could have told you it bothered me, I guess."

"We should have known," Mom says. "What's going on with us is not your responsibility to make better. It's ours, and we're going to start treating it that way. Thanks to a little help."

I come around the table and squeeze them both in a big hug. I know how hard it is to seek help, from when Mom first started managing her anxiety. But I also know how much better she feels because of it.

People aren't broken, and therapists couldn't fix them if they were. But maybe someone can make things a little better, or help them be a little happier.

"I love you guys. And I'm glad you're talking to someone."

I take my seat and resume my overeating of chips, when I see a little cassette get slid to me.

"What's this?" I ask.

"After our first date, your dad made me this cassette. This was the late nineties, so while I was thrilled—none of my high school boyfriends had ever given me one—I didn't have a cassette player anymore."

"The quality is probably terrible. I recorded them off the radio—you used to be able to do that back in the day—but we wanted you to have it."

I open the case and see a simple white cassette with a heart on it. It makes me melt, and the gift makes me need to see Leon.

"Maybe giving a cassette to someone you like is a good sign," Mom says, her grin growing wider by the moment. "If you get my hint."

"So, want to talk to us about Leon?" Dad says.

"You know—we should have him over for dinner. What kind of food does he like?"

"Oh my god," I say. "Stop! You guys are embarrassing."

"It's kind of our job," Mom says as she hooks her arm in Dad's.

After dinner, Mom and Dad decide to go to a movie. I decline, explaining that I planned on going over to hang out with Kat and Leon tonight. So after we're all overstuffed on enchiladas, they drop me off outside their place.

I stand on the other side of the Tuckers' front door and wait for the Corolla's taillights to disappear down the street. My heart races as I pull out my phone and give him a call.

"Hey, you on your way?" Leon asks.

"No," I say, staring at his front door. "I'm outside your house. And I have a proposition."

The chill of the night creeps under my cable-knit sweater, and I welcome it. It's been far too long since I've been chilly.

"My parents just went to see a movie." A pause, where the silence on the other end of the phone is deafening. "Meaning, my house is empty."

"I know what you meant. Come around back. I'll slip out."

Excitement charges through my body, and every part of me, of *this*, feels right. When I get to the backyard, he's there, the bright moon softening his skin.

He puts his arm around me as we wind around the wooded path that connects our houses. I think about how he snuck me away from reporters on the first day, how cute he was sitting on the swing next to mine, how foreign and scary everything felt.

I slip my arm around his waist. There's a moment when we struggle to fall in line with each other's gait, and it's a little awkward, but we figure it out eventually.

"I can't believe it's only been a few months since you moved here," Leon says.

"I know. It feels like only yesterday I was single-handedly saving all of NASA."

He glares at me. "Okay, I had a little help."

He plants a kiss on my cheek, and I actually blush. Embarrassing.

"I should have been there more to help you," he says. "Sorry, babe. I was so in my head about everything."

I lean my weight into him and momentarily forget how to make words when I breathe him in.

"Can we stop apologizing? I love NASA, and I'm so glad we are still here, but I'm ready to move on. Talk about new things. Think about next steps."

"Next steps?" he says with a laugh. "Always the planner."

"Seriously. No more apologies about this. I love you."

"And I love you."

"And that's all," I say. "That's *all* that matters."

We stop outside the door to my empty house. He faces me and places his hands on either side of my head. Our lips meet, again and again, until it gets hard to separate whose tongue is whose, whose breath belongs to who.

His face is pressed to mine as I get my key out and unlock the back door—a feat of which I am extremely proud—and we push through the dark house. Breathing into each other. Holding on for dear life.

I lead him to my room and press play on my tape deck. The cassette he bought for me starts turning. I bring my lips to his again . . .

And then the music starts.

EPILOGUE

Orpheus V Launch
Cape Canaveral, Florida—Eight Months Later

T-minus three minutes to launch.

"I don't know what to do with my hands," I say. "What do I do with them?"

It was an actual question, but no one's answering me. This is a surreal experience. I'm no stranger to being on camera—it's kind of my thing. But that's when it was on my phone. Now, I've got a real camera pointed at me. And a whole production team to edit the video. Oh, and the multimillion *Teen Vogue LIVE* followers to please.

I adjust the microphone attached to my face and wipe the sweat off my hands and onto my chambray shirt. It's a mild spring morning, meaning it's like eighty (mild for a Texan, at least), but my hands are ice right now.

"Three, two, one," the camera guy says, "and you're on."

"I'm standing here in Cape Canaveral, Florida, and if you can't tell by the giant rocket behind me, we are in for a spacecraft launch today. The Orpheus V launch is happening in—how long?—two minutes. Astronauts Grace Tucker, Amira Saraya, Stephanie Jonasson, Dr. Guarav Jeswani, Joseph Sedgwick, and Lloyd Osborne are in the craft, and they won't be touching Earth's soil again for 582 days. That's almost two full years in space and on Mars. It's getting loud here as we approach launch, so we're going to switch feeds and wait for blastoff."

One camera stays on me, but I turn to look at the spacecraft. There are three distinct parts: the Martian module, which will transport the full crew from orbit to the surface of Mars; the thrusters that get the spaceship out of Earth's orbit and then break away shortly after; and the command module, which houses the crew for nearly two years in space. We're so far away, but the rumble of the engine still rocks the ground under our feet. The families, alternate astronauts, and special guests all sit in stands to my right, but a thin rope separates me from the rest. I'm in the press zone.

And I have a badge to prove it that says Cal Lewis, *Teen Vogue*.

A few weeks after the broadcast that helped save the Orpheus mission aired, an editor from Condé Nast contacted me. As it turned out, Kiara actually passed my information along to her, with a recommendation. The editor said she wanted me to help with their new live programming. Which means instead of working in fast food or retail like all my new friends at school, I can technically say I'm a real-life reporter. Cue the surrealness again.

I scan the crowd, but I still don't see him. The families of the Orpheus V astronauts have been in and out of interviews and briefings all day. Finally, I spot Kat, who's leaning into her dad. Tears brim her eyes. But where is *he*?

I get a text: *"I know you're a little busy, but can I send you something?"*

I look around for Leon, wondering where he's texting from, and I'm starting to get worried. I send back a quick *"okay?"* and wait. Immediately, like he was just waiting for my response, he sends over an image. It's a screenshot. When I expand the image, I see that it's the University of Texas site, with an acceptance letter. I got my acceptance months ago, because I'm on top of my shit, but he never even told me he applied.

He said he would make a decision and apply somewhere if and when he was ready, and I told him I would support him no matter what.

I'm not done here. I'm staying in Texas for a lot of reasons. For one, the UT at Austin journalism school is one of the best in the country. But with Dad's mission slated for two summers from now, I don't want to leave. I want to be here for all the highs and lows of training—not, exactly, here . . . but close enough that I can get here if anything exciting is happening. I want to be close to the astronaut families and still attend parties. I'll end up back in New York eventually, but for now, I'm okay in Texas.

Hell, I'm *happy* in Texas.

A warm hand is on my back. I jump at the touch.

"Leon," I say. "You . . . aren't allowed here, babe."

"I don't think they can kick me out. Benefit of being an Astrokid on launch day is everyone treats you like you're super fragile."

Like we've done thousands of times in the past nine months, we kiss. We kiss with all the highs and lows of a relationship behind us, and in front of us too. I don't know what the future brings, but I don't care as long as I'm here. Here, with him.

"You got into Texas?" I ask. "You didn't even tell me you applied."

"Was going for the surprise factor. Or . . . being sneaky in case I didn't make it in."

I put my palm on his shoulder. "You have better grades than me."

"I'm not famous."

He's got a point there. Starting a new school for your senior year is a strange experience. I tried to stay in the background, finish my studies, make a few new friends, and see Leon and Kat every chance I got. But everyone kind of knew me already. If they weren't following me on Flash, they'd heard of me thanks to the NASA-saving video. Whether people were intimidated or they thought I was too full of myself, they left me alone. And I put my head down and worked toward the only things I really cared about: becoming a real journo and spending time with Leon.

"Should you get back to your dad?" I ask.

"I'd like to stay here, if you don't mind."

I don't. And he's right—none of the journalists are going to kick him out of here. Even the *Teen Vogue* cameraman squats low to get us both in the shot.

The countdown starts. It trails from fifty seconds to forty to thirty, then down one by one until we get to the last ten seconds. The rumble of the engine gets louder. Deafening. But I can't cover my ears or my eyes. I hold my breath, and Leon clutches my hand. He squeezes hard, and I squeeze back.

"I love you," I shout into his ear.

The earth shakes underneath us, and Leon loses his footing. He leans into me, and I hold him steady.

The spacecraft rises, slowly at first, steadily getting higher in the air, until it shrinks to a small but vibrant light piercing through the already bright sky. I close my eyes and force myself to remember this moment. To capture the hope, the dreams, the happiness.

I bring Leon's hand to my lips and give him a light kiss. And we enter a new era.

AUTHOR'S NOTE

Dear Reader,

Being a Certified Nerd™, I've always been fascinated by accounts of the space race and the missions that followed. I've read dozens of astronaut/engineer memoirs, watched every documentary I could find, and I've even been known to raid antique shops in my search for *LIFE* magazines from the era. In a way, the research I did for this story goes back more than a decade.

While I've always been charmed by the science and technology behind the Mercury, Gemini, and Apollo missions, one thing always called out to me in the background of these stories. The astronaut families unexpectedly became celebrities of this era, gracing the covers of magazines and giving interviews for national news outlets. This meant the astronauts' spouses and children had to be immaculately dressed, polished, and ready to entertain, all while not knowing if their husbands or fathers would come home alive that night. In *The Gravity of Us*, I wanted to capture this brilliant tension while also showcasing a contemporary queer love story.

Like so many authors, I've always loved reading. From the historical fiction diary series Dear America, to the creepy sci-fi Animorphs series, to—of course—the world of Harry Potter, I couldn't get enough. My tastes were always changing, and by high school I found myself getting into cozy mysteries, reading all forty of the Agatha Christie books that were available at my school library in the span of a year. As a quiet, closeted queer kid growing up in a farming village in Ohio, books became my everything.

But even in the world of fiction, the safe space I'd built for myself, I never got to *see* myself in these books. Sure, I could relate to Hermione getting picked on for being a bit of a know-it-all—yep, I was that kid—but I never saw a gay boy on the cover of any books. My experience wasn't on the page, and it felt like it never would be. But now, there are so many fantastic queer books on the shelves, and I'm so lucky to be able to write the books I'd have needed most as a teen.

Thank you for reading.

All my best,
Phil Stamper

ACKNOWLEDGMENTS

The Gravity of Us has only one name on the cover, but if I listed everyone who had an influence on this book—and my career—it'd take another hundred pages. I know every other author says that, but it's true. There's no way I could have done this alone! Because of all your help, some thank-yous are in order:

To Brent Taylor, the best agent in the biz, for being a steadfast champion of my work. There's no one out there who works harder for their clients, and I consider myself very lucky to be represented by you. And an extra special thank-you to my agent sibling Whitney Gardner, who first connected me with Brent. You're the best cheerleader I could have had through this process.

To Mary Kate Castellani, my brilliant editor, for having a wealth of faith in me—and Cal!—from day one. You pushed me, you caught me *every time* I cut corners, and helped me create a book I'm unbelievably proud to call my own. To all of Bloomsbury Children's—Claire Stetzer, Courtney Griffin, Lily Yengle, Erica Barmash, Oona Patrick, Danielle Ceccolini, Donna Mark, Melissa Kavonic, and Cindy Loh—and to my illustrator Patrick Leger for their creativity, insight, professionalism, and enthusiasm throughout this process.

To Chelsea Sedoti and Jenny Howe for your early critiques. You were the first people to get to know and love Cal, and your excitement for his journey built my confidence as I readied the book for the submissions process.

To Josh Hlibichuk for being a fantastic friend through all this. You were the first person I told about my book deal, which makes sense, as you were the first person I complained to about every single step of the submissions process. And to Jo Farrow for coming up with the title of the book, and for all your support and friendship over the years—I hate to expose this secret, but you're a softie at heart and everyone needs to know it.

To the amazing authors who blurbed this book: Becky Albertalli, Adam Silvera, Karen M. McManus, Jeff Zentner, Shaun David Hutchinson, Caleb Roehrig, Julian Winters, Chelsea Sedoti, and Adib Khorram. Having read and loved your books *so much*, I was beyond honored to have your support.

To Adam, Caleb, and Kevin—with special guests Ryan and Kosoko. By the time this book is out, the snake (me) will have already been revealed and destroyed our chat. We're probably sworn enemies now, but know that I'll always have a special place in my heart for the Real Housewives of YA. *twirl*

To Beth Revis for her magical query critiques and constant guidance. To Caitie for being an advocate for my work. And to all my writerly friends who haven't already been mentioned, including Lilah, Kristine, Greg, Rachel, Anna, Katie, Katelyn, Jess, Leann, Marley, Morgan, Tasha, Annie, Melissa, Kim, and Nic.

To Amanda Bennett for originally (and continually) encouraging me to write novels. And to Ali, Laura, and Meghan for taking me in when I was twenty-two and had no business making adult decisions for myself. Without you all, I wouldn't be the person I am today. Especially you, Laura. *crash*

To Heather Croley. From fast getaways with the parking brake on, to "415 Miles for Ronnie Day," the only reason I'm able to write such real, meaningful YA friendships is because of everything we had . . . and still have!

To Ali and Reuven Szleifer for your friendship through the most stressful and the most exciting years of my writing career to date. There's no one else I'd rather share a bottle (. . . or two) of celebratory rosé with. To Diana S., Kiersten M., Greg M., Caitlin P., Jasmine B., Elizabeth M., Megan L., Nicole A., Chloe F., Hannah A., and Whitney D.—your friendship and support over all this time have been priceless.

To my husband, Jonathan, for being by my side through the many highs and lows of this process. Over the years, you've stepped into many roles—editor, manager, therapist, and cheerleader—and without your support and input, there's no way I'd be the writer (or the person) I am today. I love you!

To Andi and Bruce, Rachel and Greg, and the rest of the

Stein family for all the love and support you've given me over the years.

To my parents, Karen and Phil (Sr.), for always encouraging me to pursue my creative and nerdy passions. Whether it was a community theatre performance, marching band show, or piano recital, you always made sure you had a front-row seat. You've been cheering me on every step of the way, and I'm so happy I make you proud. To the rest of the Stamper and Lamb families for all the love you've given to me (and this book!) over the years. I love you all so much!

To Ella Lamb, my granny, for everything you did to make me who I am today, from buckets of Lee's Famous Recipe Chicken to the countless games of Euchre, Yahtzee, and *Vegas Stakes* we played over the years. I'll always be your buddy.

CATCH UP WITH CAL AND LEON IN THIS EXCLUSIVE BONUS CHAPTER!

There's a light drizzle when I step out of the subway. I didn't bring an umbrella, but the drops of water that scatter around don't annoy me much. I mean, how can they? I'm finally home. *Home.*

New York freaking City.

As soon as the thought crosses my mind, there's a little nagging feeling that maybe this isn't home anymore, but I suppress it immediately, because I can't handle that kind of self-treason.

I step to the side and get my bearings, even as the rain gathers on my collarless denim button-down. As soon as my gaze meets the street sign, I find myself lost in what lies beyond it: Times Square.

A full year has gone by, and everything's changed. The ads are different, the buildings look different. I wasn't even in the city to see that ball drop. (Not like I'd ever *be* in Times Square for the actual dropping, but it still felt weird not to be in proximity of it.)

I'm different too. Leon and I are about to celebrate our first anniversary. But we also don't know exactly what anniversary we should celebrate—should it be the first time we met, when he saved me from those reporters? Or should it be the first time we kissed, when we were packed into the cockpit simulator, our lips finding each other, when a silent pact was made that it was us against the world. Against StarWatch. Against NASA.

Realistically, though, our anniversary is the night before the satellite launch . . . or rather, the *failed* satellite launch. We shared so many unforgettable firsts that night, but I replay one moment in my head every single time:

"Can we . . . make this official?" Leon asks, his body pressed fully into me.

I try to look at him, really look at him, but it's past midnight and the room is pitch black. I feel my defenses tighten up, but I decide to be honest with him:

"I'm scared. It's so fast, all of this. But I . . ." I don't tell him I love him, which I'm now three-hundred percent sure I do. "I think it's real. I want to be your boyfriend."

His lips are on mine again. His arms wrap around me, and I don't take another breath the entire night.

When I break free from the daydream, I can feel myself getting hard in the middle of one of the busiest streets in Manhattan. Great. Cool. Normal. At least the sky is literally giving me a cold shower right now.

We're running behind schedule. But riding the train with

Deb and Leon proved to be an adventure I wasn't remotely ready for. Leon's inability to swipe into the turnstile on the first—or even fifth—time is something I didn't anticipate, and it took all my patience not to lose my mind about it.

I'm trying to be a kinder, more patient person, I swear, but there are some things a lifelong New Yorker cannot handle.

"Did you hear me, Cal?" Leon says. "Dad said Kiara, *Star-Watch Kiara*, is coming back to cover the Orpheus VI launch for her new job."

Deb scoffs. "I don't even know her, but after watching that 'special' of hers, I can officially say I hate her."

"We could tell Donna," Leon suggests. "I bet we can stop her."

"Guys . . . I'm tired." I sigh. "It's not that I don't care, but I want to focus on me. On *us*. It's time to let go and enjoy college and worry about things that aren't NASA for once."

"I hear that," Deb says. "Even my FlashFame followers don't seem to care about the drama anymore. Everyone's just waiting for his mom to land on Mars."

"Yeah," I agree, then look to Leon. "We'll let them deal with it?"

He nods. "You're right."

"So what's next?" Deb cuts in.

I point at the glowing city in front of us. "Times Square, Empire State Building, Strand Bookstore for some souvenir shopping, then back to Brooklyn for pizza."

We take our time winding through the city, and despite the rain, things do feel right here. I show Leon where I started all my broadcasts and we follow the path down Broadway, stopping by all my favorite places. But the falafel cart I used to go to has moved, the street vendors I'd pass every day are gone, and everything feels different.

The city's changed over the last year, but for the first time, I haven't changed alongside it.

"I feel so out of the loop," I tell Deb as Leon steps away to show his sister all the hectic glory that is Times Square on FaceTime. Seeing his excited and overwhelmed expression makes me smile.

"Well of course you do. You've been gone for a while," Deb says. "For light years, in New York time."

"Light years measure distance, not time," I say quietly.

"*You* certainly haven't changed, know-it-all."

She throws me a wink and I laugh. Of everyone, she knows how I've changed. Sure, I'm still as fashionable as ever—though, I did ultimately donate my John Mayer hat when going through my closet last month—but I am different.

"I'd like to think I'm kinder," I say. "Less selfish?"

"You are. You're a better friend now, and I like that. And you gave me your media empire in New York, and my wallet loves that. Like with that StarWatch girl coming back to Houston, the old Cal would've written this whole exposé and interviewed fifty people by now to try and put a stop to it."

"Think I'm losing my spark?" I ask, feeling immediately vulnerable.

"Never. You're not a spark anymore. You're more like . . . a steady flame."

I pause. "Oh god, you're just being nice to me so we can get vegan doughnuts on the way back, aren't you?"

"I mean . . . if you wanted to . . . I wouldn't, like, stop you . . ."

Leon wraps me in a hug from behind. "Did I hear doughnuts?"

I curl into him and breathe in his warmth. I'm surrounded by so much love right now, and maybe she's right. If I'm a steady flame, these two are the ones who'll never let me burn out.

— —— —

We return to Deb's Brooklyn apartment *soaked*. New York City in rain has a sort of charm to it, but that charm fades quickly. Dirty rainwater streams down the streets, tree boxes start to flood, and all the passersby are even more erratic than usual.

But we're here, and it's calm and quiet. This neighborhood is still bustling by Clear Lake standards, but there's a marked difference between here and the touristy areas of Manhattan.

Her brick building sits on the corner of a busy intersection. It's eerily similar to the one our parents lived in, back before Dad got the job at NASA, before she and her family had to relocate too. When we take the stairs to her fifth-floor walk-up, I hear Leon panting behind me.

"I thought you were a gymnast," Deb says with a laugh.

"Surprisingly, stair climbing is not an official gymnastics event," he replies between heavy breaths. "Besides, I'm a gymnastics *teacher* now."

She lets us into her apartment, its soft pinks instantly

reminding me of her old place. It's a small two-bedroom she shares with a girl she met on Craigslist, but she's been able to make it all her own.

"Who's this?" I ask while looking through the many photos on the fridge.

For some selfish reason, seeing Deb with her arms around this group of girls brings out this hollowness in me. Yes, there are plenty of pictures of us here too—on our old stoop, at vegan restaurants or cassette shops—but those fade into the background.

"Well that's my roommate," she points to a girl in an oversized crew neck sweatshirt. She's cute, artsy. "And those are her friends from Pratt. You'd love them."

I smile and nod as I sort through my feelings.

"I left you when you needed me," I say to the fridge, because I can't justify looking at her. Tears well up in my eyes. "This is all so weird. You've got this whole life, and I've got mine, and I just feel like we'll be drifting farther apart. I'm sorry."

"We FaceTime, like, three times a day. We're not growing apart," she says. "What we had when you lived here was complicated and messy and so much fun, but we were too dependent on each other. We both needed to grow up, on our own, away from each other. And yeah, you did fully ghost me when I needed you, but I figured it out, and I'm better for it. *We're* better for it, too.

"As for me?" She puts her arm around my waist and pulls me in tightly. "I'm neither new nor improved—I just find myself at fewer creepy cassette shops without you."

"We can make up for that tomorrow," I say. "There's a shop down in Red Hook which I know is really far away, but I—"

"No!" She plugs her ears. "I will *not* support this habit anymore."

When we return to the living room, Leon's on the couch flipping through dozens of selfies he took on our mini-tour of the city.

"He's gotten vainer since you met him, right?" Deb asks, and Leon shoots her a glare.

"*Actually*, I'm choosing the photo I want to send my mother, who is floating in a metal tube millions of miles away from us right now." He dons a serious look before breaking into a smile. "Sorry, too intense? I'm trying to get this banter thing down, but you two are hard to keep up with."

Once we're settled in Deb's apartment, she goes out to pick up a pizza—one New York thing that the rain can't even ruin—and for the first time in twenty-four hours Leon and I are alone. We take our seats on the couch, browsing through Deb's Netflix. I lean into him, slightly, and he puts his arm around me. And I'm so perfectly content.

With the challenges of transitioning from literal world fame to quiet solitude (okay, I still have my million-or-so FlashFame followers), I started seeing a therapist, like Mom and Leon do. I could never enjoy quiet moments like this, when I have nothing on my agenda. No worlds to save.

It hasn't always been easy. For me, for Leon, or for us.

"Deb's Netflix queue is terrifying," Leon says. "She really likes murder documentaries. Like, maybe *too* much."

"That's . . . a new development," I reply.

"Is it weird for you to be back? Like, back in New York, back with Deb?"

I nod. "Everything's changed. Deb and I have changed. And that's good, but if all this can change in a year, what happens after?"

"After four years in college?" Leon asks. "New York will still be here. And if we move here, we can make it our own."

"You'd actually move here?" I ask, a little surprised that the overwhelmed guy wandering the streets could see a life here.

He shrugs. "Maybe. I don't know what I want to do with my life yet—"

"—oh I *know* you don't."

"*But* whatever it is, I can probably do it in New York. And honestly, I see you struggle in Texas sometimes. You'll thrive in college because you'll join every group, quadruple-major in something, you'll have enough. But once we graduate, what'll be left for us?"

"I don't think I need to move back here," I say. "Assuming we're still together, I'd want to build a life with you somewhere. And being with you as full-blown adults, building our careers and taking on the world . . . that's the exciting part. If it's New York, then great. But I can be flexible."

He holds me tighter.

In four years, the Orpheus missions will have come to a close. His mom will have taken humankind's first steps on Mars, with my dad's flight not far behind her. We could be anywhere.

"I'm baaaack!" Deb announces, giant pizza in hand. "I

swear, this vegan pizza place is better than Roma, just you wait."

"I highly doubt that," I say. Many things have changed in New York, but me being a Roma Pizza stan is a constant. "But I'm always willing to try the best *vegan* pizza in New York."

She grabs a big picnic blanket and a bottle of champagne from her fridge and leads us out her window. The fire escape is slick as we take the metal stairs up to her roof which, officially speaking, should not have any guests on it. The rain's stopped and it looks like we're heading for a clear night.

The sun hangs low, disappearing just beyond the buildings, and I almost expect to see some sort of iconic skyline when I hit the roof—the Chrysler Building or even the Matchstick—but we're surrounded by the neighborhood's high-rises, some office buildings, and a whole lot of construction.

She lays the picnic blanket down, pours us each a glass of champagne, and ceremoniously opens the pizza box. Smells of tomato sauce and herbaceous beauty hit my nose and for the first time I *truly* feel like I'm home.

Home . . . it isn't New York. Home is laughing at Deb's jokes and curling into Leon's arms. I look into the night sky as Deb proposes a toast.

"To us?" she asks.

Leon smiles as he shouts, "To us!"

I take a sip, and I'm reminded of all our nights together. All the nights left to come. Deb and I fight over the biggest slice of pizza, while Leon's laugh echoes off the buildings around us.

I'm finally home.

Read on for a glimpse at Phil Stamper's next novel . . .

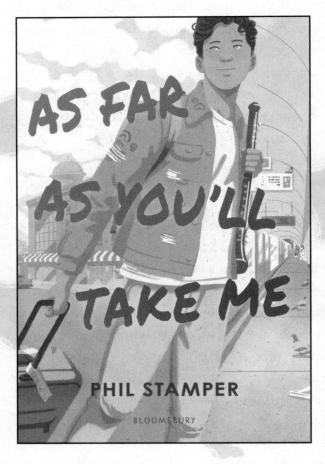

AS FAR AS YOU'LL TAKE ME

PHIL STAMPER

BLOOMSBURY

"A beautiful tribute to every queer kid who's ever had to leave their home in order to find one."

—Leah Johnson, bestselling author of *You Should See Me in a Crown*

AS IT TURNS OUT, I'm pretty good at lying.

On paper, there's nothing about me that says I'd be a great liar. I follow whatever obscure rules have been set by fake authority figures—*No running near the pool! Turn off your phone in the theater!* I won't even jaywalk. I was shoved into Christian youth groups for most of my upbringing, and, well, the Bible is pretty clear on what happens to liars.

But maybe that's why I'm so good at it. I'm incognito. Why *would* Marty possibly lie? The answer, of course, is simple:

I'm gay, and I'm suffocating.

I came to a realization about the former a long time ago, but the suffocating? That crept slowly into my chest, shortening my breaths until I realized I wasn't breathing at all.

"You're being melodramatic." Keeping one hand on the steering wheel, Megan flips her long hair out the car window so strands sway and tangle in the wind.

She has a habit of doing that. The hair flip *and* the dismissal. Like my worries don't matter. Like my *looming international trip* is nothing.

"My flight leaves in five hours. I don't have a return ticket. My parents don't *know* I don't have a return ticket." I grip the oh-shit handle harder. "I'm freaked."

"I can tell. You're panting harder than when we did that hot yoga class."

"God, don't remind me."

"You've got to believe me when I say this. You know how I hate giving compliments, but this is just fact. You are the most competent seventeen-year-old on the planet."

Her voice puts me at ease. It's a suspended chord—unsettling at first, both soft and harsh, followed by a clear resolution that feels like home. I lift my double chocolate Oreo milkshake out of the cup holder and wipe the French fry crumbs off the bottom of the cup, these now-ancient reminders of all the fast-food adventures we've gone through in this car. Megan in the driver's seat. Me, the passenger.

Always the passenger.

"I don't know how I could have prepared so much, yet still feel so unprepared," I say. "It defies logic."

I know it's partly because of Megan. We've got this yin-yang thing going on. She's so chill it's like she's constantly high on pot, and I'm about as high-strung as Hilary Hahn. (Because she's a violinist. And violins are high-pitched and have strings. High-strung? Okay, never mind.)

"You graduated early," she says. "You saved money working

at that shit diner all year. You performed in about every ensemble in the tristate area to beef up your resume. You figured out your dual citizenship and visa process in the middle of Brexit." She lowers her voice to a whisper, the wind in the car taking away the words as soon as they leave her mouth. "You've been trying to escape Avery for years. You're more than prepared for it, Marty."

Her words sting and soothe at the same time. Is she bitter that I'm abandoning her? My best of two friends—no offense to Skye. But a lot of history is there. It took me ten years to meet her, five years to stop hating her, and two years of hanging out near constantly to get where we're at now.

"I'm not escaping." Of course I'm not escaping.

"Finish your milkshake," she says. I do. "We've got two more ice cream stops before I roll you into the airport."

PHIL STAMPER is the author of *The Gravity of Us* and *As Far as You'll Take Me*. He grew up in a rural village near Dayton, Ohio. He has a BA in music and an MA in publishing with creative writing. And, unsurprisingly, a lot of student debt. He works for a major book publisher in New York City and lives in Brooklyn with his husband and their dog.

WWW.PHILSTAMPER.COM
@STAMPEPK